G000135607

Someone Like You

Karly Lane lives on the mid north coast of New South Wales. Proud mum to four children and wife of one very patient mechanic, she is lucky enough to spend her day doing the two things she loves most—being a mum and writing stories set in beautiful rural Australia.

ALSO BY KARLY LANE

North Star
Morgan's Law
Bridie's Choice
Poppy's Dilemma
Gemma's Bluff
Tallowood Bound
Second Chance Town
Third Time Lucky
If Wishes Were Horses
Six Ways to Sunday

Karly
LANE

Someone Like You

ALLEN&UNWIN
SYDNEY · MELBOURNE · AUCKLAND · LONDON

First published in 2018

Copyright © Karly Lane 2018

All rights reserved. No part of this book may be reproduced or transmitted in any form or by any means, electronic or mechanical, including photocopying, recording or by any information storage and retrieval system, without prior permission in writing from the publisher. The Australian *Copyright Act 1968* (the Act) allows a maximum of one chapter or 10 per cent of this book, whichever is the greater, to be photocopied by any educational institution for its educational purposes provided that the educational institution (or body that administers it) has given a remuneration notice to the Copyright Agency (Australia) under the Act.

Allen & Unwin
83 Alexander Street
Crows Nest NSW 2065
Australia
Phone: (61 2) 8425 0100
Email: info@allenandunwin.com
Web: www.allenandunwin.com

 A catalogue record for this book is available from the National Library of Australia

ISBN 978 1 76029 689 6

Set in 12.4/17.6 pt Sabon LT Pro by Bookhouse, Sydney
Printed and bound in Australia by Griffin Press

10 9 8 7 6 5 4 3 2 1

MIX
Paper from
responsible sources
FSC® C009448

The paper in this book is FSC® certified. FSC® promotes environmentally responsible, socially beneficial and economically viable management of the world's forests.

For Lyn

Friends are the family we choose for ourselves

One

Hayley Stevens packed the last box into the back seat of her candy-apple Audi Coupé, shutting the door quickly before everything tumbled out. She leaned against the side of the car and looked at the house where so many memories had been made.

She'd already said her goodbyes to the neighbours. Mary and John next door had been more like grandparents to her over the last seven years and had been the hardest to farewell. She'd allowed herself to cry yesterday, but today was the start of a new chapter in her life. She'd shed enough tears over the last twelve months to last a lifetime. No more.

As she left the city behind and moved out onto the freeway, Hayley felt her spirits begin to lift. She'd miss

Sydney and all its conveniences, but it was time for an adventure, a fresh beginning.

After her marriage of five years had ended a little over twelve months ago, Hayley had found it difficult to settle back into normal life. Everything she'd believed in had turned out to be a lie. For the last two years of her marriage, her husband and best friend had been having an affair. Hayley had quite literally stumbled upon the truth, discovering Paul and Lisa in bed together. She'd lost not only her husband but also the only true friend she'd had in a very long time. Life as she'd come to know it had ceased to exist.

As an author, working from home had been both a blessing and a curse. At least she hadn't had to go out and face people every day, but spending all day alone, surrounded by memories, hadn't exactly been conducive to moving on. Her only escape had been in her writing and in that regard the break-up had been a boon.

In the early days of her writing career she'd written in the early mornings and on weekends and in her time off from her real job as a receptionist in a real estate agency. After finding a publisher for her first book, it had been disappointing to discover that, contrary to popular belief, authors didn't actually make enough money to buy a private island with their first book deal. It was only after her third book had sold well that Hayley had decided to leave her job to write full-time.

She'd thought Paul would be happy, since the hours she kept in order to write while working full-time meant they hardly spent any quality time together and he made no secret of the fact he found this frustrating. She went to bed hours after he did and was up early in the morning, squeezing in as much writing time as she could before heading off to work. However, strangely, giving up her job only seemed to alienate her husband even more. He seemed to resent the fact she could stay at home whilst he had to go out to work. As her books began to gain popularity and her fan base grew, she found herself working twice as hard to meet the demand for new releases, and she and Paul spent even less time together.

In this respect, she knew she'd contributed to her marriage's problems. She was preoccupied with her new career and always seemed to be going to one writers' festival or another. Between travelling and writing, she barely had time for anything else. However, that was where she drew the line of blame. Her husband deciding to sleep with her best friend was all on him.

So, at thirty years old, she suddenly found herself alone. She'd always thought of herself as a happy, optimistic person, but it'd been a long time now since she'd been happy. As the big three-o had approached, Hayley knew she needed to make a change.

She took an exit off the freeway and the landscape began to change dramatically. As she followed the winding Hawkesbury River, towns gave way to open pasture and livestock. Horses and cattle grazed lazily in their green, grassy paddocks. Already she felt a million miles away from the city. Okay, so as far as grand adventures went, moving approximately two and a half hours away wasn't such a huge deal, but Lochway and Sydney couldn't be more different.

Lochway was a small village in a valley established around the time of the first settlers. It had once been a bustling town and a vital agricultural centre, being so close to the newly established Sydney settlement and easily accessed via the river. However, after the railway had opened the Great Dividing Range to the rapidly expanding settlement, development had ceased and the valley had been all but abandoned. It was later dubbed the Forgotten Valley. Over recent years, however, it had undergone a resurgence in popularity with an influx of city dwellers restoring the old buildings and turning them into B&Bs and boutique accommodation. For the most part, Lochway itself had avoided the gentrification of its neighbouring villages, dominated as it was by farms that had been owned by generations of the same families.

Hayley had first discovered the area when she'd been invited to the writers' festival in nearby St Albans a few years previously. She'd been so captivated by the history and sheer beauty of the region that she'd brought Paul back a few months later. They'd stayed in a convict-built stone farmhouse in Lochway. She'd been racing to meet a deadline and had tried to combine their getaway with writing, which hadn't gone down terribly well with Paul and, looking back, had been the turning point in their marriage. It had been shortly after getting home from the trip that Paul and Lisa had started their affair.

The book she'd been writing then had coincidently been released just prior to her thirtieth birthday a few months ago and had set off an avalanche of emotions. She felt a need to escape, to start over someplace else and remembered the solitude Lochway and its surrounds had offered. Hayley spontaneously searched real estate listings online and purely by chance discovered the little stone farmhouse in Lochway was listed for sale.

That was eight weeks ago.

She hadn't told anyone she'd bought it without having made a trip out to view it again after staying there. It sounded crazy and maybe it was. She didn't know anyone. All she knew was she needed a change and this was it.

Beside her on the passenger seat was a manila envelope with copies of the paperwork she'd signed last week and various other bits and pieces from the real estate agent. It was really happening. A little bubble of excitement rippled through her. This was her new beginning.

'You have reached your destination,' the ever-serene voice of her GPS informed her at the same time as she spotted the number on the letterbox.

Thick bush blocked the house and the rest of the property from view, making it completely private. The five hundred metres of driveway wound its way through the bushland till it broke out into a clearing to reveal a beautiful sandstone cottage with a bull-nosed verandah behind a white timber fence.

Hayley parked her car outside. A Colorbond shed in the same shade of sandstone had been built a few metres from the house and would provide storage for anything she couldn't fit inside, as it was considerably smaller than her old one. But what the cottage lacked in size it more than made up for in character. Hayley loved everything about the cosy place. The gardens had been painstakingly designed and meticulously cared for. The rear verandah had the most gorgeous view over a rose garden and an arbour covered in wisteria. The plump, purple flowers hung in clusters and the gentle drone of bees happily buzzing about them filled Hayley with memories of lazy summer days and warm sunshine. Beyond the arbour hedges on three sides created a courtyard feel to the garden.

Hayley walked towards the small gate in the far back corner of the hedge. She hadn't ventured this far when she and Paul had stayed here. She knew from the contract that there was a small overseer's cottage and some sheds out here but previously there had been a sign marking this area as private.

The overseer's cottage had been built from the same convict-hewn sandstone bricks as the main house and had apparently been the original homestead. It was tiny: just one bedroom, a bathroom and small kitchen. There was a front verandah with only enough room for two chairs and a side table. The cottage would make a wonderful writing space, or perhaps even accommodation for paying guests.

Across from the overseer's cottage was what the title documents described as the shearing shed, but judging from its condition and the remaining infrastructure, there was very little internally that resembled a shearing shed now. It reminded Hayley of a defiant old man who'd weathered more than his fair share of storms and, although battered and bent, still remained upright, refusing to give in and topple over.

The sides and roof were made of tin covered in varying shades of rust and old paint. Inside, the frame seemed to be made from roughly sawn timber logs—in all their knobbly, curved glory—with a few large slabs supporting the bulk of the weight. It was open at the front, with a wide walkway through the centre and the remains of old stalls along the sides, although most no longer had any gates on them.

There were a few other sheds of different sizes in varying condition, most looking like machinery sheds and none looking new. Beyond the buildings was open pasture. It was divided into three paddocks that ran down to the river forming the boundary of the property. There was a little over twenty hectares of land, approximately fifty acres in the old scale. The original property had been subdivided and sold off over the years but had once been over two hundred acres of prime grazing land. Small mercies, Hayley thought. She wasn't sure how she was going to keep fifty acres under control, let alone two hundred!

There wasn't time to explore down by the river today, but she decided to do it first thing tomorrow. For now she needed to unpack her car and set up the blow-up bed so she had a place to sleep tonight. The removalist truck was scheduled to arrive at lunchtime tomorrow, which meant she'd only have to rough it for a night.

Hayley unpacked the kitchen essentials she'd brought with her: a coffee machine and toasted sandwich maker. You could exist pretty much forever on good coffee and toasted cheese sandwiches. She knew, because for a great deal of the time since Paul had left, that's what she'd lived on. With work consuming her as it had, and no one to complain about the lack of groceries in the house, she had stocked little more than the bare essentials. She might not have eaten a balanced diet but the last two books in her series had been written in record time and her publishers were ecstatic.

She'd fallen into her unique genre of action, suspense with a dash of romance thrown in quite by accident. She'd started writing traditional romance but had been met with rejection after rejection from publishers. It was only out of frustration that she'd decided to let off some steam one day and begun writing a dark yet hilarious character named Chance Delaware, a tough ex-detective with a trail of bad decisions and dysfunctional ex-husbands who continued to reappear in her life just when she seemed finally to be getting herself together. She always fought for the underdog. Maybe it was the hot men or Chance's take-no-crap-from-anyone attitude that kept readers coming back for more, but whatever it was, her three-book series had turned into five and didn't seem to be finishing any time soon.

She'd had the first book in the series, *Chance is a Fine Thing*, optioned by a movie producer, and although it was exciting, she knew that more often than not optioned films were never made. So far they'd held the option for two years and there still wasn't any word on whether they were going to go ahead with making the movie or not.

She wrote under her maiden name, H.B. Alexander, and not many of her acquaintances even knew she was a writer, let alone what her pen name was. Since her divorce she'd stopped doing publicity or interviews, and while her publishers had been understanding, she knew they were eager for her to start again now that the popularity of the series was growing so quickly. She'd never particularly enjoyed that part of writing. While she loved her readers, standing up in front of a crowd was not and never would be something she felt comfortable doing.

Hayley dug through the esky and got out the coffee beans and milk, finding the familiar ritual of preparing coffee soothing after her long day driving.

Later, after a quick toasted cheese sandwich, she changed into her pyjamas and hopped onto the blow-up bed, which creaked and protested every time she moved. She closed her eyes, forcing her overtired mind to rest. Tomorrow was the start of her new life.

Two

Luke Mason kissed his grandmother hello before moving to the other side of the kitchen to greet his mother, swiping some icing from a cupcake as he went and dodging his mother's wooden spoon.

'Thank you for doing this, darling,' his mother said, watching as he leaned against the kitchen counter. 'I couldn't postpone these clients, they're planning a huge wedding.'

'That's okay, I've got some stuff to do in town anyway. Are you ready, Gran?' he asked.

'Ready as I'll ever be,' said the old woman, picking up her handbag. 'I'm quite happy to cancel this silly doctor's appointment, you know. There's nothing wrong with me.'

'You are not cancelling, Pearl. You know that you can't miss your check-ups,' his mother told her pointedly.

'Waste of time,' his gran muttered, pushing her walking frame with a huff as she moved towards the back door.

'Hold up, Gran,' Luke said, hurrying after her.

Outside, he manoeuvred her around to the passenger door of his mother's BMW. While he could appreciate the leather seats and smooth ride of his mother's pride and joy, he was far more comfortable in his reliable four-wheel drive ute that usually smelled of lucerne, old fuel cans and dog hair. However, he was fairly sure Gran wouldn't be nearly as comfortable in his monstrosity of a vehicle, so his mother's car it was.

They drove in silence for a short while.

'So, tell me,' his gran asked eventually, 'how are you?'

He gave a surprised chuckle. 'Gran, you see me every day.'

'Yes, I know, but we haven't sat down and talked about anything of much importance in a long while. You always say you're fine, but I want to know how you *really* are.'

He sent her a swift sidelong glance. 'I *am* fine,' he said.

'Are you?'

Luke wanted to shrug off his gran's doubt, but she'd always had the knack of seeing more than he liked to reveal. It was unnerving, to be honest. 'I'm doing okay,' he relented. 'The market's been good. It's just been a bit hectic with the brewery and restaurant starting up, and Dad's been stressed about taking on more risk, but it's all looking positive.'

'But that's not what's troubling you, is it?' Gran said knowingly.

'There's nothing troubling me,' he frowned.

'You feel as though there's something missing.'

Luke clenched his jaw. 'I've told you and Mum before, Lucinda and I just didn't work anymore. I'm fine with it. I've moved on.'

'Yes, I know, dear. I told you she wasn't the one for you,' Gran said serenely. 'But it's all right, she'll be along soon.'

'Who will?' Luke asked, confused. He was beginning to regret offering to take Gran to her appointment.

He glanced over at his grandmother and saw a soft smile playing on her dry lips. 'Everything will work out the way it's supposed to, in time,' was all she said, turning her head to look out the side window without bothering to elaborate further.

He should be used to Gran's ways by now. She'd never been any different—always a little eccentric, and fond of dabbling in angel cards and the tarot. But he couldn't shake the slight feeling of unease her statement left him with. Who was coming and what did it mean?

The bright sunshine streamed in through Hayley's window the next morning. While the bed hadn't been the most comfortable, at least she'd managed to sleep—mostly due to the fact that she'd gotten little sleep in the days leading up to her move with so much to think about. One look at the view outside though had made all the stress worth it. A kookaburra somewhere nearby gave a cheerful belly laugh and a chorus of magpies joined in just for the fun of it. Outside her bedroom window in the bottlebrush a noisy argument broke out between a group of lorikeets that screeched and chattered. She smiled. Country life. This was what she'd dreamed of waking up to every morning. Fresh air, the soft calls of nature and the soothing sounds of . . .

The loud rumbling of a truck gearing down and braking scared off the kookaburra and was enough to cut short the magpies mid-song.

She walked from the bedroom into the lounge room at the front of the house and gaped as a large removalist truck crept its way up the drive.

They weren't supposed to arrive until later in the day. She'd been planning to give the entire house a good clean before they started unpacking everything. Still, she thought later as the two men began to bring in the trolley of boxes, at least she could get a head start on setting everything up.

While the removalists unloaded the furniture, Hayley went outside with her coffee, doing her best to stay out of their way but remaining within earshot in case they needed her. She intended to head to the old table and chairs that had been left under the big tree by the previous owners, but curiosity got the better of her as she spied the small stone building just off the old overseer's cottage. It had a small step leading to a door and a dusty window that looked like it hadn't been cleaned in years.

There wasn't a lock, so she turned the doorknob and pushed open the reluctant door. It was empty and dark inside, with a strong musty smell of old, cold places. Two more windows on the far side let in a bit of light, but it was still gloomy and the dust in the faint shards of sunlight swirled around her eerily. She thought she remembered from her previous stay that it had once been the old kitchen, back when settlers had separate buildings for cooking to keep smells out of the house and as a safety measure in case of fire.

This of course would have been the upgraded building, the original kitchen would have likely been a wattle and daub hut, but it was still old—at least as old as the cottage itself. Hayley felt a small tremor run through her and decided she'd been in there long enough. It gave her the creeps actually, and she had no idea why. She retraced her steps to the door and closed it firmly behind her.

Thanks to the early arrival of the removalists, Hayley hadn't had a shower all day—she hadn't been able to bring herself to get naked while two strange men were wandering around her house. But now they'd left she searched out her fluffy bathmat and towels from the packing boxes and stepped out of her grubby clothes into the shower stall, anticipating the soothing feel of hot water easing her sore muscles.

She turned on the tap and waited. Nothing happened. 'What the—' she muttered and suddenly a gush of icy cold water exploded from the showerhead, drenching her.

She was pretty sure her scream could have been heard all the way into town and she half expected the police to show up on her doorstep with reports of a woman being murdered.

Teeth chattering, she grabbed her towel and wrapped herself in it, then stepped back and tried to adjust the water temperature. The water was now flowing reasonably normally and slowly it lost its arctic coldness. What felt like ten minutes later, steam finally began to billow above the shower stall and she stepped under the water gingerly.

Find a plumber, she made a mental note as she dried herself and got dressed. *Have also found a possible solution to running out of caffeine,* she added, not having felt this awake since . . . well, ever.

The small village of Lochway had only two shops, one being a convenience store that had a small post office agency and a limited variety of groceries, but stocked the basics like milk and bread. The other was a feed store with two bowsers out the front, one petrol and the other diesel.

She hadn't stopped in the village on her way through yesterday and she was running low on milk and needed to stock her new pantry.

There was a bell above the door that gave a cheerful tinkle as she opened it, and a few minutes later a woman in a floral shift-style dress shuffled in through a rainbow of plastic strips hanging in the doorway behind the counter.

'Morning,' Hayley said, summoning a smile. 'Beautiful day out there.'

'You lost or something?' the woman asked, eyeing her suspiciously.

'No, at least, not yet. I'm Hayley Stevens. I've just moved into Abby Cottage.'

'Ahh,' she said, nodding as though to confirm something to herself. 'The city woman.'

'Yes, well . . . not anymore,' Hayley said lightly.

'We'll see.' The ominous comment was not exactly confidence-boosting. 'What do you need?'

'Just some milk and . . .' She gave the uninspiring shelves a quick perusal before grabbing the first thing she came to—a couple of packets of cup-a-soup and a box of tissues—before moving across to the small fridge. 'Do you have any skim milk?'

'Nope. Full cream or light. No idea why a person would want to drink skim milk anyway. May as well just grab a bottle of full cream and tip most of it out then fill it up with tap water.'

Hayley was pretty sure that wasn't how they made skim milk, but she let it pass. 'Light will be fine,' she said with a smile, carrying her purchases over to the counter where the woman stood waiting. It seemed she wouldn't be able to do her weekly shopping here; the range of groceries was dismal.

On the way out of the store, a piece of paper flapping on a noticeboard caught her eye. It was an advert: *Donkey, free to good home.*

Don't be ridiculous, she thought, shaking her head.

She went to turn away but stopped as the corner of the paper flapped wildly as a breeze picked up. Hayley stared at the handwritten note warily for a few moments before putting down the plastic bags in her hand and reaching up to take out the drawing pin and shoving the notice in her pocket. *It would only have blown away,* she told the voice making a *tsk* noise in her head.

It wasn't until later in the evening, after she'd had enough of unpacking for one day, that she remembered the note and dug it out of her pocket. She'd just call, see what the story was; no harm in that. The phone was answered with a brusque, 'Hello?'

'Ah, hi. I was just calling about the notice at the grocery store . . . about the donkey?'

In the background, Hayley could hear loud yelling and squealing children—a lot of children if the noise was any indication. She had to wait while the woman yelled out for everyone to shut up.

'Have you found a place for it yet?' She wasn't sure how long the notice had been up for.

'No. It's still available.'

'Oh. Okay. I've only just moved to town, I—'

'You bought the B&B out on Macdonald Road?'

Hayley was taken aback. 'Um, yes,' she stammered. How did the woman know that? Hayley had only arrived yesterday.

'Okay, great. When do you want it?'

'Oh. Well, I thought maybe I could come out and take a look at it first,' she said, not liking how fast the conversation was going.

'Yeah, well, I don't know, we're going away for a few days—' A loud crash sounded in the background. 'What did I tell you kids about climbing up there? Look, I have to go.'

'Yes, no, sure. You go. I'll call back—' the phone clicked in her ear and Hayley was left listening to the beeps '—later,' she said to nobody.

She put the phone onto the coffee table and leaned back against the cushions. Maybe it hadn't been such a great idea after all. A donkey was a big responsibility. Maybe she'd start with a goldfish and work her way up from there.

Three

The sound of chirping woke her bright and early the next morning. The noise grew louder as the birds screeched at each other. Hayley staggered to the window and stared out, expecting to see thousands crammed into the small bush outside, but counted roughly fifteen. *Nature was nice,* she thought as she pulled the window shut firmly, *but not this early in the morning.* She climbed back into bed and dozed off.

Later, as she yawned and stretched in bed, a loud revving sound caught her attention, mid-stretch. At the sound of a groan and crunch of gears, she threw back the bedcovers and hurried from her room. As she made her way to the front of the house, kicking her toe on the corner of the chair as she went, she heard a bang, followed by raised voices, mixed with an unfamiliar animal noise that set Hayley's nerves on edge. What the hell was that racket? She'd just reached the front door and stepped outside when the truck revved loudly once more and took off down the driveway in a cloud of dust.

'What the heck?' Hayley muttered, unable to catch much more than a glimpse of an old red truck. She was about to head back inside when a God-awful noise started up nearby. The braying, wheezy cry increased in decibels as she ran down the two steps and along the front path towards the side fence, almost skidding to a halt when she came face to face with a brown and white donkey with a grey snout, making the loudest racket Hayley had ever heard in her life.

'Hey,' she said, unsure how to proceed. What on earth was a donkey doing tied to her fence? She glanced back down the driveway, even though she knew the truck was gone. For the briefest of moments she wondered if the donkey had somehow fallen off the back, until she rationalised it would hardly have tied itself to the fence.

'Okay, I know you're upset, but you need to knock off that noise,' she told the donkey, striving for a firm tone. The animal stopped briefly, but then quickly started again.

This was ridiculous. Maybe if she fed it the donkey would shut up, she thought, turning away to run back inside and find something suitable. The noise got even louder. 'I'll be right back,' she yelled over her shoulder, then shook her head. As if it understood a word she was saying.

What the hell does a donkey even eat? She grabbed her phone and googled the question. Hay. Well, that wasn't helpful, she didn't have any hay in the fridge. Carrots and apples. 'Jackpot!' she said, grabbing a carrot before running into her bedroom and changing out of her pyjamas.

She raced back outside, following the racket.

'Okay, calm down. Here,' she said, walking cautiously towards the animal, the carrot held out in front of her as a peace offering. The noise stopped as the donkey sniffed at the carrot before mouthing at it timidly. 'That's better, isn't it,' she said, relieved. 'There's a good . . . donkey.' She realised she had no idea if it was a boy or a girl. Now that the immediate hysteria had eased, Hayley began to make sense of the situation. It was too much of a coincidence that she'd called about the free donkey last night and this morning it had somehow miraculously turned up outside her house, but why the hell would someone dump a large animal like this and leave without even talking to her? She'd said she was *thinking* about it, she hadn't agreed to take it.

What was she going to do with a donkey? Gingerly she reached out and touched the fur on its face, encouraged when it didn't try to bite her hand. With a little more confidence she scratched between its ears and it leaned its head into her touch. 'Wow, those are some big ears,' she said quietly as she continued scratching. 'What are we going to do with you?' She looked back over her shoulder a little desperately. There was no help there; whoever had owned it before was long gone. There was the old shearing shed out the back that had the stalls, she supposed that would be the logical place to put it for now. She couldn't just leave it tied to the fence.

Moving slowly, she untied the rope and, whispering a silent plea for the animal to cooperate, led it around the back of the yard, dangling the rest of the carrot in front of its nose.

As they neared the shed the animal became a little more wary and slower to move. 'It's okay,' she said, hoping she sounded encouraging. She let the donkey take a bite of the carrot before urging it forward inside the nearest of the old gated stalls, dragging the rickety old gate closed.

'What am I supposed to do now?' she asked, leaning over the gate as it finished eating the carrot. Almost as though answering, the animal began baying once more. Food. In order to shut it up, she was going to need to feed it something more satisfying than a carrot. She needed hay.

When she walked into Lochway rural supplies a combined smell of animal feed, fertiliser and who knew what else hit her. A stocky man wearing dirty jeans and a polo shirt strode into the dim interior, followed by another man wearing a saggy, faded hat and muddy work boots. Both men glanced at her but didn't stop their conversation.

Hayley waited patiently as they discussed the weather and the stocky man dug a pair of glasses from his pocket, perching them on the end of his nose as he searched the computer at the front desk for something.

Hayley couldn't say she'd ever been inside a feed store before; there wasn't anything overly interesting, unless you were a farmer, she guessed. There were lots of pipes and parts, a whole wall of fittings for things she couldn't identify. There were bottles of insecticides, treatments for worms, fleas, ticks and buffalo fly, whatever that was. There were big bins of seeds and bags of feed for what looked like every kind of animal under the sun.

'Can I help you?'

Hayley turned and found the man from the counter standing nearby.

'I'm after some hay.'

'What kind of hay?'

Hayley stared at him blankly. How many kinds of hay could there be? 'Ah, I don't know . . . what have you got?'

'Lucerne, oaten, grassy, barley.'

'Umm, what would you recommend for a donkey?'

'Grassy,' he answered.

'Then I'll get some grassy hay, please.'

He turned and headed back to the desk, typing in something, before telling her the price.

'I only wanted one,' she said slowly.

'That is the price for one,' he said.

'Oh. Okay. That's fine.' She handed over her card and waited for him to process the payment. Maybe it was going to be cheaper to feed the damn donkey on carrots and apples after all. Without a word, the man headed out of the store and Hayley hurried to follow him as he disappeared into the depths of a large shed attached to the store, reappearing with a bale of hay and heading towards her car.

He opened the boot, and before she could say anything he dropped in the bale and slammed the lid shut. Her lovely clean carpet in the back was not designed to carry hay. 'Thank you,' she said weakly as he turned and walked inside the store without a backward glance.

Hayley gave an irritated sigh as she stared at her car boot when she got home. It was going to take forever to clean. If the hay was baled up, how come so much of the damn stuff had fallen out? Grabbing hold of the blue twine, Hayley heaved and managed to lift the bale of hay up onto the edge of the boot, bracing herself to get it the rest of the way out.

She was going to need a better way of doing this next time, she thought as she struggled to take more than three steps at a time. She staggered into the shearing shed and dropped the bale to the ground, then sank onto it for a well-deserved rest, picking stray bits of scratchy hay from inside her bra. 'You better appreciate this, donkey,' she muttered, turning sideways to glare at it for added measure, only to jump to her feet in alarm. It was gone!

The long rickety gate she'd pulled across the front was now slightly ajar, and despite the evidence before her eyes, Hayley searched the rest of the shed hopefully, but there was no sign of her noisy, unexpected guest. A dark shadow darted across the floor in front of her and Hayley shrieked. 'Bloody mice!' she shuddered, hurrying back outside to continue looking. There was no sign of the donkey anywhere, but as she stood at the edge of the paddock, she heard a familiar noise. The heehaw wheezing was faint, but it was distinct.

Hayley followed the sound as best she could, realising that it was leading in the direction of the neighbouring property. She climbed through a fence and picked her way across the paddock. The grass wasn't too long for the most part, but it was thick and still long enough to hide snakes. *Boots,* she thought, mentally putting them on her growing list of things she needed to buy sooner rather than later.

By the time she reached the final fence, she was breathing heavily. Exercise. *Better add that to the list too.* She hadn't realised just how out of shape she'd gotten. Hermits were probably an unfit bunch in general. Well, now she had no excuse. Here she could get outside and still not have to see anyone.

There was a faint mechanical droning somewhere in the distance. It floated to her in the breeze that rustled the tops of the few tall trees scattered across the paddocks.

The braying had gotten louder so she knew she was on the right track, but she also knew that the stupid animal was no longer on her land. She gave an irritated sigh as she squeezed through the barbed wire fence and swore silently as her shirt was snagged. She had to reach back awkwardly to unhook herself. As she made her way through the paddock, she could see the source of her irritation braying from down in a gully . . . smack bang in the centre of a small dam.

'What are you doing?' she demanded, glaring at the animal from the edge of the water.

As soon as the donkey saw her, the braying increased. 'All right, I heard you! The entire valley has probably heard you,' she added as she eyed the water cautiously. It clearly wasn't very deep, considering the animal was standing up, but the water was up to the tops of its legs, which would be thigh high on Hayley. Naturally the halter was just too far enough out of reach for her to be able to lean out and grab it. She really didn't want to wade out into the dirty-looking water. She tried calling the donkey, patting her knees and forcing a cheerfulness she was far from feeling into her voice, but the hairy beast just bellowed more.

'Oh, for goodness sake!' she said after a few minutes of unsuccessful coaxing. She was going to have to go in. She considered taking her sneakers off, but the thought of going in barefoot was not an option. Tiptoeing one foot in slowly, to test the water, Hayley soon discovered that the bottom of the dam was soft and extremely squishy. Carefully she took another step and let out a startled gasp as her foot slipped, barely managing to right herself. 'Come on, get over here,' she called, reluctant to go out further. She was having second thoughts about the entire rescue mission now she had discovered how muddy the bottom of the dam was; her feet were beginning to sink and she wasn't at all confident that she was going to be able to get the stupid animal out on her own.

If she could just reach the halter, she might be able to tug it towards her; at the very least she'd have something solid to hold on to. She lifted one sodden foot with a great deal of effort and took another step, but halfway through the movement her shoe slipped and she lunged forward, sinking to her knees and slipping sideways into the dam. Cold water plastered her shirt to her skin and took the air from her lungs.

For a long moment Hayley could only stare at the animal as she dripped, until the uncomfortable sensation of being fully clothed, wet and smeared with stinky muddy water snapped her out of her surprise and she let out an outraged shriek. The donkey increased the volume of the heehawing, throwing in its opinion of the situation for good measure.

With a defeated sigh, Hayley closed her eyes, dropping her head forward briefly before throwing her shoulders back with renewed determination. 'Right, you,' she snapped as she surged forward and grabbed hold of the halter. 'Come on.' She pulled as hard as she could, but there was no budging the animal. 'You can*not* be that stuck,' she muttered, sloshing her way closer, checking the position of the animal's legs, but it wasn't looking good. It was, in fact, very stuck. She wasn't game to go out any further in case she sank as well.

'Wouldn't that just be my luck,' she muttered. She could see the newspaper headlines now: MISSING AUTHOR'S REMAINS FOUND NEXT TO THE UNGRATEFUL ANIMAL SHE TRIED TO SAVE.

She was so busy trying to figure out what she was going to do that she didn't immediately register the new sound until it was almost upon her. Hayley turned just as a white ute pulled to a stop and a man in a hat and sunglasses climbed out.

Just great, she thought, trying to ignore the clinging fabric and smell of mud, *a witness to my inept attempt at donkey rescue.* Not to mention what she must look like . . . Could today possibly get any worse?

Four

The man stopped at the edge of the dam, his hands on his hips. 'You all right?' he asked. Hayley stared at him. *Seriously? When would it be all right for a woman to be knee-deep in a dam with a stuck donkey?*

'Not really, no,' she said. 'My donkey's stuck in the mud and I can't get it out.' Hayley wondered if maybe he could talk and help at the same time; her wet clothes weren't getting any less uncomfortable. 'Can you give me a hand?'

'Hang on.' He turned and walked away.

He came back from the ute with a long length of rope, and Hayley gaped as he strode straight into the water. Clearly he had no issue with mud and cold water. 'I don't keep the cattle in this paddock for this reason. It's a bog pit.'

'I'm not sure how it got over here. I had it in the shearing shed but it escaped.'

'The fence is probably down somewhere. We had a big storm a week or so ago and I haven't been over this way to check if there was any damage.' He secured the rope, tying it around the animal before sloshing back out of the water to the vehicle. 'I'm just going to back up so there's enough tension to get some traction—you better move out of the way,' he said, indicating she should stand up on the bank.

Hayley had no reason to believe he didn't know what he was doing, but she worried about the rope ripping off the donkey's limbs in the process. Much to her relief, as he backed up the ute slowly, the donkey clambered and splashed about in the water until it managed to exit the dam, with little grace but successfully nonetheless.

'Thank you,' Hayley said as their rescuer came back down to the dam, where she'd just caught the rope of the troublesome donkey. 'I'm not sure what I would have done if you hadn't arrived when you did.'

'No worries. Luke Mason,' he said, introducing himself.

'Hayley Stevens,' she smiled, wiping her hand on her muddy shirt before extending it towards him.

He slipped his sunglasses off his face and hooked them on the front of his buttoned work shirt before taking her hand in his. Two blue eyes held hers, the colour intensified by the suntanned skin that crinkled attractively around them. The flash of white teeth wasn't helping her concentrate either. *Pull yourself together.* 'Thank you.'

He grinned. 'You already thanked me.'

God. 'I'm just really grateful.' *And acting like an idiot!*

'So, how'd you end up with Errol?'

'Who?'

Luke nodded his head towards the donkey. *Errol?* 'You know him? Wait . . . *him?*'

'Everyone knows Errol, and yeah, it's a he.'

'Well, maybe *you* can tell *me* how I ended up with him. Someone in a red truck left him tied up to my front fence.'

'That'd be Alfie Provost. He's been trying to get rid of Errol for the last two years.'

'I saw the ad on the noticeboard at the grocery store and called to enquire yesterday, and this morning there he was. I didn't even tell them my name.'

'It's not hard to figure out. You're the only newcomer.'

'How do you even know that? I only arrived three days ago.'

'Word gets around. We knew weeks ago the place had been sold.'

So much for keeping to herself.

'Well. Thanks again,' she said, then winced. *Stop thanking the guy.* She made to move away but then remembered she wasn't sure how to get the stupid animal back home. 'Ah. I didn't actually see any gates . . . I'm not sure how to get him back through the fence.'

'You lead Errol and I'll take the ute for a drive along the fence line and see where its down. That way I can fix it while I'm here.'

'I'm sorry to be a nuisance.'

'Nah, it's okay. It has to be fixed anyway.'

He waited until she'd got the wet, bedraggled donkey moving before climbing into his ute and driving slowly towards the fence.

Left alone, Hayley found herself processing the whole ridiculous fiasco in between coercing the reluctant cause of the whole thing into walking forwards. Way to meet the neighbours. She plucked at the damp, muddy shirt and gritted her teeth against the disgusting sensation of walking in wet clothes. The hot water better be working by the time she got home.

She saw the ute stop and Luke walk around the rear of the vehicle to take something out. By the time she'd begged, pleaded and threatened Errol to reach his side, he was already busy dragging a large branch off the sagging fence.

'Found the problem,' he said, coming up to take the rope from her hand and carefully lead the animal over the loose wire for her. 'There you go.'

'Thanks. I'll try to figure out a way to make sure he doesn't get out again.'

'I can come and take a look at it after I finish this if you like.'

'Oh no, I couldn't get you to do that. We've already imposed too much.'

'Nah, it'll be right. I'll probably beat you there at the rate old Errol moves.'

Hayley gave a small unamused grunt in response. It *was* going to be a slow walk home and she didn't have time to waste standing around arguing when clearly the man had decided he was coming around.

'This isn't a very good start to our relationship, Errol,' she said after they'd been walking a while, stepping over sticks and negotiating the thick green pasture grass. 'Why would you try to escape? You didn't even stick around long enough to get to know me.' She looked back at the donkey, who seemed to be wearing a rather bored expression. 'I know I don't have much of an idea what to do with you,' she admitted, 'but I'm sure we can figure it out. There's always Google, you know. Or Luke.' *Or not,* she added silently. She couldn't keep running to other people for help every time something went wrong. She was going to have to start learning how to do things for herself. The last twelve months had been a big learning curve—who knew there'd been so many everyday mundane things that needed taking care of? Things she'd never really thought much about because Paul had been there to do them.

She'd had amazing neighbours. She'd barely had to lift a finger. Max from next door would mow her lawn for her, despite the fact she'd told him she'd do it herself, or get a lawn service in. He'd just shake his head and wave off her protests saying that he had his mower out, and it wasn't any more trouble to do her tiny yard while he was doing his own. At first she'd just been grateful that it was something she didn't have to worry about, but after a while she began to feel helpless. She knew they didn't mean to make her feel that way at all—quite the opposite, they were just trying to help—but one of the things brewing in the back of her mind about moving had been that she wanted a fresh start, so she could reclaim her independence. She needed to.

Somehow along the way she'd lost something . . . other than her marriage. She'd lost part of herself. She needed to start taking control of her life again.

As they neared the house, Hayley felt a tiny glimmer of victory. She tied Errol to a post inside the stall and peeled off a chunk, or *biscuit* as she'd discovered it was called, of the hay to keep him occupied until she could sort out a way to keep him secured.

Hayley was just tugging out an old rusted gate from behind the shed when she heard a car pull up. She dusted her hands on her already disgusting jeans and went to greet her neighbour.

'You made it back, I see,' he said, nodding at the donkey eating hay contentedly as though he were the perfect animal and hadn't just almost drowned in a muddy dam.

'Yes, thank goodness.'

'This'll be fine to hold him once we fix the gate,' Luke said, indicating the old shearing shed. 'But he'll need his own paddock to graze in through the day. If you fence off some of the bigger paddock behind the shed, that'd be perfect.'

'Okay. I'll look into finding a fencing contractor. I don't want him roaming around the rose garden near the house.'

'No, probably not the best idea,' Luke agreed dryly.

'I found this old gate behind the shed. I'm wondering if we could use it to replace the dodgy timber one he managed to push through?'

'Should do the trick,' he said, inspecting it. 'I'll have a scratch around and see what I can find to put it up.'

He came back a few minutes later with some tools and Hayley blinked in surprise. 'You carry all that stuff with you?'

'You have to,' he said, moving past her to drag the gate into position. 'Something's always breaking down or needing to be fixed when you're too far from the house to go back.'

'Like a boy scout. Always prepared,' she said.

'Something like that.'

'Can I do anything to help?

'You can hold that end of the gate for me if you like.'

Hayley stepped closer and took up position where he showed her, glad she had something to do instead of stand and watch him . . . *work,* she added quickly. She was only watching him work. He worked very well in those denim jeans. *Would you stop it?* What was happening to her? She didn't normally ogle men. She had absolutely no desire to find a man, and she doubted she'd even know what to do with one anyway. She firmly ignored the helpful suggestions her overstimulated mind offered at this thought and cleared her throat. 'How long have you lived around here?' *That's good. Nice, friendly conversation.*

'All my life. Born and bred. What about you? Where did you grow up?'

'Mainly in Sydney. We moved from the central coast when I was about nine, so pretty much most of my life.'

'So what makes a city girl want to buy a place like this?' he asked, squinting up at her as he continued attaching the gate to the post.

'I wanted a change of scenery. I came here for a weekend once and I couldn't stop thinking about it. When I saw it online for sale, it was like a sign or something . . .' Her words trailed off as she saw him watching her thoughtfully. He probably thought she was some city slicker jumping into something without a second thought. He actually wouldn't be too far off the mark. It had been a very spontaneous decision, but she couldn't shake the feeling that somehow it was meant to be. What were the chances that *this* property would have just been placed on the market *literally* the day before she started looking?

'Are you a big believer in fate?' he asked, momentarily throwing Hayley.

'I don't know . . . I haven't been in the past,' she admitted. 'What about you?'

He gave her a lopsided smile and Hayley felt something shift inside her. For the briefest of moments she felt a flash of recognition, something so familiar that her heart actually ached, then it was gone.

'My grandmother is a big believer in all things fate and destiny. Me? Not so much. I personally think we make our own choices and choose our own path.'

'Your grandmother sounds fascinating.'

'She's a character—a bit of a legend around these parts.'

'Does she live nearby?'

'She's your next-door neighbour,' he said, smiling. 'The Masons are one big happy family. All three generations are currently living there together.'

His dry remark made her smile. 'In the one house?'

'It's a pretty big house,' he admitted, 'but no. Thankfully there are enough houses that we can all have our own space.'

'So, how many of you are there?'

'My parents, Gran, my brother and his wife, their kids and me.'

'Wow. That's a lot of people. Do you like living there with your family?'

'Sometimes it feels a bit crowded, but mostly we all do our own thing, except for Sunday lunch—that's always up at the main house with everyone. Not what you're used to, I take it?' he asked, looking around. 'Aren't you going to get lonely here all by yourself?'

'How do you know I'm living here alone?' she asked, more curious than offended.

'Word's got around, you bought this place on your own. No sign of a husband or significant other spotted by anyone,' he shrugged.

Hayley stared at him gobsmacked. They'd all been piecing together her life story?

He glanced at her surprised face and quickly back-peddled. 'No one meant anything by it. It's just kind of a big deal when we get newcomers to the area. People get curious.'

'Oh. Sure. I can understand that.' Well, sort of. 'I don't mind being alone. I work from home, so I'm used to the quiet.'

'What do you do?'

'I'm a writer.'

'Yeah?' he said, kinking an eyebrow in interest. 'What do you write?'

'Fiction.'

'Romance stuff?'

'Ah, no. Although there is usually a bit of romance thrown in. I write a series based on a female detective.'

'Sounds good. I might have to look for your books.'

Hayley smiled politely; that was usually the standard reply from people who hated reading but didn't want to risk offending her by saying so. She didn't take it personally.

'There we go,' he said, standing back to admire his work. 'That should keep old Errol in. You might have to make sure all your gates are kept shut, though—if he does get out, at least that way he won't be able to wander as far again.'

'I wasn't expecting a donkey to land on my doorstep or I would have made sure I had a safe place to keep him before he turned up.'

'Yeah, that's a pretty low act even for Alfie.'

'Do you know where he lives? I think I'll go around there and have a chat to him.'

'I don't think it'll do you much good. Alfie's not exactly the sharpest tool in the shed, if you know what I mean, but he can be a shifty old bastard when he wants to be. Look, if you really don't want the donkey, I can organise to get rid of him for you.'

'Get rid of him how?'

'He's getting on, it wouldn't be unreasonable to have him put down.'

'Put down?' Hayley stared at the man, horrified. 'Because he's inconvenient?'

'Because he's had a pretty crap life up there with Alfie and his tribe of feral kids and you don't want him, so it's doin' the poor bugger a favour.'

'I didn't say I didn't want him,' she said, glancing across at the now quiet animal chewing contentedly on his hay. 'I just wasn't prepared for him. He can stay. I'll just have to get his yard sorted out first before I start on anything else around here.'

'Okay,' Luke said with a shrug, no doubt confirming his theory that she was indeed some kind of crazy city person. 'Well,' he said, tapping the top railing of the newly installed gate, 'I guess I better get out of your hair so you can go back to whatever you were doing.'

She glanced at her watch and realised it was almost lunchtime. 'Would you like a cold drink? I'm pretty sure we've earned one.'

There was a brief moment of hesitation, but maybe it was surprise, before he agreed. Hayley led the way into the house and showed Luke where the bathroom was to wash the grime from his hands, then she quickly changed out of her now damp clothing and tried to get as much of the muddy-water smell off her as possible.

Hayley took out some juice from the fridge, along with some crackers and dip. It wasn't much of a lunch but it was all she had on hand. 'I've only got orange juice,' she said as he appeared in the kitchen. 'Pickings are a bit slim at the moment until I get around to doing a grocery shop. Is that okay?'

'Sure. That'll be fine, thanks.' He looked around curiously. 'The last time I was in this house I think I was about seven. I came over with my gran to bring some fruit to the woman who used to live here.'

'Really?' Hayley asked. 'What was it like back then?'

He lifted an eyebrow. 'When you say *back then*, it wasn't like a hundred years ago or anything. I'm not that old,' he grinned.

'I wasn't thinking a hundred years . . . maybe fifty or so,' she added, for some reason feeling comfortable enough to joke with a man she'd only met a few hours ago.

'Well, to answer your question, young whippersnapper, it looked like an old lady's house. She'd been living here for a long while and was a fair age when she died.'

'Died . . . as in here?'

He gave a faint chuckle at her concerned expression. 'No, in a nursing home. Her family sold the place and since then it's had a few different owners.'

He followed her outside to the table under the shady tree, glass in hand.

'Are you going to continue the place as a B&B?' he asked, stretching his legs out as he sat down.

'I'm not sure yet. Not at first. I think I just want to enjoy being by myself for a while, but maybe down the track a bit.'

'One of the things people from the city often notice is how quiet it is out here.'

Hayley smiled. 'It was one of the first things I noticed too, but I don't know, maybe it's because I'm a writer, but my mind is never quiet. I've always got so much going on, plotting a new book, characters trying to get my attention to tell me their story . . . It's never truly quiet.'

'Wow, and I thought I had it tough never escaping my family and their constant dramas . . .'

'He says, putting his glass down and stepping away from the crazy lady,' Hayley chuckled as she sipped her juice.

'You're not the craziest person I've ever met. You haven't met my family yet.'

'They sound like my kind of people.'

'They aren't anyone's kind of people,' he warned her dryly.

'I'm sure they can't be that bad.'

'Nah, they're not. They're a good bunch, most of the time. What about your family? Where are they?'

'Mum and Dad divorced when I was in my teens, and Dad's remarried and lives overseas. Mum passed away a little over ten years ago.'

'I'm sorry to hear that. Do you have any other family nearby?'

'I have a few aunties and cousins floating about, but we're not close.'

'Isn't that kinda lonely? I don't think I've ever been without family somewhere nearby.'

She'd never had a big happy family living on top of each other, it had only ever really been her and her mum. There wasn't a day that went by that she didn't think about her and wish she were still here. That kind of gap could never be filled. 'I don't think you necessarily have to be by yourself to feel alone. You can be surrounded by a whole city full of people and still feel lonely.'

He seemed to consider her answer carefully before slowly nodding. 'That's true, I guess. Is that why you moved out here? Because you were too lonely where you were?'

'I guess. Partly. It could also have been some kind of reaction to turning the big three-o as well.'

'Ahh, I see.'

'What?'

'I had a mate whose sister went through something similar when she turned thirty a couple of years ago.'

'She moved?'

'No, she took up belly dancing and travelled to India in search of her inner self or something,' he told her. 'Turning thirty somehow made her realise she hadn't done everything she'd thought she'd do in her twenties.'

'It does kind of sneak up on you.'

'I didn't really give it much thought, to tell you the truth.'

'Maybe it's different for men.'

'Maybe. Although I have to say, Mum's hints about settling down and producing grandchildren have increased noticeably in the last two years.'

Hayley gave a small smile. At least she and Paul hadn't had any children to drag through a divorce. 'I'm hearin' ya,' she murmured. That was one thing she wouldn't miss—the annual Christmas dinner with Paul's family and everyone asking when they were going to start a family. They'd be pleased now. The text she'd received from Paul and Lisa, on her birthday no less, letting her know that they were expecting a baby, had been the icing on the sad cupcake she'd bought to celebrate her thirtieth birthday, all by herself. They'd wanted her to hear it from them first. Which she supposed was them trying to be considerate of her feelings. If only they'd considered her feelings before sleeping together, maybe she'd have appreciated it a little more.

Hayley glanced up and realised Luke was watching her curiously. 'My ex-husband's family were big on wanting grandchildren too,' she shrugged.

'Ah, I see,' Luke nodded knowingly.

'Yes, now you know my deep dark secret,' she said drolly. 'I'm a jaded divorcee.'

'I wouldn't have necessarily picked you as jaded,' he said, looking at her thoughtfully.

'Give it time,' she said dryly.

'It wasn't an amicable split, I take it?'

Hayley sipped her juice. 'It was amicable enough, I suppose. Guilt apparently inspires generosity.'

'Ah, I see.'

Hayley wasn't sure exactly what he saw, and she didn't push him to explain.

'I can understand why you'd want to start somewhere new after a divorce,' he said quietly. 'It's hard to move on when everything around you is connected to your old life.'

'You sound as though you're speaking from experience.'

'I was in a pretty serious relationship with someone until about a year ago too. Till she decided she didn't want to be a farmer's wife. But I couldn't move away to start over. It was hard at first with everyone watching to make sure I wasn't falling apart.'

'I'm sorry. It obviously hurt a lot.'

Luke gave an offhand shrug, but Hayley suspected he wasn't one to reveal his feelings easily.

'That's life, hey? Anyway, I'd better get going. I have to help out in the bar tonight.'

'You work at a bar?'

'At our place. We have a microbrewery and restaurant. It's a bit of a new venture for us. My brother and sister-in-law run it, using pretty much everything we grow ourselves, from the meat and produce for the restaurant to the hops and barley for the brewery.'

'Wow.'

'Yeah, we're pretty excited about it. It's only been open for a few months, but it seems to be going great guns.'

'I'll have to come and check it out one day.'

'Yeah, you should do that. Let me know when you want to and I'll make sure we reserve the best seat in the house,' he said with an easy smile.

'I'll hold you to that.'

Hayley watched as the ute drove away and there was nothing left but the settling dust along the driveway. She turned and headed back inside. Maybe Errol getting stuck in the dam hadn't been a complete disaster after all.

Luke Mason drove home on automatic pilot. His mind was still with the new neighbour he'd just rescued. Well, not that he'd rescued *her*, exactly, mainly her donkey. He gave a soft chuckle at the afternoon's encounter. Hayley Stevens was the last thing he'd expected to find when he'd gone to investigate the strange noise he'd heard when he'd turned off the tractor engine.

He got a tiny flutter of something, a cross between excitement and interest, when he thought of her. Covered in mud, and clearly annoyed, she wasn't anything like the woman he'd been expecting. For some reason he'd assumed a woman buying a property, with no sign of a husband, would be much older, a grey-haired countrywoman perhaps. He certainly hadn't been expecting an extremely attractive woman from the city, his own age and a writer too.

In a small place like Lochway there wasn't exactly a huge pool of eligible singles. It wasn't the kind of place kids hung around in after high school. Farming was the only real industry and there were fewer farms—and farmers, for that matter—every year. His mother's wedding reception centre brought new women to town, but only briefly. Bridesmaids were an entertaining option if he needed a fix of feminine company, but relationship-wise there was very little in the way of options out here. Not that he was looking for a relationship. God, just talking about Lucinda earlier had brought back a healthy dose of 'no way, no how'. He was not a glutton for punishment. No, his next serious relationship was going to have to be pretty damn impressive to make him even think about going through all that again.

He parked the car and went back to work, his mind still on the woman with dark curly hair and big blue eyes.

Five

Hayley groaned as she woke to the now familiar squabbling of parrots outside her bedroom window. 'You have got to be kidding me.' Each morning they seemed to increase in number and the volume of their constant screeching was rising to the ridiculous.

'Shoo,' she yelled through the window, but other than a few nearby fluttering off their branch, they all continued fighting amongst one another. With a frustrated groan, Hayley closed the window and pulled the curtains across. She knew she wouldn't go back to sleep with that racket going on, so she got up and made coffee.

By now Errol was making it clear he was awake too. She tried to be annoyed by his insistent heehawing, but he really did have the most gorgeous face. His big fluffy ears just killed her. The only time he didn't bray was when she was with him or he was eating, and she'd noticed that he'd started getting destructive, chewing at his stall and the posts.

As soon as he spotted her his braying increased. She approached the stall he was in and he reached out to rub his head against her. 'Yes, I know, you missed me and you're hungry,' Hayley said, giving his big head a scratch and feeling her heart melt as large black eyes gazed up at her longingly. She broke off some hay and fed it to him, leaning against the rail and watching him devour his meal, enjoying the quiet that suddenly descended.

Only to be broken by the ringing of her phone. Damn. She'd leave it inside next time. Hayley gave a small groan as she noticed her agent's name on the screen.

'Hales, how are you? Are you still alive? How is it out there?'

'Hi, Soph. Yes, I'm still alive. They actually have electricity out here nowadays. It's all quite civilised, really.'

'I'm sure it is. I still think you're mad to give up living in the city, with everything you could possibly want at your fingertips, for a place that doesn't even have a David Jones.' Sophia sounded horrified by the idea.

'You'd be surprised at how well a person can survive in the wilderness,' Hayley said sarcastically.

'Yes, well . . . Just wanted to touch base and see how you're progressing with the manuscript.'

Hayley's good mood slipped a notch at the mention of her work in progress. Well, progress was being a tad too generous; she hadn't actually started on it yet and it was due in less than five months. 'Fine. Everything's going fine.'

'Why am I getting the feeling that everything is *not* fine?'

Hayley swore under her breath. Damn the woman and her perceptiveness. 'Maybe it's the connection . . . we're lucky to even have reception out here in the boondocks.'

'Hayley, if you need more time, I'm sure we can arrange an extension. When you're ready just send me through a few chapters and I can give you feedback.'

That was a great plan . . . if only she *had* a few chapters to send. 'Sounds great. Listen, I have to go, but I promise you'll receive some pages soon.'

'Hayley—'

'Talk soon, bye,' she said, disconnecting the call. She let out a long, slow breath. Now that she was here, she'd be able to concentrate. The peace and tranquillity was exactly what she needed to coax out a new novel. She wasn't going to panic yet.

Trust Sophia to pick up on her anxiety. Over the last few years her agent had become as close to a real friend as Hayley had. Their relationship was a business one first and foremost, but Sophia had been very supportive during the whole Paul and Lisa fiasco, and the two women had become close because of the experience.

Friendships had never come easily to Hayley. At school she'd been a loner, preferring to spend her time reading. She'd been a complete book nerd and as a result had often found herself the butt of jokes and snide remarks. It baffled Hayley that for such a quiet unassuming person, she'd seemed to ruffle the feathers of a lot of people.

Hayley's attention was brought back to the present by a gentle nudge to her elbow. 'You're all finished with breakfast, are you, little man?' She rubbed his grey face between her hands and smooched his white muzzle. 'You're just a big softy, aren't you,' she said, smiling as the donkey closed his eyes in seeming bliss. He just loved attention. *All the time.*

'I wish I could stay out here with you all day, but I'm never going to get this book written if I do.'

The racket started up as soon as she walked away and Hayley knew she had to find a solution and soon.

The lorikeets seemed to have landed en masse this morning and were straight into a hysterical fight over rights to the best of the bottlebrush nectar. Last night she'd googled how to deter birds and was now armed with an arsenal of ideas for moving on noisy feathered visitors. First thing this morning she was heading into town to buy a stuffed toy cat.

It was somewhat of a novelty to leave the house. There was no such thing as a quick drive to a shopping centre when heading anywhere other than Lochway involved a river crossing on a ferry, and depending on where she had to go, not one but *two* ferries. She was going to have to factor in waiting time, she decided as she sat in her car after having only just missing the ferry on her way into Windsor for a big grocery shop.

The sun lulled her into a sleepy kind of relaxation as it streamed in through her window. The earlier rush hour of commuters and schoolkids would most likely be hectic, but at this time of the day no one seemed in much of a hurry.

She studied the steep rock face that shaded the other side of the river. Convicts had built the roads and bridges that had made access to this part of the country possible. It was mind-boggling that men without the aid of power tools or heavy machinery had been able to cut their way through rock, carving roads and stones for building houses with what today we would consider such primitive tools.

The whole area was awash with so much history. It was one thing to live in Sydney and know that it was the first part of the country to have been settled, making it older than this region, but still, it wasn't something Hayley ever truly stopped to think about in her day-to-day life. For some reason though, here, it surrounded you. Maybe it was because it wasn't a city, and it had stayed pretty much intact and kept its quaint, rural personality. The area *was* named the Forgotten Valley after all, and even though it may have disappointed the earlier settlers when it hadn't grown into a bustling region, as they'd hoped, in those first early days, the lack of development and destruction of the natural beauty was now, over two hundred years later, its biggest strength.

Hayley glanced in the rear-view mirror and noticed two other cars had pulled in behind her. The driver of the vehicle furthest back stepped out and Hayley peered a little closer as a hat and checked shirt filled her mirror.

'Hi. Thought that was you up here,' a deep voice announced as she wound down the window to greet Luke.

'I guess there aren't too many red coupés around here, are there?' Hayley said as he hunkered down so he was on eye level with her.

'It does tend to stand out,' he agreed. 'Where you headed?'

'I'm going down to Windsor. I need some groceries and I thought I might have a bit of a look around. What about you?'

'I've got to drop off some papers in Wisemans Ferry, but I'm heading down to Windsor after that. Do you have time for a coffee later?'

His invitation caught her off guard, but she found herself excited by the prospect, slightly more than was warranted for a neighbourly meeting. 'Sure. I don't have to be anywhere in particular.'

'Great,' he said, pulling out his phone. They swapped numbers and Luke gave the top of her door a quick tap in farewell. 'I'll give you a call when I'm done.'

Hayley glanced across and was surprised to see the ferry getting ready to dock and unload its passengers. 'Okay, sure. That would be great.' She started the car and waited until the attendant waved her forward, nervously inching onto the ferry. One day maybe she'd be doing this like it was second nature, but for now she was terrified of driving the stupid car off the other end and into the water.

Windsor wasn't a huge town by any stretch of the imagination, but it did have the basics plus a bit more, and even though she'd only been in Lochway for a few weeks, the prospect of shops was kind of exciting.

The department store was her first stop. She had a list of items she needed for Operation Bird Evacuation, and she headed straight for the toy department.

Her basket was filling at an alarming rate as she strolled through the store remembering that there was nowhere to nip down to should she forget something. Two ferry rides and a long drive were not really going to be feasible when you realised you needed *one* thing. She'd have to start making lists.

At the supermarket she felt as though she was preparing for a zombie invasion, stocking up on essentials like toilet paper and long-life milk. Maybe she had been watching too many doomsday prepper shows but was there any harm in making sure you had a good supply of the basics? She thought not. She might be living somewhat remotely now but there was no way she was going to run out of toilet paper.

After placing her purchases in the car, she heard her phone announce a message and dug it out of her handbag, trying to calm the little leap her heart gave when she saw Luke's name on the screen.

A wave of butterflies fluttered in her stomach. *Oh, for goodness sake! He's just your next-door neighbour. Pull yourself together.*

ꙮ

Luke caught himself fidgeting with the small bowl of packet sugars and swore softly. He felt like a damn teenager. *You're*

51

a grown-arse man, get it together, but here he was, sweating bullets and feeling as jumpy as a cat in a room full of rocking chairs.

As the door opened and she stepped inside, sliding her dark sunglasses up onto the top of her head, he felt his mouth go dry. She was beautiful, though not in the tall and willowy way Lucinda was. She had a natural beauty, a freshness that lit her eyes and gave her a glow.

He moved to stand up but she was already pulling out a chair. He found himself watching her and searching in vain for something intelligent to say, feeling like a fool. What the hell was wrong with him?

'Did you get everything done?' she asked, folding her arms across the table and leaning forward slightly.

'Yeah,' he said, clearing his throat. 'How about you?'

'I did, and then some,' she said with a small grimace. 'I think I overbought a little. I'm still getting used to the whole remoteness thing.'

He chuckled. 'We're not that remote.'

'Well, compared to living in the city with everything on your doorstep, trust me, it's remote.'

'Yeah, I guess. I remember when I used to bring friends home for a visit when I was away at high school, they were pretty horrified about not having any shops close by,' he conceded.

'What did you do for high school?'

'I boarded.'

'Ah, private school,' she said.

He cocked an eyebrow at her. 'What's that supposed to mean?'

'It explains why you have this, I don't know . . . cultured air about you.'

'Cultured?' he almost laughed at that. His brother and sister-in-law were forever giving him grief about his lack of appreciation of the arts. They were both big fans of art galleries and concerts, things he had no real interest in himself.

'Well, I don't know, you just don't seem like the born and raised on the farm kind of guy. Did you move straight back home after high school?'

'I went to ag college for a few years and did a business degree, but I was back and forwards to the farm during that time. It's where I've always wanted to be. My older brother, Grant, stayed in the city after uni. He and his wife only just moved back six months ago to start up the brewery and restaurant.'

A young waitress came over to take their order, momentarily interrupting the conversation.

'So you always wanted to be a farmer?' Hayley asked when she'd left.

'Yep. For as long as I can remember. It's been in the blood for generations. We can trace the property back to the first land grant issued in the area.'

'That must be really something, having your family own that one piece of land for so long. So much history.'

'It's pretty special,' he agreed. 'It hasn't all been smooth sailing—like everyone else on the land, we've had to diversify to keep it profitable and able to support us all. That's the problem with a lot of farming now: there's not enough profit to support the parents and the adult kids who want to go into the family business. Not like there once was.'

'I think it's fantastic how you've managed to work together as a family.'

'It took some planning and Dad wasn't a hundred per cent sold on the idea of diversifying at first.' Bit of an understatement, he thought silently. His father might have given up arguing about the new ventures, but he sure wasn't thrilled about it all.

'Why not?' He saw her glance up and smile at the waitress as she placed their coffee in front of them.

He couldn't believe it, his heart actually hitched . . . What the hell was that? When had he even started thinking of hearts hitching? He blinked and realised she was waiting for him to answer. 'Dad's pretty old-school. He deals in cattle and crops. Mum turning the place into a wedding reception centre and Grant and Olivia wanting to open the brewery was a big shift in his way of thinking.'

'But he's come around now?'

'To a certain degree. I think he was surprised at how it's taken off. Oh, that reminds me, Mum texted earlier, she wanted to know if you'd like to come over on Wednesday for afternoon tea.'

'Sure. That'd be lovely.'

They talked about her books, and, despite what she thought, he really was interested. Sure, he couldn't remember the last book he'd read for pleasure, but maybe it was time he started again. He'd loved reading once.

'I probably should get going, I've got groceries out in the car,' Hayley said when they'd finished their coffee.

He seriously couldn't remember the last time he'd felt so at ease with a woman. Not even with Lucinda.

'Yeah, I should too. I didn't realise it was that late.'

They both stood and walked towards the counter. When Hayley went to reach for her purse, he casually stepped in front of her and handed his credit card to the waitress. 'I asked you out,' he said when she protested.

'Thank you,' she said, and tucked a stray strand of hair behind her ear.

He followed the action and had to force himself to look away in order to stop staring. 'My pleasure.'

He tucked his wallet into his back pocket as he followed her outside to her car. 'Wow, you did do a big shop,' he said, eyeing the pile of plastic bags on the back seat.

'I figure I'll be busy hibernating once I get back into writing.'

'Hey, I'm not judging,' he grinned. 'You should see when my mum and sister-in-law go on a shopping spree.'

She turned the key in the ignition. 'Thanks again. I guess I'll see you around.'

He watched as she waved and pulled out, disappearing down the road. For the strangest moment he felt the urge to run after her, afraid he might never see her again. Luke gave a harsh grunt and forced himself to turn away. Maybe this was some weird side effect of going too long without sex—you suddenly became obsessed with a stranger.

He hadn't been entirely celibate since the break-up with Lucinda—there was that weekend in the Hunter Valley for a mate's bachelor party, and he had called on a few casual acquaintances in the city—but he hadn't been seeing anyone seriously, and no one at all in the last six months. He just didn't have the drive to go out and meet someone new. It hadn't helped that he'd been busy setting up the restaurant and brewery with Grant, but still, if he'd felt a need to find love, he could have found a way.

He frowned. What did love have to do with it? He wasn't ready to sink his entire life into a relationship again. Not now, maybe not ever. *Maybe you just haven't met someone you were really in love with yet,* a little voice reasoned. Hayley's smile flashed into his mind. There was something about her, he couldn't explain it—something about Hayley Stevens stirred emotions in him that he hadn't felt in a long time, if ever. It made him a little uncomfortable. As though her arrival in Lochway was going to shake everything up.

Six

Hayley stared out the window the next morning and gave a disheartened sigh. So much for the stuffed cat theory. Looked like she could cross that one off the list, she thought as she watched the birds jumping up and down on the soft toy's head and swinging off its tail. Either it looked too cute for the lorikeets to take seriously or these birds didn't realise they were supposed to be terrified of a cat. Admittedly, a stuffed cat really didn't pose that much of a threat, but there wasn't any ethical way to tie a real cat to the bush in order to scare away the birds.

Hopefully she'd have more success solving Errol's problem. It seemed from her research that the reason for his clingy, needy behaviour was that he was lonely. Donkeys apparently needed the company of other donkeys or animals.

Her quest to find Errol a friend, and in doing so find some peace and quiet for herself, led her to a small farm half an hour away which had listed a miniature donkey for sale on a community buy, swap and sell site.

Hayley pulled up at the farm and was greeted by a smiling woman in her mid-thirties.

'Have you ever owned a mini before?'

'No. I have a bigger one currently. I'm after a companion for him.'

'Well, these make great companions. We got ours as a baby for the kids, but they've outgrown their donkey love in favour of dirt bikes,' she said dryly, as the droning of a motorbike sounded somewhere further down behind the house.

Hayley heard the familiar sound of a braying donkey as it spotted them walking towards its pen.

'When the kids played with him all the time he never made a peep, but lately it's been getting worse, which is why we've decided to sell him. He's lonely and it breaks my heart to hear him crying out for some attention.'

The donkey wasn't as small as she'd imagined a miniature donkey to be, but he was smaller than Errol by probably half a metre. Hayley followed the woman into the pen and immediately the animal came up to them for a pat and a cuddle. Where Errol's back came to about chest height, this little guy was at hip level. His light grey fur was fluffy and he had two caramel-coloured splodges around his eyes and a white muzzle.

'What's his name?' Hayley asked, rubbing him behind his long ears.

'Flynn.'

Hayley's gaze snapped up. 'You're kidding.'

The woman looked across at her quizzically. 'No, that's what the kids named him. They were obsessed with the movie *Tangled* when we got him. Why?'

Hayley felt a smile creep across her face. Maybe there was something to this fate business after all. 'My donkey's name is Errol.'

The woman's eyes lit up and she laughed, 'Errol . . . Flynn.'

'I think that's a sign if ever I saw one,' said Hayley, looking back into the big dark eyes.

∽

It was too nice a day to write. She couldn't seem to settle; everything distracted her and her focus wasn't on the story. Hayley looked out the window and made a sudden decision. She was going to go exploring.

Thanks to Errol's escape she'd seen the paddocks surrounding the house, but she hadn't seen much of the rear of the property and she decided there was no better time than right now. She went into the spare room and searched the remaining boxes for the stash of bags she hadn't gotten around to unpacking; right at the bottom of the last box she found her old canvas daypack. She pulled on the closest thing she had to acceptable footwear—a pair of joggers—and headed back to the kitchen to grab a bottle of water, some fruit and a muesli bar.

Outside, she was struck by the absence of heehawing. Flynn's arrival had been a huge success. Hayley had been a little concerned the two donkeys wouldn't get along, but she needn't have worried, they'd become inseparable. They made a funny sight, the long and the short of it, but Errol hadn't made a peep since Flynn's arrival. The next job was to make a bigger enclosure so they could have more room to graze and wander.

She closed the first gate behind her and took a deep breath, filling her lungs with the heady scent of warm sunshine. The grass was growing rather long and she was wary of snakes. Clearly the land hadn't been used for some time; no livestock had been grazing here to keep the grass under control. She climbed up a short incline, her puffing making it embarrassingly obvious her fitness levels needed improving. At the top she had a rest, bending slightly and placing her hands on her thighs to catch her breath.

The little knoll looked over a flat open paddock. The walk down the other side was a little easier than going up had been. An old tree, or rather the remains of an old tree, lay rotting away where it had fallen who knew how many years ago. Hayley ran her hand across the sun-bleached timber, her fingertips tingling at the smooth weatherworn trunk as she imagined the stories this old tree could have told.

A cloud moved across the sun and a small shiver ran down Hayley's back. Everything slowed down. Sounds became muted, as though coming from a great distance.

What was happening? Maybe it was heatstroke. She should have told someone where she was going . . .

Her scalp felt prickly, and tiny black spots appeared before her eyes. She blinked but couldn't clear her vision; an image seemed to detach itself from the hazy heat vapour across the paddock. It was a man on horseback, cantering towards her.

Out of the corner of her eye she caught movement and turned slightly to see a woman in a long dress running towards the rider. Hayley watched as she stumbled and fell to the ground, but immediately picked herself up again and continued running, her long dress bunched up in one small hand as she sobbed. Her hair was loose, falling down past her shoulders in a dark blonde curtain.

The man pulled up his horse and slid from its back, scooping the frantic woman into his arms and holding her tightly. The look on his face was utter anguish mixed with such love that Hayley felt her own heart ache in response. Who were these people? She saw the man ease back and cup the woman's tear-streaked face in his big hands and say something. Hayley frowned: why couldn't she hear? They were standing no more than a few metres away from her and she could see their lips moving, yet she couldn't hear a thing.

This couldn't be real. She had to be having some kind of weird lucid dream. Maybe she'd fallen and hit her head . . .

The couple seemed to be having a troubled discussion. The woman was crying as she clutched at the man's black coat, then suddenly they both turned around. For a moment

Hayley's heart stopped. They were looking in her direction, but not *at her*. She slowly turned her head and followed their gaze. At first she couldn't see anything, but then she caught sight of something mounting the crest of the hill. More men on horseback. They were dressed oddly, in old-fashioned clothing like some kind of historical re-enactment group.

Part of Hayley knew it was unreal, absurd, yet she couldn't look away. She couldn't move. Her legs felt heavy.

The men brought their horses to a halt a short distance away. Hayley turned to look at the couple near the tree and saw the terror plastered across their young faces. She didn't know who these people were or what was going on, but the fear was tangible, hanging heavily in the air around her.

She wanted to reach out and do something, but at the same time she knew she couldn't. Suddenly the young woman turned and ran. Hayley saw the man shout and spin around to face the advancing horsemen just as one of the men raised his rifle and a puff of smoke exploded from it. The scene unfolded around her in terrible detail. The shot hit the young man squarely in the chest as he threw himself between the woman and the other men, but as he fell, the young woman lurched forward, a large red stain spreading across her back.

Hayley could only stare helplessly. She tried to move but her legs were too heavy, then everything went blurry once again and she blinked to find herself alone in the paddock, beside the fallen tree that had been standing only moments before.

Hayley clutched at her chest. It felt just like the time she fell from a tree in the backyard when she was small. She was gasping for air but couldn't breathe. Fear clawed at her, until in one huge rush her lungs suddenly remembered how to work again. What the hell had just happened? She wasn't asleep—she was still standing for goodness sake! She could smell the warm, earthy scent of the grass and feel pasture under her feet. The sound of insects going about their business buzzed all around her. In the distance she could even hear a cow calling out . . . but nowhere could she hear the hoof beats of retreating horsemen or see the bodies of the two young lovers on the ground where they'd fallen.

Hayley sunk onto the fallen trunk and took her water bottle from her pack. *You're losing your mind, Stevens.* It had to be heatstroke . . . or even *a* stroke. She couldn't rule anything out right now. That had been disturbingly real and she had no logical explanation for it, though there clearly had to be one.

Hayley took a long swig of water and wiped the back of her hand across her mouth as she considered the old tree she now sat on. The bark had long since fallen off and it was in a bad state of decomposition at one end but, in its day, it must have been huge if the thickness of the trunk in the middle was anything to go by. *Like the tree the two lovers had been shot under* . . . Goosebumps prickled along her arms. The tree before her had long since lost all its leaves and most of its structure, but the fork in the trunk remained. It was the same tree from her vision . . . or whatever the hell that had been.

You're a writer, she reminded herself irritably. It was probably her imagination trying to give her a story to write. But she'd never experienced anything like that before. It was as though she'd been there, had witnessed something truly horrific. It had felt so . . . real.

A hot bath and a glass of wine was what she needed, she decided. As she reached the top of the small rise, she examined the ground carefully. There was no sign of anyone having been up here, and certainly no churned-up ground from excited horses. She gave a small snort and set off down the other side. Just because she couldn't come up with a sensible explanation for what had just happened didn't mean there wasn't one. For the life of her, though, she didn't know what it could be.

Seven

Luke saw his father striding towards him as he turned off the grader. He bit back a groan. *What now?*

'Didn't I tell you to take a look at the boundary fence today?' his father demanded in lieu of a greeting. 'Why are you wastin' time in the grader?'

'Because Mum's been worried about the road in getting too rough. It's not going to be good for business if the guests are drivin' over corrugated dirt in their Mercs and Audis, is it?'

'The guests,' his father said scathingly, 'will have something more than corrugated roads to complain about if they hit a bloody cow because the boundary fence wasn't fixed. Priorities. You heard of the word?'

Luke clenched his jaw to stop the retort from escaping. He knew from experience that reacting to his dad would only end up in a big argument.

'Did you drive the water run like I asked?'

'I don't need to. I spent two days putting in those tank monitors so we can check on the water levels from the computer.'

'Doesn't show you the cattle though, does it?'

'No, but—'

'Technology won't ever replace experience. Or a pair of eyes. Driving out there and checking the cattle at the same time is killin' two birds with one stone. Knowin' how much water's in the tank doesn't mean jack if there's sick or injured cattle layin' around.'

'Dad, I'm trying to make things easier. You're always sayin' there's not enough hours in the day—well, I'm trying to help cut down some of the workload. If you don't have to drive out and check water every day then you have more time to do something else.'

'And I'm tellin' you that depending on technology to make things easier is askin' for trouble. Nothing replaces a set of boots on the ground.'

'Fine. Whatever. I'll drive out there now and check the bloody water levels *and* the cattle,' Luke snapped, climbing down from the big machine.

'I warned you that takin' on this restaurant business was going to cause trouble. You were the one who said it wouldn't interfere with the running of the place,' his father pointed out.

'And it's not.'

'Well, all these damn shortcuts you're tryin' to put in place isn't what we agreed to.'

'Dad, these shortcuts are called technology and that's the way modern farming is going. I'm just trying to keep us up to speed.'

'Seems to me you're tryin' to spread yourself too thin.'

'It's under control,' Luke bit out.

'It better be,' he said, turning away.

It was true his old man had always been stubborn, but lately he'd gotten worse. Nothing was ever right, and no matter how hard Luke tried to innovate and find better ways to do things, his father would always find a reason why his ideas wouldn't work. When Grant and Olivia had suggested the three of them set up a sustainable restaurant and brewery on the property, Luke had instantly jumped on board. This was something he could do his way—without his father breathing down his neck all day. Of course, there was still the work on Lochmanning to do, but having the sideline of the restaurant and brewery business had saved his sanity.

The trade-off, though, was that the more successful the sideline businesses became, the more inflexible his father seemed to become. There were days when his dad pushed him beyond his limits and it took every ounce of his strength to walk away without starting a fight. He knew his mother worried about their strained relationship, and rightly so. Luke wasn't sure how much longer he could keep working with his old man.

He slammed the car door and headed towards the back paddocks, leaving behind another good three hours of work he wouldn't get finished until late tonight.

∽

Hayley woke up breathing heavily and slightly disoriented. She glanced across at her bedside table: 3.20 am. With a groan, she rubbed her face and threw back her covers, getting up for a drink of water from the kitchen. She hardly ever dreamed, or at least she didn't remember her dreams, but tonight she had. She took a glass from the cabinet and filled it with water, looking out through the window at the surprisingly bright moon.

She'd been dreaming of running through long grass, looking back over her shoulder at a man. She wasn't frightened, she was laughing. She'd caught a glimpse of the man but hadn't been able to make out his features—just a flash of colour, dark hair, a white shirt and a smile. There was something about that smile. Something familiar that made her feel a little giddy. It had been sunny and warm and she'd felt happy. Then the sun had disappeared behind dark clouds and a cold wind had whipped at her hair and clothes. She'd been reaching towards something—desperately trying to hold on to whatever it was as it slipped out of her reach. Then she'd heard a deep voice call in a long, anguished cry, 'Jane!' And that's when she'd woken up, her heart racing.

In the moonlight, looking out over the tranquil garden, Hayley couldn't work out what had frightened her so much about the dream. It was silly, but she was half afraid to go back to sleep again.

∽

Later that morning Hayley reached into the pantry and caught a blur of movement from the corner of her eye. Cautiously she moved a few boxes, giving a yelp as she heard a scurrying noise. She slammed the door shut with a shudder. She couldn't stand mice. Sure, they were cute in pet-shop windows, wiping their little faces with their paws, but there was nothing cute about them racing around inside her pantry, eating holes through boxes of food and leaving their disgusting droppings everywhere. She normally went with a live and let live approach, but not when it came to rodents in her house. Nope. This meant war.

Inside the feed store Hayley paced the aisles while she waited for Ernie to finish gas-bagging with a farmer at the counter—despite the fact she had a mouse emergency to deal with. While part of her was a little envious that Ernie was having an honest-to-God conversation with someone when she was flat out getting more than one-word sentences out of the man, the fact still remained there was a community of mice currently alone in her house probably eating their way through her entire food store.

Eventually Ernie waved his mate off and turned his attention to Hayley with a notable lack of interest.

'I'm wondering what you have to get rid of mice.'

She wasn't sure how to interpret his grunt of a reply, but decided to translate it into, 'Certainly, madam, please follow me this way.'

'You got two options. Poison or live traps.'

Hayley felt herself flinch. Poison sounded so . . . painful, and she couldn't even think about live trapping without shuddering. 'Just out of curiosity, would there be a third option?'

'Get a cat.'

Now there was a possibility. 'Don't suppose you happen to stock cats?' she asked wryly, and was surprised when he turned and took a piece of paper from the front counter and handed it to her. *Free to good home. Female cat. Desexed. Good mouser.*

'No way,' she said, looking up at him suspiciously.

'Thelma Goodwin dropped it in this morning.'

'How do I find Thelma Goodwin?'

'Last house on your way out of town.'

It was too good to be true, but she ignored the little voice pointing out that if something was too good to be true then it usually was and headed to the old house at the end of the main street.

The house was timber and if it had ever been painted it had been a very long time ago. The front verandah was sagging, but there was still a certain kind of charm about the antique-looking building. Hayley picked her way across the uneven floorboards of the verandah to knock on the door and heard the shuffle of footsteps approaching.

'Hello, would you be Thelma?' Hayley asked, smiling at the red-haired woman who opened the door.

'Who wants to know?' The woman narrowed her eyes and looked Hayley up and down.

'Ernie from the feed store told me you had a cat to give away.'

'You that city woman who's moved in up the road?'

'Ah, yes. That would be me. Hayley,' she said, extending her hand. The woman eyed her warily, making no move to accept her handshake. Hayley cleared her throat and put her hand in her pocket. 'So, have you still got the cat?'

'Yeah. You want her?'

'Yes, I do. I've got a mouse problem and she sounds like just the cat for the job.'

The woman sent her another strange look and Hayley held back a frustrated sigh. Did no one in this place have a sense of humour?

'Wait here. I'll get her.'

'All right then . . .' Hayley said under her breath as the woman went back inside and shut the door. There was a series of scuffling noises, followed by a high-pitched miaow and some muttered cursing, before the front door reopened and Thelma reappeared with a cardboard box under her arm, red-faced and breathing heavily.

'Here. I wouldn't open it till you get home. She's a bit feisty at the moment.'

Hayley opened her mouth to speak but the door shut in her face, leaving her to juggle a moving box containing one very annoyed cat.

'All right, just settle down,' she said to the box as she gingerly carried it to her car. She eyed the back seat but had visions of the unhappy feline escaping the box and landing on her head as she drove. 'Sorry, puss,' she murmured as she placed the now softly growling animal in the boot and closed it securely. Why did she have the feeling she'd become the perfect fall guy for these people to offload their problem animals onto?

The box was a lot quieter when she arrived home and carefully opened the boot, half expecting the cat to have escaped and to disappear in a blur of fur, never to be seen again. Much to her relief, she discovered the box still secure. She placed it on the kitchen floor and took a deep breath as she slowly opened the lid. When nothing came leaping out, Hayley risked a look inside, seeing a small, rather skinny bundle of ginger, black and white fur cowering in the corner of the box. Her heart melted. 'Hey there. It's okay. Don't be scared,' she said gently. Her first instinct was to give the cat a bowl of milk, but she decided to err on the side of caution and start with water. Knowing her luck, the cat was probably lactose intolerant and she'd end up giving it diarrhoea or, worse, killing her before she'd even had her a day.

She filled a plastic container with some water then searched for something to give the cat to eat. She had some leftover chicken in the fridge and she cut up a small piece and placed the offering next to the box. She ached to pick up the small frightened animal and comfort her, but something told her that wouldn't be wise. This was a cat that hadn't had much human contact judging by the terrified way she eyed her. 'Okay, puss, I'm just going to leave you in here to get used to the place while I go and find you something better to eat.' She closed the kitchen door and prayed her new charge wouldn't do too much damage while she headed back into town.

Surprisingly, the convenience store had a rather impressive stock of cat food and accessories and Hayley was glad she didn't have to make a trip into Windsor to find the basics.

'You didn't mention you had a cat,' said the stern-faced shopkeeper as Hayley placed a bag of cat food on the counter.

'I only just got her today, actually.'

'Oh yeah? What kind is she?'

'Umm, I'm not exactly sure,' Hayley admitted, digging in her handbag for her wallet. 'I'm not really a cat person.'

'Oh. I see,' the woman said, not even bothering to hide her disapproval. Hayley noticed a cat saunter through the door behind the counter, then looked around and spotted another cat snoozing in the window and a third sitting in the morning sun out on the street.

'I see you like cats. How many do you have?' Hayley asked.

'Seven.'

'Seven?' She hadn't meant to sound so incredulous.

'They're better company than most people,' the woman said somewhat stiffly.

'Well, maybe you could give me some tips on what else I'll need for mine?' Hayley said, holding out an olive branch to the prickly woman.

'Depends how old she is.'

'Umm, I'm not sure . . . She doesn't look like a kitten, but she doesn't look very old either.'

'Well, the food you got is a pretty good brand, it's what I feed my younger ones after the kitten stage. And you'll be wanting kitty litter. I don't s'pose you have a tray?'

'Um, no.'

'You best follow me then,' she said in a resigned tone.

'I'm Hayley, by the way. I don't think we've introduced ourselves,' she offered, meekly tagging behind the woman.

'Bernadette,' she threw over her shoulder before proceeding to hand across an assortment of equipment and bags for Hayley to take.

Hayley was beginning to regret asking for help as the pile steadily increased, but at least she'd managed to if not break the ice then at least make a decent chip in it. She was determined to win over at least one local, even if it did end up costing her a small fortune in cat supplies.

Hayley lugged her purchases into the house and timidly peeked inside the kitchen door, breathing a sigh of relief when she saw that nothing seemed to have been destroyed. As she stepped into the room, though, she gasped as a blur of colour ran past her, brushing her leg and vanishing down the hallway.

'Okay, you go and explore the rest of the house while I set up your food,' she called after the cat, feeling slightly disheartened.

With everything in place, Hayley tried calling the animal to see if she would eat the food she'd put out, noting she hadn't touched the chicken she'd placed on the floor earlier.

'Puss, puss, puss, come on, dinner's ready,' she called, tapping the side of the tin and waiting, but there was no sign of the cat.

She walked around the house, calling out, but she couldn't find her anywhere. 'Okay, this isn't funny, cat. Where are you?' She searched under beds, looked behind furniture, even opened cupboards, as though somehow the animal had magically grown arms and could open the doors in the first place.

'Where the hell did you go?' she muttered, turning in a slow circle in the lounge room. A slight movement caught her eye and she looked up, blinking in surprise when she spotted the missing feline balanced on the top of the open door, watching her with an unnerving stare.

'How are you even up there?' she asked quietly.

The cat remained on her impossibly narrow perch, on guard against any movement from Hayley. 'Okay, if you're happy up there, I'll leave you alone. Food's waiting in the kitchen,' she added as she left the room quietly.

This was perfect: she now had a cat who thought she was a bird and liked to hang out on top of open doors. Fat lot of good she was going to be up there when the mice were in her kitchen!

Eight

Hayley was dithering over what to wear. She told herself it had nothing to do with wanting to look nice for anyone in particular, definitely not Luke. She was just trying to make a good impression on her new neighbours. But what was appropriate dress for afternoon tea?

She finally settled on a long skirt, tan ankle boots and a flowy blouse. She pulled her hair back into a low ponytail, securing it with a clip, and checked her makeup. She didn't want to wear too much and have them think she was trying too hard, then again, she didn't want to wear too little and look like she hadn't made an effort. This was why it was easier to remain a hermit.

She turned in through the impressive front gates worthy of any Hollywood home in LA, all wrought-iron curves topped with a Lochmanning Estate sign. She followed the sweeping hedge-lined driveway and pulled up outside the main house, feeling gobsmacked at the grandeur of the place. The two-storey building reminded Hayley of an old English manor, complete with circular driveway and impeccable gardens. It had apparently been built by the original landowner who'd made his fortune supplying the early settlements with meat and crops, grown with convict labour. She'd googled the property and done her homework.

Hayley could see why the place had become a tourist fixture. She'd learned it was extremely popular for weddings, catering for receptions in a rather grandly renovated shearing shed.

As she opened her car door, Luke was walking towards her along a gravel pathway that seemed to lead from the back of the house. 'That was good timing,' he said, coming over to her.

'I hope I'm not late.'

'Nope, right on time. Come on in.'

She followed him to the huge front door and walked into the house. The inside was just as impressive as the outside. The foyer was big enough to hold a large round table, and behind it a curved timber staircase swept up to the second storey. On the walls hung large portraits of what Hayley assumed were Mason ancestors staring down long noses with stern expressions. She would have liked to have spent longer looking around, but Luke was leading her through a set of French doors into a sun-filled room where several people were gathered.

'Hayley! It's so good to finally meet you!' said an older woman, crossing the room to greet her with a warm smile.

'This is my mother, Delma,' Luke introduced.

'Hello, Mrs Mason, it's lovely to meet you too.'

'Call me Del,' she said, waving away the formalities briskly. 'There's too many of us here by that name anyway,' she grinned, taking Hayley's arm. 'This is my mother-in-law, Pearl,' she said, introducing her to a small-framed elderly woman.

Pearl Mason sat on a high-back chair like a queen surrounded by her family, and while her body had a frailty to it, her eyes were bright as they held Hayley's. 'I knew you'd come back.'

Back? Hayley's smile slipped a little in confusion. Had she met this woman before? At the St Albans writers' festival maybe? She was sure she would have remembered if she had. 'Hello, Mrs Mason,' she said, recovering quickly.

'Hello, dear,' she said, grasping Hayley's hand with a firmness she hadn't been expecting from such a fragile person. The old woman's skin was thin, showing the blue veins beneath the surface, and cool to the touch, making Hayley want to grasp them between her own and rub them warm. 'Call me Pearl.'

'And this is my husband, Patrick,' Del said, gesturing towards a stouter, older version of Luke who stood up and extended his meaty hand.

'Pleased to meet you, Hayley. I hear you've inherited old Errol. You must be a bit of a glutton for punishment.'

'I guess I walked right into that one, didn't I?' she said with a small wince.

'Bloody Alfie Provost, he's a damn menace.'

'I've kind of grown attached to him. Errol, not Alfie, that is,' she hastened to add. 'And now he has a friend he doesn't make so much noise.'

'A friend? What, you got another one?' Patrick asked, surprised.

'Well, he was lonely,' she started to explain. 'Maybe if Alfie Provost had bought him a companion, he wouldn't have had so much trouble with him.'

Patrick gave a noncommittal grunt and Hayley wasn't sure if he was impressed by her solution or thinking she was proving to be a typical Pitt Street farmer after all.

'So, how are you settling in over there, Hayley?' Del asked, handing her a cup as she took a seat and pouring in tea.

'Really well. I've still got a bit of unpacking to do, but I think I'm just about there.'

'It's such a beautiful place. The gardens are wonderful.'

'They are. It was one of the things that drew me to the place. Although they aren't as spectacular as yours.'

'I can't take credit for that, I'm afraid,' Del said. 'Some of the gardens here date back to the late 1800s.'

'Lochmanning used to host the most elegant garden parties,' Pearl added wistfully. 'That's where I met my Harry,' she added with a soft smile.

Hayley saw Del reach over and gently squeeze the old lady's hand. 'Of course, it's been a long time since we hosted any garden parties. They went out of fashion. But we do have wedding receptions now, and they're just as lovely.'

'It's a beautiful location for weddings,' Hayley said.

'That's Delma's brainchild,' Pearl said proudly, smiling over at her daughter-in-law.

'It seemed a shame not to make use of the gardens,' Del said. "I always loved listening to Pearl's stories about Lochmanning in its heyday and thought we should try to bring back some of that grandeur.'

'And now we're open year-round to every flamin' tourist in the district,' Patrick muttered, but the look he sent his wife held a touch of tolerant resignation.

'Don't listen to him, Hayley. He likes everyone to think he hates the tourism turn, but he's usually the first one out there talking to anyone who'll listen about his family legacy. If we didn't have the tourists, who would you talk to about the place?' Del asked with a chuckle. 'We have lots of historical groups coming out for daytrips. They walk through the gardens and take a look through the museum. It's very popular.'

'I didn't know there was a museum.'

'Oh yes, that was my idea,' Pearl piped up proudly. 'We had all sorts of bits and pieces in the attic that the family had been storing for generations, not to mention the amount of old machinery we had scattered around the place. I said to Harry, "We need to do something with all this history. It's too valuable to keep hidden away up here gathering dust." Eventually I must have worn him down, because we turned the old carriage house out the back into a museum of Lochmanning and local history.'

'I'd love to see it sometime,' Hayley said. She was a sucker for history, and knowing the age of this place, she didn't doubt there'd be some fascinating things to look at.

'Luke can take you out there before you leave, can't you, Luke?' Pearl said, happily volunteering her grandson for the job.

'Oh, I don't mean today, I can do it another day.'

'Nonsense, you're here now, it makes perfect sense,' Pearl waved off her protest.

Luke just grinned and sent his gran a tolerant smile. 'It's fine, Hayley, I don't mind.'

'So, Hayley, you're a writer, I hear,' Del said, changing the subject.

'Yes, I am.'

'Well, our daughter-in-law, Olivia, has been raving about your books for quite some time, and she's very excited about meeting you. Unfortunately, she and Grant have had to go into the city for restaurant supplies, but I'm sure she'll be trying to catch up with you as soon as she can.'

They continued to chat and Hayley surprised herself by enjoying the company.

'I can't sit around all day gasbagging,' Patrick finally said, getting to his feet and leaning down to kiss his wife's cheek. 'Someone's gotta do some work. It was nice to meet you, Hayley, don't be a stranger. Don't forget I need that trailer unloaded this afternoon,' he said to his son in a gruff tone.

'Yeah, no worries,' Luke said, and Hayley wondered at the slight edge to his voice.

She decided it was a good opportunity to make her own move. 'I should get back as well.'

'Luke's got to show you around the museum, dear. Take her out the back way, Luke,' Pearl instructed from her seat.

Hayley thanked the two women and promised to return the invitation once she got herself settled.

'This place really is amazing. It must be so cool to live in a house this old,' she said as Luke led the way out towards the rear of the house.

'Yeah, I guess we are pretty lucky. It was a great place to play hide and seek.'

'I can imagine. How many rooms does it have?'

'There's seven bedrooms in total, six upstairs and one down here, plus a drawing room, kitchen, dining room and study, and then there's the attic and a cellar.'

She couldn't even imagine living in a house like this. They crossed a perfectly manicured lawn, went through a gate and walked across a clearing to another old building with huge barn doors.

Luke flicked on a light switch and the interior lit up to reveal a huge space housing three antique coaches of varying sizes and styles. Around the sides of the room were glass display cabinets. Some held mannequins dressed in various period clothing. There were elaborate ball gowns and maids' uniforms, and two child-size mannequins whose outfits were from 1880, according to the display.

'Everything here came from the attic Gran was talking about. It had been stored away in boxes and some of it hadn't seen light of day in almost two centuries.'

'This is—' Hayley gaped as her eyes roamed from one thing to another, '—amazing.' It was beyond amazing actually, but there were no words to adequately describe how much history was packed into this one huge room. There were open ledgers on display, showing the daily running of the sheep property in the estate's earliest years, as well as sketches and paintings depicting scenes of a thriving farming community. Other cases displayed old letters and original editions of books that had been sent to the colony from England. There was so much to look at, she didn't know where to start.

'There are museums all around the country that would kill to get their hands on this stuff,' Luke said, his arms folded as he leaned against the wall nearby, watching her.

'And to think someone had the presence of mind not to throw it away.'

'Yeah, although nowadays we call them hoarders,' he said with a crooked smile.

'I can't imagine what it must be like to have all this history around you. To walk into a museum and know that every single thing in it is part of *your* actual family history,' she said, shaking her head slowly. She watched him straighten and wander over to stand beside her, looking down at an old yellowed map of the property under glass.

'Mostly it's pretty cool, but sometimes it can be daunting. There's a lot to live up to, you know?'

She hadn't thought about that. It would be a lot of responsibility to take care of a place with past generations watching over you from every nook and cranny.

'I better not keep you any longer,' she said, remembering his father's warning about the jobs that still needed doing. 'Thank you for showing me all this. I'll have to come back again, there's just so much to see. I think I could happily wander about in here for an entire day and still not be done looking through everything.'

'Just yell out whenever you want to take another look,' he told her as they headed back outside.

'I had a lovely afternoon, thank you,' Hayley said as they neared her car.

'Glad you could come over. It was good to see you,' he said, and something about his intimate tone made her a little bit fluttery inside.

She found herself drawn into his blue-eyed gaze. And until now she'd never really thought stubble on a man particularly attractive—Paul had been the clean-cut, well-dressed type. Somehow on Luke it looked rugged and sexy. She itched to reach up and touch his jaw. His lips, manly but gentle looking, seemed to draw her closer. She could almost feel the touch of them against her skin.

'Luke!'

Hayley jumped and dropped her car keys as Patrick yelled from somewhere nearby. She bent to retrieve them but gave a howl of pain as her skull collided with something hard. Luke had bent down to pick up her keys at the same time, his forehead banging against the back of her head in a painful thud.

She heard his curse, which echoed her own, as they pulled apart, each rubbing their heads.

'Sorry,' she said, clutching the keys.

'My fault. I'd better go,' he said, backing away.

'I'll see you later.' She managed a smile but she could already feel a headache starting. Great, she probably had concussion, and Luke too. That was one way to ruin a perfectly fine moment. Smooth, Stevens, real smooth.

Nine

It had been a week since the cat's arrival and so far Hayley had only ever caught glimpses of her as she darted behind a lounge or under a bed whenever Hayley walked past. She tried not to take it personally, but it had become her mission to win the cat over, one way or another. Every day Hayley put out food and water in the kitchen and every day it was gone, so at least she knew the cat was eating—either that or the mice were going to be the size of damn elephants.

As she sat in bed reading one evening she glanced up to find her mysterious housemate hovering in the doorway. Her heart gave a small leap. The cat never ventured into the same room as her. Hayley sat still, hardly daring to breathe in case she scared her off. Maybe the cat didn't realise she was in here, she thought, waiting for her to turn and dart back into the shadows as it usually did, but instead the cat stood there, watching her for a moment before cautiously taking a step into the bedroom.

Finally Hayley's perseverance had paid off. It had taken a while, but at last she'd won her trust. She'd never wanted an indoor cat, never imagined in a thousand years she'd have any animal inside, and yet here she was, happily accepting a feline in her bedroom. Her chest filled with a mixture of pride and emotion and she found herself blinking back tears as the cat softly padded towards her and leapt up onto the bed . . . to drop a mouse on her doona.

Hayley didn't scream at first. It took a few seconds for her brain to register that the cat had brought her a mouse. *A freaking mouse.* It was only as the rodent—seemingly dead—suddenly sprang back to life and shot across the bed that Hayley's scream ripped from the depths of her chest and sent the cat screeching, the bedside lamp crashing to the floor and the mouse missing in action.

In seconds Hayley was on her feet on top of the mattress, flattened against the wall, trying to keep up with the chase between cat and mouse as it played out on the floor of her bedroom. She tried to judge the distance to the doorway, wondering what her chances were of leaping from her perch through the open door without having to touch the floor. Possibly not good, she decided as she thought back to her schooldays and her dismal attempts at long jump. Her mind was made up, though, when the cat ran under her bed and she realised she would never sleep until it caught the damn mouse again. Closing her eyes, she took a deep breath and, with a hop, skip and jump that would have made Mr Brown, the PE teacher, proud, hit the ground and managed to pull the door shut behind her in one fluid movement.

So much for relaxing before bed with a good book. She sat in the lounge room, her feet pulled up underneath her, and waited. She looked at the clock on the wall. She wasn't sure how long it would take to re-catch a mouse, but surely half an hour was long enough. Taking the broom from the hall closet, Hayley approached the bedroom door with all the stealth of a SWAT operative, reaching out to push it open and wincing as she glanced around the corner, half expecting the room to look like a murder scene, but all was quiet.

Hayley found the cat waiting patiently in the centre of the room, one paw on the dark object on the floor. With a slow blink that somehow implied scorn, she picked up the limp mouse and carried her prize, head and tail held high, past Hayley to the back door.

Hayley followed cautiously behind, on alert in case the mouse was faking again. The cat was now pointedly ignoring her, but staring fixedly at the back door, waiting for her to open it.

'You want to go outside?' Hayley asked, realising she was talking to a cat. 'Okay, that's a good idea. You take it outside and get rid of it.' She reached out to open the door while remaining as far away from the mouse as possible. She watched as the cat gracefully leapt down the back step and vanished into the night.

Hayley had just finished righting her bedroom and climbed back into bed when she heard a scratching noise coming from the back door. She got up and cautiously opened the door a fraction, only to find the cat staring up at her with an accusing glare.

'How was I supposed to know whether you were coming back or not?' Hayley said.

The cat squeezed in through the opening and, with a sassy swish of her tail, walked past her and disappeared up the hall and into the bedroom. Hayley watched from the doorway as the feline jumped up onto her bed, pawed at the mattress before circling then curling up and going promptly to sleep.

'No, please, make yourself at home,' Hayley murmured, cautiously getting back into bed and eyeing the cat warily as she pulled the blankets back up. 'Fine, you can stay there,' she told her, 'but only because you caught the mouse. And you better not snore,' she added, closing her eyes.

Tomorrow she'd set some ground rules. She was not going to be one of those crazy cat ladies who slept with a dozen cats on the end of her bed.

⁓

Hayley opened her eyes to the familiar morning racket and sat up with a renewed determination. The squawking and screeching was starting to build in intensity as she stalked across to the window. Picking up the prepared plastic water gun she'd purchased in Windsor, she took aim at the small bush and fired through the window, sending the flock of birds into a flutter of chaos.

She felt like a female Rambo as she held the trigger and watched the water blast from the end of the gun. It had been wise to go with the Megatron 2000 Ultimate Exterminator Cannon. She'd feared it might be a touch of overkill, but the ten-year-old boy in the toy aisle had assured her that this one was *lit*, which she'd assumed was a good thing.

Her triumph lasted no more than three minutes until the gang of wet, dishevelled birds regrouped and returned to continue eating. Two more attempts to discourage them also failed and Hayley slumped in disappointment. She eyed the cat, who was watching at the window, and briefly considered letting her out there to take care of the situation, until her conscience kicked in and she reluctantly let the thought go.

Damn it, she'd been sure the ultimate exterminator was going to work. There had to be a way to get rid of these bloody birds.

Hayley parked her car in front of the feed store and noticed there was a small market set up in the park across the street. She decided to have a quick look before heading in to stock up on hay for Errol and Flynn.

The first stall had a colourful display of jams and chutneys and Hayley smiled at the lady seated on the striped fold-out chair behind the table. 'Everything looks delicious,' she said.

'It's all made from what I grow in my garden,' the woman said proudly.

Hayley selected a few different jams and handed over her money before moving on to the next stall. There were more chutneys and a few tables of knitted gifts, and a stall selling fresh fruit and vegetables. Her arms loaded up with purchases, Hayley almost bypassed the last stall, but a sound caught her ear and she stopped, looking at the cages of clucking chooks.

She'd always wanted chooks, but they hadn't been allowed to keep them at her old house. *You have a farm now,* a little voice reminded her. *You need to settle down and wait before you take on any more animals,* a second voice cautioned, and she knew that was what Paul would have said. He was the sensible, rational one when it came to making decisions. He researched every purchase, from vacuum cleaners to cars. The man didn't know the meaning of impulse buy. Hayley, on the other hand, often got impatient and would have bought a vacuum simply because it was purple. She told herself it made sense to go home and research what type of chickens would be the best for her situation and weigh up the cost of feeding compared to the price of a carton of eggs from the supermarket. Yes, that would be the mature, grown-up thing to do.

'Morning Ernie,' she called out cheerfully as she walked to the counter of the feed store.

'Two bales of grassy hay?' Ernie said without glancing up from the computer screen.

'And whatever chooks eat,' she said, secretly smiling when he lifted his gaze to peer over at her. He made a few keystrokes and told her the tally, taking her card without comment.

As she drove home she kept a wary eye on the box in the passenger footwell. She tried not to feel the weight of Paul's disapproval. It had always driven her crazy. She'd never actually stopped to think about it before, it was easier to just go along with it but, on some level, she knew there'd been a building resentment. *What was the last thing she'd actually bought just because she liked it?* There was the jug, she recalled. She'd loved it the moment she'd seen it in the window of the electrical store as she'd walked past in the shopping centre.

It was the most beautiful candy-apple red colour and so shiny and new. She'd gone inside and bought it, trying not to cringe at the outrageous price. She'd brought it home, setting it up on the kitchen bench and had admired it every time she'd walked past, until Paul had gotten home and spotted it. She'd endured a lecture on impulse buying for the rest of the evening, complete with being walked through its stats online, and told how much power it used compared with the old jug, which, he'd hastened to add multiple times, there'd been nothing wrong with at all. But Hayley had stuck to her guns—it was pretty, damn it. Besides she'd bought it out of her last royalty cheque, so she hadn't even touched the joint account.

Three months later the stupid thing blew up. She'd been expecting another dressing down, but Paul didn't say a word. That annoyed her more than a lecture would have.

She'd pulled out the ugly boring white jug they'd bought when they'd first gotten married, and nothing more was ever said about it. There'd been quite a few occasions where she'd felt like a naughty child in their relationship instead of an equal, contributing adult.

Hayley pushed the thought away. She hated feeling petty. He was gone and she didn't want to think about stupid things that didn't matter anymore.

The old shearing shed was becoming a hub of activity. Errol and Flynn had their enclosure and a temporary paddock coming off the rear of the shed, and the bits and pieces stacked behind the old building provided a treasure trove of useful things. After a quick look through it, Hayley came up with enough mesh to construct a temporary cage in one of the far stalls for her three new lodgers. She sat down to watch them scratch through the hay she'd spread on the floor as they explored their new surroundings.

She was going to need a proper chicken coop for them, somewhere they had room to explore but with a sheltered area for them to sleep and lay their eggs, which the man who'd sold them to her had assured her they should start doing within the next month or so.

There was also the growing concern about keeping the grass in the paddocks under control. Luke had mentioned he'd do some slashing next time he was over this way, but she really hated depending on favours. However, she wasn't sure she was brave enough to buy a tractor and do it herself, so she was a little stuck.

She smiled as she switched her glance between the donkeys happily munching in their enclosure and the chooks clucking quietly. It felt good. This was her making her own decisions, doing what she wanted, being happy.

She stood up and dusted off her jeans. Okay, so she bought the hens on impulse, and been landed with a donkey, but the cat and Flynn had been bought after careful consideration. Well, sort of. Who cared, she thought with a silent huff, it wasn't the end of the world. Tomorrow she was going to find herself a handyman. She was realistic enough to know she wasn't going to turn into a DIY expert overnight, but that didn't mean she was some helpless damsel. She could use a phone. There were people who knew how to do the things she couldn't and she fully intended to find them.

She walked back towards the house, passing the caretaker's cottage. The old stone outbuilding still bugged her for some reason. She had no idea why. She loved old buildings, but every time she went near it she felt . . . Hayley shook her head irritably. It was nothing. Just the lingering uneasy feeling that had come from her afternoon in the bottom paddock. She'd done her best not to think about it again, but she was fooling herself if she thought she could forget something like that.

She hated that it managed to intrude on her happiness. This was her home, her little piece of paradise, and nothing was going to ruin it.

Trust you to pick a haunted house to buy, a little voice sniggered in her head, and she mentally stamped her foot in frustration. 'It's not haunted,' she said and realised she'd said it out loud. Maybe if the place was haunted that would at least explain what had happened; after all, tourist places made a fortune from ghost tours and staying the night in haunted accommodation all over Australia. But somehow, she didn't think that was it. She didn't feel weird around any of the other buildings. It was just that one outbuilding . . . and the bottom paddock, of course, but she blocked that out of a habit she'd developed ever since coming home that day. *Just don't think about it,* she told herself firmly. After all, that was how she usually handled anything unpleasant in her life. Her marriage, for example. Maybe if she'd been brave enough to confront Paul at the very first inkling that something wasn't right—his absences that were a little suspicious, the meetings that ran a little too long, a little too frequently—maybe they could have saved their relationship before things had gone beyond repair.

But nope, she'd pushed it aside and ignored it, hoping everything would just go away. That was her, Cleopatra, the Queen of De Nile.

Ten

'It's a bunch of bullcrap, that's what it is. Flamin' bureau-crats gone crazy,' Patrick Mason bellowed, slamming his fist on the table in the kitchen.

'Patrick, calm down. Remember your blood pressure,' Del admonished before sending a searching look at Luke seated across from her. 'So what on earth does all this biohazard stuff mean for the business?'

'Biosecurity,' Luke said calmly. 'Well, there are going to have to be some changes. For starters, we'll have to fence off areas and put up signs telling guests they can't go in certain places.' He turned the computer to show them the examples.

'What! I'm not putting one of those hideous things up at the front gate,' Del gasped as she stared in horror at the glaring red sign that warned visitors this was a biosecurity area. 'My God, that would make you want to turn your car around and go straight home.'

Luke ignored his mother's outburst. 'We're also going to have to make a direct road to the reception shed and designated parking areas. All vehicles coming onto the property have to be hosed down and cleaned if they go anywhere near the livestock, so it'll mean putting up more fencing and signage. It'll have to be monitored.'

His mother pulled the computer closer and read from the text. 'Biosecurity zones or checkpoints?' she said, looking over at her husband. 'It sounds like some kind of army compound. Who on earth will want to get married in a prison camp?'

'It's probably not as bad as it sounds,' Luke said wearily. It *was* as bad as it sounded and somehow he was going to have to figure out how to implement it.

'What's this about access to certain areas?' Patrick asked.

'It means we have to control movement around the property. We can't have people, namely *guests*, traipsing all over the place.'

'But what about the photo shoots? The riverbank. The old dairy? They love that old rustic ruin in wedding photos,' Del said with a worried frown.

Luke shook his head. 'The whole reason for biosecurity is to limit the spread of potential contamination.'

'Oh, for goodness sake! What do they think wedding guests are going to bring in?'

'I don't know, Mum. I don't think they had wedding guests in mind when they made the rules, but they're still visitors and it says here that all visitors have to be signed in and out and have limited access.'

'I am not signing my guests in and out like . . . well, like prison visitors,' Del snapped.

'Nah, we're not doing this crap,' Patrick said, leaning back in his chair and folding his arms across his chest.

'Dad, it's enforceable. Not only that, but they've said that there can be random audits at any time. That means they can come here and check that we're following procedure and, if we aren't, fine us.'

'I've heard enough of this rot. I'm not having any part in it,' Patrick said, pushing away from the table with a loud screech of his chair and leaving the room.

Luke slid his hands onto his head, linking his fingers as he stared at the barrage of information on the computer. As if he didn't have enough to deal with already. 'Dad's right, it is shit,' he muttered to his mother. 'It's going to mean a lot of stuffing around and more paperwork—like we aren't already snowed under as it is.' He glared at the computer screen. 'But it has to be done.'

'I suppose it does. You'll work it out, you always do,' his mother said, standing up to kiss the top of his head before leaving the kitchen.

Great, yep, leave it to Luke, he'll sort it out.

With a long, low curse he opened up a new document on the computer to start sorting out a plan.

⚭

'Come on, puss,' Hayley called after tapping the can of cat food for a few minutes with no response. The last few days the cat had become decidedly less interested in food, whereas the previous week she'd been a virtual eating machine. She hoped it didn't mean there was something wrong; it was a bit of a trip to take a sick animal to the vet around here. She'd wormed her on arrival and had been impressed by her rapid weight gain, to the point that she'd considered cutting back on feed because of the rather noticeable bulge that had been forming.

Putting the can down, Hayley went in search of the missing cat. There hadn't been a mouse sighting in weeks and for that alone Hayley was willing to overlook the fact her rule of no cats in the bedroom was constantly ignored. 'Where are you?' Hayley called, searching each room. A tiny noise caught her attention as she walked down the hallway and into the laundry.

At first she didn't see anything, until she poked her head around behind the hot water system and saw two big eyes blinking at her. 'What are you doing in here?' she asked, before she spotted three tiny mouse-like creatures snuggled protectively under the cat's belly. They weren't mice though, they were . . . kittens.

'Holy cow,' Hayley breathed, looking back at the cat, who was wearing a what-the-actual-hell-is-happening-to-me look.

As the initial shock wore off, Hayley did a double-take. 'Hey! That's my favourite shirt,' she said, eyeing the stained

T-shirt the four cats were lying on. 'How did you even get that?' Although she did recall leaving clothes on the floor of the laundry the other day. 'Oh gross.' Correction, it *was* her favourite shirt. 'Well, you can't lie there in that,' Hayley said, grimacing at the mess, her hands on her hips as she considered her options.

Heading out to the shed, she found a cardboard box and a bag of old clothes she'd put out to go to Vinnies and took it all back into the laundry. When she'd made a comfy bed, she carefully sat the box next to the little family and reached for one of the tiny creatures. When she didn't get mauled by their mother, she gently gathered the first one up and transferred it to the new bedding. She did the same with the other two, mother cat shadowing her final transfer and settling herself into the box around her babies.

'There, I bet that feels better,' Hayley said, feeling rather satisfied with herself.

She moved the cat food and water dishes closer to the box and sat down to watch them for a few minutes. She wasn't sure how long it had been since they'd been delivered, but considering they'd still looked a little damp, and the stains on the T-shirt were still wet, it couldn't have been more than a few hours.

'Desexed my arse. I seriously must have sucker stamped on my forehead,' she said to the cat, who was busy nuzzling her new babies. A reluctant smile tugged at Hayley's face as she watched. Okay, so that made it pretty damn hard to resist, but seriously? Four cats? Well, on the upside, it should mean the end of any future mouse problems.

Later that morning she scooped up the car keys from the dish on the kitchen counter and headed for the back door. She'd been planning on leaving earlier for her shopping trip, until she'd got sidetracked playing cat midwife. But she wasn't going shopping for groceries. Today she was shopping for a car.

Once she would never have considered parting with her Audi—she loved it—but the reality was, it just didn't suit her needs anymore. It was a city car; it wasn't designed for carrying hay and animals. As much as she'd love to keep it as a second car, it wasn't practical to own two vehicles. It would sit in her shed for months on end without use. No, the time had come. She was going to have to trade her baby in.

New beginnings. That's what this was, she thought as she drove along the winding roads, savouring the last time she'd sit in her zippy little red car.

The Audi had been the first new car she'd ever owned and had been bought from her first decent-sized royalty cheque. Hayley swallowed past a tightening throat. Sometimes thinking about the past caught her off guard. She needed to think of something else.

Hayley found her thoughts once again turning to what had happened out by the old tree. She still had no logical explanation, but when she was away from the farm she seemed to have more perspective. It was almost as though the more distance she put between herself and the property, the more breathing room she had.

It had to be the stress of moving and packing up her old life. She must have fallen asleep or something . . . except she didn't recall waking up. Part of her was tempted to return to the spot to see if anything strange happened again, but her inner coward—the part of herself that wouldn't watch scary movies or go outside at night to investigate strange noises—kept her from following through. A shiver ran through her body now as she remembered. Nope. She was not going back there alone again anytime too soon. Whatever she'd experienced, it still made her incredibly uncomfortable.

⁂

'Morning, Ernie,' Hayley said as the poker-faced man walked out from the office to serve her. While she'd waited for him to finish on the phone, she'd been reading the notices on the small board beside the counter. 'What do you know about miniature belted Galloways?' she asked him curiously.

'They're small and they taste good,' Ernie shot back, already typing in her usual order of hay and laying pellets.

'They're the black ones with a white stripe across their middle, aren't they?'

'They can be dun or red sometimes too.'

'What's their temperament like?'

'I dunno, they're cows. They eat grass all day, crap and eat more grass.'

'Are they quiet?'

'Reasonably. They're still cattle though, not dogs,' he warned. 'Why?'

'I'm thinking of getting a few.'

'Doesn't surprise me,' he said dryly.

'Do you know the people who are advertising them?' she persisted, ignoring his usual world-weary tone. 'Is there any reason they're selling them?'

'They're city folk who come up on the weekends to play farmer. They've managed to overstock their property, apparently.'

It seemed like an ideal situation. They needed to get rid of a number of cattle and she needed to buy a few to help keep her grass under control. But she'd need to fix and add a few fences first.

'I don't suppose you'd know of anyone who does fencing, maybe a handyman who could build me a chicken coop too?'

'I might know a bloke,' he said, before tallying up her feed bill and taking the money. 'Jason Weaver,' he said. 'Lives just up the road from you. Inverness is the name of his mother's place. He might be able to do something.'

'Thanks, I'll drop in on my way home.' She followed him back out to her car and waited for him to load the feed into the back.

'Traded in the Audi,' he said with a small grunt as he heaved the feed into the back of her shiny black four-wheel drive. 'About time,' he added.

'Yeah, well, trying to vacuum bits of hay out of my boot was getting annoying.'

She was still getting used to the size of the monstrosity she'd just bought. She missed her snazzy little Audi. Driving this one around she felt like a kid wearing her father's boots. There was so much space and she almost had to use a stepladder to climb into the damn thing, but it was safe, economical and practical—she'd done her homework this time.

'Might make a farmer out of you yet,' he said in his now familiar gruff tone.

Hayley blinked. Was that a compliment?

'Or at least look the part,' he added, closing the tailgate with a thud before walking back into the store.

Ah. Nope. False alarm. Still, she thought with a satisfied smile, she was slowly chipping away at that tough exterior of his. One day she'd win him over. Or die trying.

The weatherboard house sat in a clearing surrounded by a brown timber fence, both looking to have been freshly painted judging from the ladder still resting against one side of the house. Hayley climbed out of her car and opened the gate. She'd walked three steps when the sound of hysterical barking reached her, followed immediately by two small fox terriers racing towards her at alarming speed. Hayley paused, trying to decide if she should run back the way she'd come or run towards the house and pray someone was there to let her in. Instead she did neither, only froze in place and closed her eyes tightly as the two animals barked and yipped around her.

A loud, piercing whistle ripped through the air and the barking instantly ceased. Hayley opened an eye and saw a figure moving towards the path from the house. She breathed a sigh of relief and hoped she didn't look too ridiculous.

A man with shaggy hair and stubble that had gone a shade past *I forgot to shave for a few days* hobbled towards her and Hayley mustered a smile of greeting. 'Hi. I'm Hayley Stevens. I've just moved in up the road. Are you Jason?' When he didn't return her smile or comment straightaway, she rushed on to explain. 'Ernie at the feed store gave me your name. He said you might be interested in doing some work for me.'

'What kind of work?' he asked, eyeing her frankly. Up close, she was surprised to see he was younger than she'd first assumed.

'I've got a chicken coop I need building, and I'd like a bit of fencing done. Is that something you'd be interested in?'

He stood with one hand on his hip and rubbed his jaw with the other. 'Yeah. Maybe. When do you need it done?'

'As soon as you can fit it in.'

'Yeah. All right. Leave it with me. I'll drop over and take a look at the job and measure up.'

'That would be great, thanks.' She wasn't sure when she'd be seeing him; hopefully leaving it with him wouldn't mean six months from now.

Jason lifted his hand from his hip in a brief farewell, or he could have been waving her off like an annoying fly; either way, he then turned and hobbled back inside the house, leaving Hayley to return to her car and drive home with a mix of satisfaction and curiosity. Who was this Jason person? And what was with his limp?

Eleven

Hayley sat at her desk inside the small overseer's cottage she'd made into her office and dragged her eyes from the window. She found herself continually distracted by the garden. It beckoned to her to come out and enjoy it instead of sitting inside staring at her computer screen, and maybe if she'd had anything to show for a morning of work she'd have agreed she deserved the break. Sadly, though, seventy words wasn't exactly productive.

'Come on, Chance. Give me something to work with here,' Hayley said, tipping her head back with a frustrated sigh. She'd somehow lost her connection with the tough-talking ex-detective. While it wasn't ideal, Hayley wasn't alarmed. It happened. Occasionally Chance disappeared without warning and refused to come back until she was good and ready.

But Hayley knew Sophia was still waiting on those chapters from her, so she decided to call Chance's bluff. Taking a deep breath, she straightened her shoulders and poised her fingers over the keyboard, ready to force out some creativity. She began typing.

The door swung open. A large threatening shadow filled the doorway. She wasn't sure she could fight him off another time. Her skin began to crawl as he stepped through the doorway and stopped behind her. She shivered as she felt his foul breath against the back of her neck. Her hand tightened around the knife handle and she squeezed her eyes shut.

Hayley stopped typing and frowned at the screen. Where was this scene fitting into the plot? The words seemed to flow from her fingers, but she had no idea where it was going. *Seriously? The first real writing you've done in weeks and you're going to complain?* She gave a quick shake of her head and set her hands on the keyboard once again.

'Dinner won't be long, sir.'

'It's not food I be wantin', girl, and you know it.'

'Please, sir,' she heard the quiver in her voice and tightened her grip on the knife.

'I told you, girl—if you want to be treated nice, you have to treat me nice. Play your cards right and I'll sign that letter to the Governor for your ticket of leave.'

She hated him with every fibre in her being, but he was her master and was so much bigger than her. A tear ran from the corner of her eye as she thought of Edward. She jumped as his hand touched her waist and moved up across the thin material of her white shift. Her stomach lurched as she remembered the last time he'd cornered her in the barn. No! She wouldn't allow him to touch her like that again. She was in love with Edward. As he jerked her roughly back against his fat body and lifted her skirt, a fierce anger exploded inside her. She turned to push him away and froze as his body jerked upright then stilled. She watched in horror as his wide eyes stared at her in disbelief, before his grip on her slackened and he crumpled to the ground at her feet.

A large red stain seeped through his shirt front and she looked down at the bloodied knife she held in her fist.

'What have ye done, you stupid girl?' Cook's voice came from the doorway.

For a long moment the two women stared at each other and then down at the man on the ground, before her hand began to shake uncontrollably and she stumbled away towards the kitchen. Behind her she heard the blood-curdling scream of the Master's wife.

Edward. She needed Edward. He would make everything all right.

Hayley stared at the screen, re-reading the words, and felt that now familiar dizzy feeling as it began to creep through her. She pushed away from the desk and stood up, noticing her hands shook slightly.

What. The. Actual. Hell.

She'd seen the whole scene unfolding inside her head—had smelled the metallic, sharp scent of blood in the air and felt the churning dismay. Her skin crawled, still feeling Mr Mears's hands on her skin. Hayley took two unsteady steps away from the laptop. *Mr Mears?* Where the hell had that name come from? Why was she even writing this scene? It had nothing to do with Chance Delaware. Since when did her hardened ex-detective suddenly work as a kitchen maid? How did she even know this woman *was* a kitchen maid?

Hayley forced herself to walk back across to the desk to close the computer, then gathering it up she hurried out of the office and across the garden into the house. She placed it on the kitchen bench and poured herself a glass of wine. Leaning against the opposite side counter, Hayley eyed the computer warily. What on earth was going on?

Twelve

Hayley knew she should probably just have called Luke, but she needed to get away from the cottage for a while. She needed a distraction and she wanted to get his advice about the miniature Galloways, which she was pretty sure could have been done over the phone or by text. It certainly wasn't an excuse to see him again. She'd almost talked herself out of it in fact, seeing as the chances of turning up unannounced and finding him home instead of out in the paddock was pretty unlikely, but she'd thought that if he wasn't home she'd just go for a drive instead.

She pulled up at the front gates and noticed they were locked. Frowning, she was just about to turn around when a ute pulled up beside her and the window wound down.

'Hi,' Hayley said, feeling a little flustered as she caught Luke's lopsided grin. 'I'm sorry to turn up uninvited like this,' she started, then pointed at the padlocked gates and the sign about a biosecurity area partially camouflaged by a newly planted shrub with huge bright red flowers. 'It looks like you're not expecting visitors.'

'Oh yeah, that,' he nodded, and judging by his tone, he wasn't impressed with whatever *that* was. 'A new lot of rules and regulations.'

'I should have called.'

'You don't need an invitation to drop by,' he assured her. 'We're just supposed to keep the gate locked. Anyway, what do you need?'

A good-looking farmer would hit the spot right now. Hayley swallowed hard. *Don't even go there, girl.* Forcing her wayward mind back on task, she gave him a calm smile. 'I was wondering if I could ask your opinion on something.'

'Sure.' He started to climb out of the ute. 'I'll just open the gate. Come on up to the house.'

'Oh no, I don't want to interrupt your work, it won't take long.'

'It's almost smoko anyway. Good timing,' he grinned over at her.

As she waited for him to park and walked beside him towards the house, Hayley asked him about the cattle.

'I guess it depends on what you want to achieve. I've heard a bit about these miniature cattle, and the Galloways are a pretty old breed, so they have a lot going for them. They're fairly versatile. If you were wanting to raise cattle specifically for beef, I'd probably go for a bigger animal. But I'm assuming . . .' He glanced across at her and they swapped a smile.

'I really only want them for lawnmowers. I need to keep the paddocks under control.'

'That's what I figured,' he said, tucking one hand into his pocket casually. 'In that case these would probably do the job. They're a smaller build so a bit easier to handle, although I still wouldn't recommend you try doing much handling alone. I'm happy to lend a hand whenever you need it.'

'Thank you, although I'm hoping to learn how to do some of it myself.'

'I can teach you whatever you want to know.'

Hayley's smile widened. She didn't know where this sudden love of farming had come from.

'You want to try to get a mix of different aged heifers. A couple of older ones are good to have in a herd to teach the younger ones how things are done. You don't want steers.'

'Why not?'

'They're for eating.'

'Oh right.' She knew that . . .

'Although I guess since you're only using them for pasture control, it wouldn't matter if you had a couple, but ideally having a few breeders would be a good idea.'

'I wasn't really thinking of breeding them . . . I guess I'd need a bull for that,' she said cautiously.

'Not necessarily. Well, I mean yeah, you need a bull to breed, but you wouldn't have to buy one. You could lease one for a month or so, or there's always AI.'

'AI?'

'Artificial insemination.'

'Oh.'

'It's pretty standard nowadays.'

'I haven't thought that far down the track, but good to know,' she added, suddenly realising there might be a bit more to owning cattle than she'd first assumed. 'Do you know the people selling them? Ernie said they came from the city.'

'I know the place. A mate of mine manages it for the owners. I'm happy to go with you and take a look at them if you like.'

'If you wouldn't mind, that would be really helpful. Maybe let me know when you've got time. There's no rush.' She felt a lot better knowing she had someone on her side who knew what they were doing.

Luke opened the back door for her and they walked into the kitchen, the smell of fresh baking wafting through the air. The kitchen was open and roomy and even though it looked like it had every conceivable modern contraption, it still kept its early Australian charm with a brick chimney built around a large old-fashioned oven.

'Hayley! What a lovely surprise,' Del smiled as she set a tray of scones on the kitchen bench.

'I just stopped around to pick your son's brains about cattle. I didn't mean to gatecrash your morning tea.'

'Neighbours don't need an excuse to drop over for a cuppa. Go on through with Luke to the other room and I'll bring this in.'

'I can help,' she offered, still feeling as though she was intruding.

'Nope, I have it all under control. Take her inside, Luke,' his mother said, ushering them out of the kitchen.

∽

Luke's grandmother sat reading in her armchair and looked up as they walked into the sunny front room. She put aside her book to accept a kiss on her cheek from her grandson.

'Hello, Hayley, this is a lovely surprise,' she said, reaching out to gently squeeze her hand.

'Hello Mrs—' Hayley started but quickly corrected herself, 'Pearl.'

'Mum's bringing in tea,' Luke said, taking a seat beside Hayley and stretching out his long legs. Hayley tried not to let herself be distracted by the jean-clad thighs beside her and wished the Masons had decorated their room with larger lounges. These ones made it almost impossible not to feel the warmth of his leg as it touched hers.

'Is it that time already?' Pearl asked. 'My, the day is flying.'

'It does have a habit of doing that. I often start writing in the morning and get a shock when I realise I've missed lunch and it's almost time for dinner.'

'Oh, I'd love to be able to write a book,' Pearl said wistfully. 'I don't know how you manage to write that many words, I'd struggle to write more than a few pages.'

'Some days I don't know how I'm going to manage to write that many words either,' she admitted ruefully.

Del and Patrick appeared in the doorway carrying trays, and Hayley was passed her cup and offered a scone as Patrick asked how Abby Cottage was going.

'I'm thinking about getting some cattle. I came over to ask Luke a few questions.'

'What are you planning on running?'

Hayley blinked and glanced across at Luke. *Running?*

'She's looking at some mini Galloways. The stud on Fitzsimons' old place is selling some off.'

'Ah, yeah, I know the ones,' Patrick nodded as he bit into a thick scone. 'Toy cattle.'

They *were* cute, but even so, something about his attitude irritated her. 'As long as they eat grass I'll be happy.'

'Yeah, they're fine for hobby farms,' he granted. 'Not as many steaks on one of them as you'd get on one of my Herefords though.'

'Maybe not,' Luke chimed in casually, 'but I've read there's a boom in miniature cattle. They're small enough to fill an average-sized family freezer, whereas a larger beast usually needs to be divided between a few, so these smaller breeds are more economical with less waste.'

Hayley nodded agreeably as she listened but didn't understand the discussion about carcass weights and meat marbling. She just needed help controlling the grass on her property.

'How's the writing going?' Del asked, putting a halt to the farm talk.

'It's at a standstill at the moment. I think maybe the move has played a bit of havoc with my creativity.' *Unless you count the historical novel that seems to have sprung from nowhere,* she added silently.

'Well, that's understandable. I'm sure things will settle down soon and you'll get back into the swing of things,' Del said sympathetically.

'I haven't really stopped writing for the last twelve months, so maybe it's a good thing.'

'Will this be a new book or part of your series? Olivia's got me hooked,' Del admitted.

Hayley smiled. It never got old, hearing people tell her they enjoyed her books. 'I'm not exactly sure. I thought I'd be writing another Chance Delaware book, but there's so much history in this area, I think that seems to be influencing this next book.'

'If history's what you're after, you can't go past Lochmanning,' Pearl chimed in. 'Finish your tea and I'll give you the grand tour. I think you'll find it fascinating.'

'Now, this is Wilfred and Henrietta Mason,' Pearl announced, as professional as any museum tour guide. 'They came here in 1806 and built Lochmanning.'

The two large frames hung side by side over the staircase in prime position, watching over their domain. The paintings had obviously been commissioned later in life as the couple looked to be rather old. Wilfred seemed to be a stern man, and the artist had caught a cold look in his eyes that put a trickle of ice down her spine. The expression on Henrietta's face was somewhat severe too, but somehow in the depths of her gaze the painter had managed to show the pain and grief this woman had experienced, along with a quiet pride for all she'd endured. Henrietta, like many women of the era, had undertaken a long voyage from her homeland. Hayley tried to imagine what it would have been like to say goodbye to family knowing you would most likely never see them again, to start a new lineage with a husband in a faraway, relatively uncivilised and isolated new world. Henrietta had not only survived, she'd left a family legacy that was still here today, as strong as ever in the generations that followed her.

Hayley walked on slowly beside Pearl, dutifully nodding as the old woman explained who each person was, the most recent being her late husband. Hayley noted the empty space beside it. 'That'll be for my portrait when I'm gone. I've already picked it out, but it won't be hung until I've passed,' Pearl said matter-of-factly, smiling wistfully up at her husband, who looked dashing in his World War Two army uniform.

'Why's that?' Hayley asked curiously.

'Well, family folklore says it's bad luck. Two Masons who hung their portraits early both died within a few months of the hanging. So we like to err on the side of caution.'

They made their way further down the hallway and the portraits took on older, sterner appearances, and Hayley had to stop herself from rubbing her arms against a weird chill. Maybe she needed to write a cheery children's book—clearly writing thrillers was having some kind of detrimental effect on her.

While Pearl talked about a rather humourless looking woman with a huge bun on the top of her head, Hayley's gaze scooted on to the remaining picture that was tucked away in the darkest corner of the hall. This portrait was a sketch, unlike the others which were oil paintings. When she stepped closer, she was momentarily distracted by the detailed pencil lines that shaped and shaded the face, until her gaze fell on the eyes. Eyes that stared back at her with such unexpected familiarity that she gasped and jerked away. They were the same eyes she'd seen in the vision by the old tree that day.

'Are you all right, dear?' Pearl asked.

Hayley turned away from the image to find the old woman watching her intently. She wasn't sure which gaze unsettled her more—the picture on the wall or the one belonging to Luke's grandmother.

'I . . . Yes. Sorry. I just thought for a moment . . .' Her words trailed off as she shot a quick look at the portrait again and felt yet another shockwave as she took in the entire face. This was not possible. It was the man she'd seen holding the woman by the old, dead tree. Hayley felt the room tilt.

'I think you better sit down, dear, before you fall down,' Pearl murmured beside her.

Pull yourself together, Stevens.

'What is it, dear?'

'I'm sorry, Pearl, I don't know what's going on with me. I haven't really been myself lately.'

Pearl tilted her head like a small inquisitive sparrow. 'Tell me.'

'Oh, it's nothing.' *I'm just losing my mind. Seeing visions, the usual everyday kind of thing. Nothing to be alarmed about.*

Pearl seemed to consider her thoughtfully for a few moments before she turned her body slightly to look up at the drawing on the wall. 'This handsome young man is Edward Mason. He was the youngest son of Wilfred and Henrietta Mason and his was a tragic tale.'

'What happened?' Hayley asked hesitantly.

'He fell in love with the wrong woman,' Pearl said sadly.

'Why was she the wrong woman?'

'She was a convict, dear.'

While Hayley was trying to wrap her head around that piece of information, Pearl continued, lowering her voice slightly, 'And a murderer.'

It was hard to see this rather dashing young man in the sketch falling for a murderer. 'What happened? To him?'

'He was found dead. Shot through the heart. They say it was a lover's quarrel. The convict woman was found dead beside him.'

Shot. Two people. Hayley didn't need a mirror to know that her face was probably going an alarming shade of white. She could feel her blood draining away from her head and a cold clamminess settling on her skin. In her vision, a man who'd looked just like Edward Mason had been shot alongside a woman dressed in a simple white shift. 'Why did they think she did it?'

'Because she'd killed the man she'd been interned to. They'd found him dead on the property. He'd been stabbed. The cook had witnessed the girl holding the knife and standing over his body. Jane Carney was her name. She ran off and the authorities went looking for her. They say that she went to young Edward demanding that he help her escape, and when he refused, she killed him, and then herself.'

Jane. Hayley's mind flashed back to the nightmare. That was the name someone had been calling . . . No *way. It was too weird.* Then she recalled the strange scene she'd written and felt the hairs on her arm stand up. It couldn't be. How could she have written a scene so similar to the story Pearl was telling now? Similar, she corrected dully, but not the same. Jane hadn't killed Edward. Oh my God, what was she saying? She didn't even know if the people she'd seen that day *were* Jane and Edward, although she knew it was a pretty feeble attempt to dismiss it. 'Mears,' Hayley murmured as she recalled the scene she'd typed.

'What's that, dear?' Pearl asked, eyeing her curiously.

'The name of the man . . . Jane—' she stumbled slightly saying the name aloud, '—stabbed. Was it Mears, by any chance?'

'Yes, it was.' She seemed surprised. 'Gilbert Mears was the original owner of your Abby Cottage, not that it was known as that back then, of course.'

She must have read the name somewhere. Maybe it was on the contract or the land title, despite the fact she figured she'd have remembered if she'd seen a list of previous owners going back to the convict era.

'Help me back to the drawing room, would you, dear?' Pearl said, cutting into Hayley's chaotic thoughts.

'Of course,' Hayley murmured, realising how long they'd been on the impromptu history tour. She allowed the older woman to lean on her as they retraced their steps back to the large, sunny room. She waited until Pearl was seated in her favourite chair. 'Can I get you something?'

'Del will be along shortly with lunch,' she waved off Hayley's offer distractedly. 'Give me your hand.'

Hayley looked at her in surprise but slowly extended her hand. Pearl immediately reached out and took it in hers, turning it face up and tugging it towards her, to peer down intently. 'Yes,' she nodded without looking up. 'It's just as I thought.'

'Pearl? What are you doing?' Del's exasperated voice interrupted them. 'Leave the poor girl alone.'

'It's right there on her palm,' Pearl said, looking up at her daughter-in-law with a satisfied smile. 'Just like I told you.'

'What is?' Hayley asked nervously.

'Your fate line, look, right there, see it?' Pearl said, holding Hayley's hand up close to her face.

'See what? I don't know what I'm looking for.'

'Right there, see how that line crosses over the other one? That's your fate line.'

'Okay,' Hayley said slowly.

'Where it crosses over is where you've reconnected.'

Hayley stared blankly at the old woman, unsure whether Pearl was losing her mind or she was. 'Reconnected . . . with *what*?'

'Not reconnected with what, dear. With *whom*.'

'Pearl,' Del tsked. 'Don't worry about it, Hayley. It's just old wives' tales.'

'Old wives' tales!' Pearl said, raising her voice with surprising firmness. 'You tell me when anything I've said *hasn't* come true.'

Hayley saw Del exchange a meaningful look with her mother-in-law, which Hayley found hard to interpret.

'All right, let's have our lunch, shall we?' Del said briskly, placing the tray of dainty sandwiches on the table in front of them, and Hayley got the feeling she was doing her best to play down the situation.

Pearl let go of Hayley's hand and eased back in her chair. 'You'll remember,' she said confidently.

Hayley felt a headache coming on. She tried to protest about staying for lunch but Del wouldn't hear of it, and so Hayley forced down a few of the sandwiches to be polite. If there was one thing she'd figured out it was that you didn't argue with a Mason woman. When she did finally manage to make an exit, her headache was in full swing and the last thing she needed was to sit in front of a computer screen. There was too much to think about and all of it hurt her pounding head. She took a couple of paracetamol and hoped somehow they would magically make everything suddenly make sense.

Thirteen

Hayley opened her eyes and glared at the ceiling above her. 'Un-freaking-believable,' she muttered as the usual morning screeching session started up just as the sun was rising. 'That's it,' she said, tossing the blankets off and getting to her feet.

It wasn't enough that she'd tossed and turned for most of the night after her encounter with Pearl, but she was also waking up at the crack of dawn every damn morning because of the insistent squabbling of noisy lorikeets. Well, enough was enough.

She pulled on the gumboots at the back door and headed for the shed. As she rounded the corner of the house and approached the bottlebrush bush, the lorikeets lifted in a cloud of irritated colour, protesting loudly as they hurled bird abuse at her from the roof and nearby trees.

'You brought this on yourselves,' she said, lifting the axe and hearing the first satisfying *thunk* as it connected with the trunk. 'If you could have just eaten without making enough noise to raise the dead, we'd have had no problem,' she said, bringing the axe down again. It took another ten swings and a few swearwords, but finally the shrub toppled and Hayley dropped the axe to the ground and caught her breath.

Her feathered nemeses continued to chirp and squawk angrily at her, and she had a moment of conscience as she bent to pick up the trunk, barely the width of both her forearms together. It wasn't a big tree; in fact, it was barely a tree at all. How so many birds could hope to fit on one small bush was beyond her, but she vowed to replant a dozen more to replace it . . . somewhere far away from her bedroom window.

Dumping the bush down behind the shed, Hayley had barely walked more than a few steps before the first of the birds landed. By the time she was back inside, the squabbling was no more than a distant hum and she kicked her boots off with a relieved sigh.

∽

Hayley was cleaning out the donkey pen, enjoying their company, when she heard the sound of a car door closing. She rounded the corner just as the visitor was knocking on the front door.

'Hello,' she called out as she approached.

The man at the door turned and spotted her, and Hayley realised it was the handyman, Jason Weaver.

'I've come to look at that job you wanted done,' he said.

'Oh. Great.' As he limped back down the verandah stairs she spotted his prosthetic leg. The first time she'd met him he'd been wearing jeans, but today he was dressed in a faded T-shirt and long cargo-type work shorts. *That would explain the limp.* She dragged her gaze away and waited for him to reach her side before leading the way around the back of the house.

'I want to enclose the orchard with a fence and build a chook pen inside that, so I could contain the chickens but they could still be free range,' she said, looking over at him to judge his reaction as they walked.

He asked about the size of the pen she wanted built and Hayley gave him a rough idea. 'You think that would be okay?'

Jason gave a shrug as they reached the site. 'Can't see why not.'

Wow. That was easier than she'd been expecting. 'Also, I have some fencing I need done. The donkeys need a bigger yard off the back of the old shearing shed over there, and I'm in the process of getting cattle, so I need to fence off the back paddocks so they can't get up around the house yard.'

He didn't seem fazed about the extra jobs. 'I'll measure it all up and price the materials. Give me a few days to get it all together.'

'Okay. Great.'

He moved across to where the fruit trees were growing and Hayley followed. When he turned to look back at her she came to an abrupt stop. 'I'm just going to measure it up.'

'Oh. Okay. Do you need me to help?'

'No. I got it,' he said stiffly, turning away without further comment.

'Alrighty then,' she said under her breath as she walked back to the shed. Now and again she looked over and watched him pacing out distances and jotting down notes on a piece of paper. His movements were a bit awkward, but he looked like he knew what he was doing.

As she stood, hose in hand, waiting for the donkey's trough to fill with water, her thoughts returned to Lochmanning. How was it that she'd seen Edward Mason before? Perhaps it had been a family resemblance to Luke that made him seem so familiar, but that didn't explain why she'd seen him that day by the old tree, and in actual fact Edward Mason didn't look much like Luke at all. *They have the same smile,* a little voice pointed out, and Hayley began to concede the point until she suddenly stopped. How did she know that? In the portrait Edward hadn't been smiling. Nor had he been smiling down by the tree. Yet in her dreams she'd looked up into his smiling face and it was the same as Luke's.

'Oh, for goodness sake, it's just a stupid dream,' she muttered aloud.

'Sorry?'

Hayley gave a small start when she looked up to find Jason standing beside her, and swore softly as she looked down and saw the water spilling over the sides of the trough. *For a guy with only one leg, he sure could sneak up on a person.* 'I was . . . Never mind,' she said, quickly turning the tap off.

'Okay, well, I'll be in touch,' he said, turning away before she could open her mouth.

So much for small talk. Clearly he wasn't the sociable sort. Well, as long as he could build her chooks a permanent home, she supposed it didn't matter if his customer service skills weren't up to scratch. Still, would it kill him to at least smile?

∽

Hayley opened her laptop, her finger hovering nervously over the file she'd saved, selecting it quickly before she lost her nerve. Every time she sat down to start the book she was supposed to be writing, a niggling sensation urged her to return to the strange scene she'd written earlier in the week. Out of pure desperation, she decided that maybe if she just wrote it, she'd get it out of her system and it would free her mind to concentrate on the book she needed to write—the one she was due to send to her publisher in only a couple of months. The one she still hadn't started.

She hadn't opened the file since that day and part of her was hoping she'd discover she'd dreamed the whole thing and hadn't actually written anything at all.

Her hope was short-lived. There it was, right in front of her. Undeniable proof she'd somehow written an account of Jane Carney's encounter with Gilbert Mears that had resulted in her stabbing him to death.

As she reluctantly re-read the scene, inspiration began to grow inside her and her fingers took over the keyboard.

Hayley looked up from the screen and realised with a start that it was getting dark outside. How had that happened? It had been a long time since she'd been so preoccupied with a story that she'd sat for hours without a break. She glanced at the time and realised it had been five hours since she'd sat down.

She blinked and eased her cramped back with a stretch as she looked at the word count at the bottom of the page. She did a double-take. She couldn't possibly have written that much. Hayley scrolled back through the pages in open-mouthed disbelief. The words were there, she recalled writing them, but at the same time she felt as though she were only now waking from a trance.

The scene she'd first written about the stabbing was no longer the opening paragraph. The story actually started further back, in Ireland. Jane was a young woman who sacrificed herself for her sister, who'd stolen a pair of earrings from the woman she and Jane worked for near their village of Ballycastle, in County Mayo. Jane found the earrings and took them back, hoping to replace them before anyone discovered they were missing, but the authorities had already been called and were there when she arrived, catching her red-handed with the stolen goods.

The months in prison were horrific, the trial a mere formality, but the voyage to the colonies was beyond anything Hayley could imagine. The disease and filth they lived in, the lack of clothing and the terrifying voyage in treacherous weather made it almost a welcome relief finally to arrive at their destination and endure the next seven years of slave labour.

The story unfolded before Hayley's eyes as she read. She knew there would be parts she'd need to flesh out, but she had the bare bones of a book here, a book unlike anything she'd ever written. She'd told it through Jane's eyes and it was so real that Hayley could almost smell, taste and feel everything she had described.

Jane was eventually sent to work for a man who lived in the recently opened Hawkesbury region. Gilbert Mears had been making his fortune off crops from the fertile land he'd been granted and he needed convict labourers. He had other convicts, men who helped with the heavy work of planting, ploughing and clearing land, but he also had two female convicts: an older cook and Jane, who was to help around the house as well as out in the field when needed. It was while she was here that she met the youngest son of the wealthy landowner next door, Edward Mason, and the two fell in love.

Edward was different. He had a kind nature; he didn't believe in many of the things that the other landowners, including his own father, had been doing since their arrival, particularly in relation to local Aborigines. He was interested in the law and had been vocal about the landowners reneging on the deal made by the governor with the local tribes. The governor had made a treaty with the Aborigines, promising that they wouldn't settle any more land lower down the river. However, a few years later, as the demand for land grew, this agreement was ignored. More land was cleared as settlement moved further down the river and, in doing so, destroyed the areas the local tribes depended on for hunting and gathering. When tensions started to rise and the Aborigines began fighting back, a group of settlers formed an unsanctioned posse to attack an Aboriginal camp. Edward vowed to bring the matter to the attention of the governor, despite his own father and brothers being involved in the incident.

When Gilbert Mears found out about Edward and Jane's secret love, he threatened to expose them and have Jane returned to a workhouse in Sydney unless she allowed him to have his way with her.

Jane finally snapped one day, stabbing the landowner and killing him. She ran, knowing no one would believe her or even care if she'd told them what he'd been dong to her—she was a convict, a worthless nobody with no rights, and Mears was a free settler and a landowner. She managed to evade the search parties for two days until she finally got word to Edward to meet her at their special place beneath the old tree.

Hayley found herself reading the next part with goosebumps rising on her arms.

A group of men arrived on horseback before Jane and Edward could escape. These men had been involved in the slaughter at the Aboriginal camp along with two of Edward's brothers. Jane knew they were here for her, but she also knew they were not going to allow an opportunity to deal with Edward pass them by either. He'd become an embarrassment to his family and a threat to their way of life. Jane knew they were both about to die, but Edward still fought to protect her, telling her to run. Promising her he'd follow her.

Hayley slumped back in her chair and stared at the last line of what she'd written. *I'll find you, Jane. I promise. Always and forever.*

A shiver ran up her spine. For some crazy reason, those words felt like a prophecy.

'Not reconnected with what, dear. With whom.'

Pearl's words floated back to her and she quickly stood up from her chair, moving away with a tired shake of her head. She needed a break from all this. And a stiff drink.

Fourteen

Luke parked his vehicle and walked to the front door, knocking briefly. When he didn't hear any sound coming from inside, he walked around the side of the house, leading to the old overseer's cottage he knew Hayley used as her office. He saw her staring intently at her computer screen, so intently that she hadn't noticed him. He moved to the open door and stuck his head around the corner. 'Hi.'

Hayley screamed and he automatically held out his hands in a calming gesture. 'Sorry, I didn't mean to startle you,' he said.

She lifted a hand in dismissal; the other was still clutched protectively against her chest.

'Are you okay?' he asked, giving the room a quick survey.

'Yes. Sorry, just deep in thought. I wasn't expecting someone to appear.'

'I didn't mean to interrupt. I was just passing by and . . . It was stupid of me, I should have known you'd be working.' *Idiot. Why would you think she'd want you to barge in on her uninvited?* He'd been trying to decide whether he should stop or keep driving and had found himself wheeling his car into her driveway at the last minute. He'd had the urge to see her ever since her last visit to Lochmanning. Who was he kidding—he had the urge full stop when it came to Hayley Stevens. He hadn't been able to stop thinking about her since he'd helped pull her stupid donkey out of his dam. It didn't help that he'd been dreaming about her too. He frowned slightly as he recalled the night before. They weren't dreams as such, more flashes of images.

The last time he'd been this consumed by a woman he'd been a teenager, completely infatuated by his maths teacher. Although in all fairness he hadn't been the only one—half the male population of his high school had fantasised over Miss Appleby. She'd left under a cloud of controversy involving an affair with the headmaster, and sadly maths had never held the same appeal after that.

This was different, though. It wasn't the hormone-driven obsession of a teenage boy, it was something very different. Hayley was important. That was the feeling he got when he dreamed about her. How could someone be important to you when you didn't even know them very well?

'No, that's okay. I've just been reading some stuff . . .' Her voice faded as she glanced briefly at the screen before coming back to him looking embarrassed. 'I could use a distraction . . . I mean a break. I could use a break,' she muttered, closing her laptop. 'Would you like a coffee?'

'That'd be great. If you're sure I'm not interrupting your work?'

'No, it's fine,' she said, leading the way back to the house and in through the back door to the kitchen.

The sound of high-pitched meowing made him stop and ask, 'What's that?'

Hayley smiled, beckoning him to follow, opening the laundry door quietly. Inside he found a tortoiseshell cat sprawled in a box with three kittens clambering over her. She turned her head to give them both a dismissive glance before returning her attention back to her offspring.

'When did you get a cat?'

'When the mice started moving inside.'

'So you naturally got one with dependants?'

'She didn't have dependants when I got her . . . They just miraculously turned up a few weeks later.'

'What are you going to do with them?'

'I don't know,' she shrugged, stepping back out of the laundry to leave the cat in peace. 'Probably keep them.'

'Four cats?' he said doubtfully.

'What? They're great at keeping the mice away.'

'You hear stories about people being found months after they've died, their bodies eaten by their cats,' he warned.

'You think I'm some crazy cat lady?'

'Well, not yet, but you seem to have the starter kit . . .'

'Thanks a lot,' she said dryly.

'I'm just sayin',' he shrugged. 'It starts with one, and before you know it the house is overrun with cats.'

'I'm pretty sure I've reached the limit of my cat addiction,' she assured him.

Luke chuckled and watched her take down cups and switch on her coffee machine. 'How's the writing going?'

She glanced at him. 'Not great. I've kind of been sidetracked by another project.'

'Oh yeah? What are you working on?'

'I really wish I knew,' she said, shaking her head as she measured coffee grounds. 'Your gran got me started on it. It was something she mentioned when I was there the other day, a story about one of your ancestors and a convict.'

'Edward?' he said, surprised.

She looked up. 'Yes. That's him. She told me the story about how he died.'

'Yeah, she likes telling that story,' he said dryly. He'd grown up with the stories passed down about the Masons and their long history with the early settlement of the valley. While he was proud of his family's legacy, he also realised that the history that was told publicly glossed over some pretty shameful parts. He'd researched his ancestor Wilfred Mason for a history assignment at school. It was the first time he'd bothered to expand his search outside of family stories, and the information had been unsettling.

Settlement of this area hadn't come without sacrifice or bloodshed from both the settlers and the Aborigines. The local Aborigines often raided homesteads, angered when farmland was cleared and their traditional hunting areas were destroyed. Retaliation parties would be then sent out to deal with them, which only resulted in strike-back action from the Aborigines. The arrogance of the English during this time was abhorrent; they dismissed the indigenous people as nothing more than animals. The general consensus was to move them on and, if they refused to go peacefully, to eradicate them completely. Reports of massacres—government sanctioned as well as unsanctioned by landholders—were not spoken of and yet were widely known.

Luke was realistic enough to accept that this had all happened in a very different time in history. Even so, he was sickened by the actions of his ancestors. They'd knowingly taken part in the slaughter of men, women and children in order to acquire the land they'd built their family fortune on. Blood stained their hands and it was difficult to stomach the family's pride in its history when he knew the cost of it.

'Have you ever looked in to it?'

'His murder?'

'Yes.'

There was something about the way she held herself, almost as though she were trying to hide the fact she was keenly interested in his answer. 'Not really. There's not that much to go on. It was back in colonial days.' He watched her suck her bottom lip in and chew it a little. 'Why?'

'No reason. I just found it interesting. I've been thinking about it a lot.'

'Is this the project you're working on?'

Her surprised look answered his question.

'I can't seem to stop thinking about it.' She slid his cup across the bench and moved into the front room.

'Gran's the one to talk to.'

'Yes, I might see if she'll sit down with me one day.'

'I don't think you'll have a problem getting her to talk. Good luck getting away.'

She gave him a small grin and instantly he had a strange sensation of déjà vu that left him momentarily breathless.

Hayley looked at him oddly. 'Are you okay?'

'Sorry?' he asked, clearing his throat.

'Are you okay?' she repeated, peering at him.

'Yeah. I just . . . No, I'm good.'

She didn't seem overly convinced but at least she didn't press him on whatever had just happened.

What *had* just happened? One minute he was sitting here drinking coffee and the next he was lying in a field of long wispy grass, looking down at Hayley wearing that same shy grin. Only it hadn't been Hayley. She'd had different colouring. But it was her. Somehow. Oh yeah, he was making all kinds of sense.

'Actually, I dropped by to ask you if you'd like to come over to the restaurant for dinner on Saturday night, you know, check out the brewery,' he said, racing to cover his awkwardness.

'Sure,' she said. 'I'd love to.'

'Great,' he said, drinking the remainder of his coffee and ignoring the fact it burned a little on the way down. 'I have to get back to work, but I'll see you Saturday. Did you want me to come and pick you up?'

'I can drive over, I don't want to put anyone out.'

'No, it's all good, I invited you, remember,' he added. 'Besides, if you plan on taste-testing the beer, you don't want to be driving home afterwards.'

'Okay then. Sure, that would be good.'

He headed back to his car with a spring in his step. He felt like a bit of an idiot for getting so excited by the prospect of spending Saturday evening with her, but he was glad he'd suggested dinner. It was a small stroke of brilliance, he congratulated himself as he headed back home.

Later that night, after putting up a measly fight to talk herself out of it, Hayley gave in to temptation and decided to further investigate the story of Jane Carney and Edward Mason. Yes, she could have taken Luke's suggestion and asked his gran for more information, but last time they spoke about Edward and Jane, well, the whole situation had been unsettling. No, she wasn't ready to revisit the topic with Pearl just yet.

Hayley opened her laptop and typed Jane Carney into the search bar. She dismissed the various Facebook links, but a few lines down a tag caught her eye: *Women transported to Australia. Convict ships.* She clicked on the link and it took her to a list of women's names on a ship's manifest, with their age, previous profession, crime and sentence recorded.

Jane Carney was listed as being Irish, seventeen years old at time of sentencing, and convicted of larceny. Hayley jotted down the name of the ship she came on and dates of birth so she could narrow down her search. When she typed in the new details there were several more links to local heritage and family history sites that gave a few more clues and enabled her to verify that this was likely the Jane Carney she was looking for. On a different web page, she found a Jane Carney listed as a maid, indentured to Gilbert Mears, and she knew she was on the right track.

Delving deeper into online archives she managed to find a newspaper transcript from 1816. Despite her desire to get answers, Hayley took time to appreciate the wonder of being able to read through such historical artefacts. Halfway down the page, she located the article relating to Jane:

A murder most foul has occurred in the Hawkesbury district on a remote farm in the Upper Macdonald River region. Convict Jane Carney brutally stabbed to death her master, Mr Gilbert Mears, fleeing the scene after being confronted by the cook, who came upon the young woman standing over the deceased bloodied body.

The despicable woman managed to evade a hunting party for two days before members of the local constabulary located the murderous fiend, sadly arriving too late to stop the second murder, that of Edward Mason, son of Wilfred Mason. Where it is believed that in a fit of rage and despair, Carney then took her own life before she could be taken into custody.

The article mostly fitted in with Pearl's version of the story, but it didn't fit in with the things she'd experienced.

The events reported in the paper and passed down through local folklore were wrong. Admittedly she couldn't prove that; she was fairly certain telling someone she'd had a vision about it wouldn't exactly count as solid evidence and yet . . . how could she have known all this and with such detail? Even now if she closed her eyes she could smell the hot summer day in that paddock and the scent of soap and leather on Edward's shirt. She could smell the damp coldness of the kitchen and feel the sticky warmth of blood on the handle of the knife and metallic scent of blood hanging heavy in the air.

Hayley closed her computer and put it aside as a cold clamminess broke out on her forehead. She concentrated on taking a deep breath. Maybe she had malaria or something, she thought hopefully. A disease would explain the queasiness and sweats. Maybe she could google exotic diseases and see if there was any mention of visions or hallucinations as symptoms. Then again, googling medical issues was never a good idea. Maybe she'd just have to accept the fact that she wasn't ill, she was just losing the plot.

Fifteen

Hayley pulled on her sneakers and grabbed an apple as she went through the kitchen, heading out to get the mail. It wasn't as easy as walking a few steps out the front door; checking the mail out here involved a pretty decent hike. Usually she checked it whenever she drove past in the car, but she hadn't left the house for the last few days.

The sound of her footsteps on the dirt driveway was a rhythmic backbeat to the birds calling to each other high up in the branches of the gum trees overhead. She took a deep breath in and savoured the clean, bush smell—a mix of eucalyptus, wattle, dried leaves and earth.

When Hayley reached the letterbox, she found herself only a little bit out of breath. She was getting fitter. Amongst her mail—bills mostly—was a slightly bent and grubby envelope that had nothing written on it. Curious, she ripped it open and found a handwritten invoice for the quote on her chook pen.

'Really?' she wondered aloud. Surely that couldn't be right? Reaching for her phone in her back pocket, she quickly dialled the number on the invoice.

'Weaver.' The abrupt answer caught her off guard and she had to think for a moment why she was calling.

'Hi, Jason. It's Hayley. I've just received your quote.'

'Good.'

'I'm just checking. Is this for the entire job? The chook pen plus the fencing?'

'Yes.'

'It just doesn't seem . . . well, enough.'

'You want me to charge you more?' he asked slowly.

'Well, no . . . unless you made a mistake or something. I just wasn't expecting it to be this . . . reasonable.'

'I can charge you more if it makes you feel better,' he said, and for the briefest of moments Hayley thought there was something that sounded a lot like humour in his tone.

'No, that's fine,' she said hastily. 'I just wanted to double-check you'd quoted for it all. But that's all good. I'm happy for you to go ahead whenever you have time.'

'I'll be there in the next day or two.'

'Great, see you th—' The phone clicked in her ear. 'Then,' she finished, giving an annoyed huff.

He was a prickly one, that was for sure. And she'd noticed he avoided eye contact. Normally that would be a sign of dishonesty in a person, but Jason didn't seem shifty, and Hayley was usually good at reading people. No, there was something hanging over Jason, something she thought must be related to the trauma of losing a limb. There was loneliness and anger in him—not so much violent anger, more an anger at the world. And sadness. She felt that roll off him in waves. She didn't think he'd be an easy person to get to know; he'd built a substantial wall around himself and it wouldn't be easy to breach.

∽

Hayley was just putting on the jug, still blurry-eyed after a restless sleep, when a car pulled up outside early the next morning. She blinked and peered through the window. Ever since Errol had been dropped off at her gate, she was suspicious of unannounced early morning visitors, and she hurried to the door, hesitating only briefly before heading outside in her pyjamas.

'Jason. Hi,' she said, awkwardly crossing her arms as she realised how uncomfortable it was to find yourself talking to your builder without a bra. 'I didn't know you were starting today.'

'I finished the other job earlier than I expected,' he said, walking around the back of his vehicle to lift out a heavy toolbox. 'I've got a truck delivering supplies later this morning.'

'Oh. Okay. Well, if you need anything . . .'

'I won't,' he said, heading around the back of the house.

'Right,' Hayley said as he vanished from sight. 'Good talk,' she added, heading back into the kitchen. As she passed the hallway mirror, she caught a glimpse of her hair and gave a fatalistic sigh. She looked like a damn scarecrow. No wonder the poor guy didn't feel like hanging around for a conversation. Oh well, she thought. It was his own fault for turning up unannounced and before her morning coffee.

∽

Hayley finished hanging out her washing and carried the empty basket back inside. All morning the place had been a hive of activity. A truck had arrived an hour or so after Jason and dropped off a load of timber, then another ute had pulled up and unloaded wire and bags of cement. Engines revved and men shouted over top of it all. This was not her usual quiet little haven.

As she settled down with her computer out beneath the tree in the yard, things had more or less settled back down. Breathing a sigh of relief, Hayley opened a new document and began to type.

Chance Delaware strode into the room . . .

The annoying blink of the cursor taunted Hayley as she stared blankly at the screen. This was getting beyond a joke. It had been weeks now since she'd been able to write about Chance. Chance was her *thing*. Chance was what sold books. What if moving from the city had somehow messed up her writing mojo? What if she couldn't write Chance's stories anymore?

'Don't be so bloody ridiculous,' she muttered aloud.

A loud banging started nearby and Hayley tipped her head back and growled. This was getting her nowhere.

Bringing up her web browser she typed in *How to over-come writers block* and started reading through the list of suggestions. Surely with modern technology someone would have found a way to overcome it by now? Then she brightened suddenly—maybe there was an app for it?

#Go for a walk.

Okay, she could do that . . . only not down the back paddock, that was definitely off the list of walking tracks for a while.

#Eliminate distractions.

Yeah, right. Where did she even start with that one? Between the guy making enough noise to be building a skyscraper behind her and the weird things that had been going on around here lately, distractions pretty much made up her entire environment at the moment.

#Do something to get your blood flowing.

Instantly an unexpected image of Luke popped up in her mind and she caught herself nodding in appreciation. *That would get the blood flowing.*

#Change your environment . . .

Now that was so crazy it just might work. She could pack her laptop and go for a drive to find somewhere else to work for the day. Maybe a change of scenery would bring Chance back.

When she had everything she needed, she glanced at the plate of Anzac biscuits she'd baked in an attempt to distract herself from her writer's block. It hadn't worked. But seeing as she was about to let Jason know she was going out for a while, she decided on impulse to take him a couple of biscuits and a glass of cold water.

She took a short cut through the hedges in the garden and out the back gate. Jason was working with his back to her, and Hayley stopped, staring at the unexpected sight. He'd removed his shirt and was thumping a large metal thing over the top of a fence post being hammered into the ground. Each time he lifted the contraption his muscles flexed and Hayley found her gaze following the movement. She hadn't taken much notice of his body in their earlier encounters; she knew he was reasonably fit-looking, but his faded T-shirts and dirty jeans had given little warning of the muscular physique beneath. He finished driving in the fence post and threw down the metal instrument, turning and catching her staring at him.

Swallowing down the awkwardness of the moment, Hayley fixed a smile on her face and moved across to where he was working. 'I just thought I'd bring you something to eat. I wasn't sure if you had a morning tea break or not.'

'I brought my own,' he said, indicating the small esky sitting in the shade of a nearby orange tree.

'Oh. I'll take them back inside,' she said feebly.

'No, it's okay. I'll eat them. Since you've already brought them out,' he added almost gruffly.

'You've done a lot.' She dragged her eyes away from his naked torso. *Not naked. Uncovered*, she corrected quickly. Good grief, up close she could actually *see* the small rivulets of sweat running down his chest.

'Yeah, once you get going it flows pretty well,' he said, reaching for a biscuit off the plate she held. 'The biggest hold-up is usually waiting on materials, but we got that all delivered this morning, so it's just a matter of getting it up.'

Don't even go there, she warned her overactive mind, which was somehow operating at gutter level at the present moment. 'Well, good job,' she said with a decisive nod. 'I'm heading out for a while. Do you have my number in case you need me?'

'Yeah. From when you called the other day,' he said, biting into another Anzac biscuit. 'These are pretty good,' he said between mouthfuls.

'Thanks. I'll just leave them here,' she said, placing the plate on the top of his esky. 'I wasn't sure if you needed a drink or not,' she said, holding the glass and wondering where to put it. He solved the problem for her, taking it and downing its entire contents in one long chug before handing it back.

Right. 'I'll get going then. See you later.' She did an abrupt turn and headed back to the house, depositing the glass in the sink and grabbing her car keys.

Maybe she had been celibate too long. It *had* been a long time since she'd been with a man, and when she said man, she meant her husband.

At first she hadn't realised how far she and Paul had drifted. She'd been so busy, and for that she did take some of the blame. But in all fairness, she didn't think Paul's attitude had helped. He hadn't bothered hiding his growing resentment of her career success. He resented the fact she could make her living staying at home. It didn't seem to matter that she still had to do housework and shopping, as well as fit in all the other time-consuming chores that arose like taking cars to the mechanic or sitting on a phone to sort out anything Paul was too busy to do. Looking back, she realised he had been jealous, maybe not of her writing career but the fact she'd made the decision to follow her dreams. He'd hated his job, and for years she'd told him to leave and find something new, but his cautious, practical nature had stopped him. It was ironic that when he had decided to follow her advice it had been to have an affair. When she'd suggested finding something new, she hadn't meant a new *woman*.

Being with a man wasn't something Hayley had really missed for the last twelve months or so since she'd been on her own. Her life had been turned upside down, so it was little wonder she hadn't had time to think about sex until now. *No, not until now,* she corrected herself angrily. She *wasn't* thinking of having sex, and certainly not with someone she'd just hired to build her a chook pen. Good grief, imagine if that got out? Still, it might make finding a tradesman a lot easier in the future. She gave herself a mental slap and told herself to behave.

Sixteen

She was getting used to the winding, narrow roads out here, and it really was an incredibly beautiful part of the country. She drove into the picturesque village of St Albans and parked her car in front of the old inn. If only buildings could talk, she thought, before a shiver ran through her and she quickly changed her mind. On second thoughts, that was probably the last thing she needed at the moment.

She intended heading over to the park across the street but decided to have a coffee first. The benches outside looked inviting, and she would have a beautiful view of the white blossoms on the trees out front.

She slipped her sunglasses onto her head and walked into the pub's dim interior. The place had been built in 1836 and the thick sandstone walls and small windows didn't allow much natural light inside. The smell of wood smoke from the huge fireplace permeated the air despite the fact it probably hadn't been lit since the end of winter.

A young girl, around fourteen or so, was wiping tables down and looked up at her arrival.

'Hello,' Hayley said before a woman in her early fifties came out from a back room. She carried a tea towel in her hand and she smiled welcomingly at Hayley. 'Hello, love. I thought I heard someone come in. What can I get you?'

Hayley glanced up at the menu and settled on a cappuccino, then added a raspberry muffin on a whim. 'Is it all right if I sit out the front and write? I'm having a bit of stuff done at my place and I need some peace and quiet to work.'

'Absolutely, sweetheart,' she said, handing over her change. 'Knock yourself out. So you've just moved to the area then?'

Hayley nodded. 'I've not long moved into a cottage over in Lochway. Hayley Stevens,' she said, introducing herself.

'Oh! Abby Cottage.' Her smile widened. 'So you're the new owner. We're the Dekkers. I'm Trudy,' she said, 'and this is my daughter, Indiana.' She put her arm around the teenage girl she'd noticed earlier. 'She helps out around here on the weekends.' Trudy then turned her head and bellowed, 'Pat. Come out here.'

Hayley heard footsteps from behind the bar area then a man with a rather large beer belly came through the doorway. 'This is my husband, Pat. This is Hayley, she's the one who bought Abby Cottage. The author,' she added.

Hayley never ceased to be amazed by the rate at which news travelled in the area.

'Ah,' he said, looking Hayley over with curious interest. 'Nice to meet you. Hey, you might find this interesting, being a writer and all.' He lowered his voice conspiratorially. 'Did you know this place is haunted?'

Oh no. 'Really?' Hayley asked, hoping she sounded interested.

'Come with me,' he said, leading the way into the dining room. An odd assortment of memorabilia decorated the mantle above the fireplace and the rough stone walls and exposed beams of the ceiling, along with the sooty bricks of the fireplace, made the room feel trapped in time.

'We've had people visit who swear they've felt something when they stand near that far corner,' Pat told her solemnly. 'One lady described it as someone putting their hands around her throat.'

'Well, that's . . . disturbing,' Hayley said, eyeing the corner of the room warily. *Please don't let me see anything,* she begged silently. The last thing she needed right now was to encounter a strangling ghost, but she couldn't see anything out of the ordinary. Still, the room gave her the creeps and she breathed a sigh of relief when Trudy called out that her coffee was ready.

It was as lovely as she'd imagined sitting outside in the warm morning sun, and after a few minutes of soaking in the view, Hayley opened her laptop and prepared herself to be inspired.

Luke drove past the old inn and did a double-take, pulling over to park before getting out of his ute. 'Hayley?' he said as he crossed the empty road. When he'd first noticed her, he'd felt a lightness in his chest and undeniable excitement flow through him.

She looked up from her computer and smiled. 'Hi.'

'If you get to hang out at pubs all day, I reckon I might be tempted to give being a writer a go.'

'See? It's all about finding the positive.'

'So what are you doing here?'

'I'm trying to find my muse,' she said with a sigh.

'What's it look like? I can help search if you like,' he offered drolly, hitching his booted foot onto the bottom rung of a nearby seat.

'Funny,' she said, pushing aside her computer. 'I just can't seem to get my head into the book I'm supposed to be writing and it's too noisy at my place today.'

'Errol?' he asked.

'Jason Weaver.'

'Sorry?'

'Jason Weaver. The handyman guy from a few farms down,' she explained.

'I know who he is, but what's he got to do with your place?'

'He's building my fence and chook pen,' she said hesitantly and he realised his face must have been giving away his concern.

'I wish you'd told me before you hired him.'

'Why?'

'He's not exactly the most stable guy in the district.'

'What's that supposed to mean?'

'He's had a few issues. Ever since he came back.'

'Back from where?'

'Overseas. He was serving in the army when he got his leg blown off.' He felt bad when he saw how shocked she seemed.

'I didn't know that was how it happened.'

'He kind of lost the plot after he came home. Started drinking too much and got banned from the pub after he started one too many fights. Since then he's became a bit of a recluse.'

'Well, he seems okay to me—a bit standoffish perhaps, but he certainly doesn't seem unstable.'

'All I know is a lot of guys come back from over there messed up. Apparently he has PTSD. Or at least that's what I heard.'

'I wouldn't have picked you for someone to listen to gossip,' she said and he felt the sting of rebuke in her tone.

'It's not gossip if it's true. The guy has a short fuse and you need to be careful.'

'He's just building me a chook pen. I think I'll be okay.'

'Look, I'm not trying to be a dick here,' he said, feeling somehow insulted by her offhand response. 'He's got issues.'

'Maybe this is what he needs then. Someone willing to give him a chance to prove himself.' She shrugged. 'I can't see any harm in that.'

Well, when she said it like that, he *did* sound like a complete dick, but she didn't know Jason the way he did. He knew Weaver better than anyone, or at least he had once. 'Are we still on for Saturday night?' he asked hesitantly, half expecting her to come up with an excuse to back out after he'd insinuated she couldn't be trusted to pick her own handyman.

'Of course. I'm looking forward to it,' she said, and he was relieved when she smiled.

'Okay then. I better let you get back to your writing. See you Saturday.'

He pushed away from the seat and headed back to his ute. He didn't want to damage the fragile friendship they'd forged and something told him he'd been treading on thin ice back there. Clearly it'd been too long since he'd had to deal with the whole new relationship minefield. *Relationship?* Was that what he wanted? It wasn't really something he'd been looking for, but all of a sudden, the opportunity had presented itself in the form of a woman covered in mud, trying to drag a donkey out of a dam.

Did he want a relationship? The question came back around again as he drove along. It was a little unnerving to realise it was a moot point. The *real* question was, could he let Hayley Stevens walk out of his life *without* trying?

Seventeen

Hayley was unexpectedly nervous as she waited for Luke to arrive on Saturday night. When he pulled up and got out of the car, she had trouble dragging her eyes from his R.M. Williams catalogue shirt and jeans look. She caught the subtle whiff of a masculine cologne. She'd always been a sucker for a nice-smelling man. They made small talk on the drive to his place and she got the feeling that he wasn't quite as cool, calm and collected as he looked. Which made her feel slightly better about her own attack of nerves.

They pulled up in front of a huge shed that looked new compared to the heritage buildings scattered across the rest of the property. Two enormous doors led into the brewery and Hayley walked inside, pleasantly surprised by the warmth of the interior. A long bar ran through the middle of the open area, its beautifully polished timber top gleaming under drop-down lights. A rustic brick half-wall created a divide between the bar area and the huge stainless-steel vats where the boutique beer was made.

At the other end of the shed was a kitchen with lots of stainless steel in an industrial-style, open-plan design, and in between were scattered timber tables and chairs. A barrage of scents hit Hayley all at once. There was a sweet malty scent, and strong brewed coffee, mixed with fragrant, herb-like smells and something mouth-watering cooking at the other end of the establishment where she could see three people busily working in the kitchen.

'Wow, this is impressive,' she said.

'Yeah, it's come up great. It's been about two years in the planning.'

'I'd say all that planning has paid off.' It was still early but already there were half-a-dozen tables occupied.

'Do you want a tour?'

'Can I?'

'Sure. I know the owner,' he said with a wink.

They walked into the brewery and the smell of hops, barley and malt was stronger than out the front but not unpleasant. Huge steel vats dominated the space.

A man came out from a side room and headed over with a friendly smile. 'I really should look at hiring security to keep out the riffraff,' he said.

'Hayley, Grant, my older, uglier brother. Grant, this is Hayley, our new neighbour.'

'So you *do* exist,' Grant said, reaching out to shake Hayley's hand. 'I figured he had to be imagining any woman who'd give him the time of day.'

Hayley wasn't entirely sure how to respond to their sibling banter, but their relaxed attitude indicated that it was something they did frequently, so she smiled and said nothing.

While there was a definite family resemblance between the men, the two brothers were complete opposites in appearance. Grant had a well-maintained but impressive beard in a trendy lumberjack fashion. His clothing was designer labelled, not from an R.M. Williams catalogue like his brother's, but very urban LA. His swanky leather shoes alone would have cost a small fortune, and when he turned away briefly to toss a cleaning cloth into a nearby sink, she caught a glimpse of a man bun. No self-respecting lumberjack would have hands that clean or well maintained, she thought with a silent snort of amusement.

'I thought we'd give Hayley a tour of the place before dinner.'

'Sure, always happy to show off our brainchild. Have you ever been inside a brewery before?' Grant asked.

'No, never. It looks impressive.'

'Thanks. It's taken a fair bit of research and time setting it up, but we're pretty happy with the result.'

'So how does it work?' she asked, looking around.

'The first stage happens out the back in the grain mill where the barley, wheat and corn we've grown is put through the malting process. The grain is wet down and allowed to germinate, then it's dried and tumbled to knock the beginnings of the roots off. Next it's kiln-dried and, depending on what we want to do, for instance, for our porters and stouts, we caramelise or roast it to create dark malts, that kind of thing.' The passion for his craft resonated through Grant's voice and Hayley found herself caught up in his enthusiasm. 'After that it's brought in here and put into the hopper above the mash tun,' he pointed to a large cone-shaped steel vessel, 'where it's milled and added into the tun with hot water. From there the enzymes break down the starch and we strain the liquid part of the mash, which is called the wort, into the kettle and add the hops and then it's boiled.'

Hayley followed the process as they walked around the various equipment and machinery, finding it far more interesting than she'd imagined.

'It cools as it passes through this radiator-looking thing where a heat exchange takes place and the yeast is added before it goes into this,' he tapped another large vat. 'It's called the fermenter and it'll sit in here for about a week. After that we add the hops and sugars and leave it all to settle and mature for another three to seven days before it's filtered and most of the yeast removed. Then it's carbonated and either bottled or kegged, ready to drink.'

'Wow,' Hayley said, seriously impressed by the complexity of the procedure, even though she was fairly sure he'd given her the layman's tour. 'What an awesome initiative.' She looked around slowly, taking in everything with a new appreciation.

Grant and Luke both wore satisfied grins as they followed her gaze around the room.

'You've managed to combine a little bit of everyone's strengths,' she said, looking at Luke. 'You and your father's love of farming, Grant's obvious passion for brewing, Olivia's cooking and your mother's function-organising skills. It's amazing.'

'We just had to be a little bit creative,' Luke told her. 'People on the land have always been good at that. If one crop isn't bringing in much, you swap to another for a while until something else picks up again. You have to be able to diversify in modern farming if you want to stay afloat. This is just an extension of that.'

'What a fantastic asset to the region. You must be bringing in a ton of tourists,' Hayley said.

'We're averaging about three bus tours a week, plus the city daytrippers on the weekends. We're getting there,' Grant agreed before he glanced over as some customers came up to the bar. 'I better go. It was nice meeting you, Hayley. I'll catch up a little later.'

'Thanks for the tour,' she said as they all walked over together.

'Can I get you a beer?' Luke asked.

'Sure.'

'What would you like?' he asked, gesturing towards the large chalkboard on the brick wall behind the bar. The choices were mind-boggling and Hayley gaped at some of the combinations listed.

'I seriously have no idea. What do you suggest?'

'How about we do a sampler?'

'You're the expert,' she said, giving him free range to order on her behalf.

'You pick a table and I'll be right there.'

Hayley found a table for two off to one side and a few moments later Luke came across carrying a long board with round holes that held a dozen small glasses of beer. They varied in colour from light straw to amber and gold to one that was almost black.

'Now this is what I call service,' she said, peering down at the glasses.

'This is our beer-sampling paddle. It's the best way to taste all the most popular brews.'

'So, what have we got?' she asked a little hesitantly.

'We've got ginger, chilli, this one's lime,' he said pointing along the row. 'There's a chocolate stout and a coffee stout and that one's a watermelon wheat.' He went on to list the remainder of the beers: blueberry, guava, pumpkin, lamington, passionfruit and an apple cider.

'I had no idea you could have these kinds of flavours in beer.'

'Beer's an amazing base for all sorts of flavours.'

'How did you come up with them all?'

'That's all on Grant and Olivia. They sit back there and experiment with different ingredients. I'm more of a traditional kind of guy when it comes to beer, but I have to admit some of these are pretty cool to try.'

A woman with dark hair pulled back in a tight ponytail came out from the kitchen and made her way towards their table. 'Hello there—finally, I get to meet our mysterious neighbour.'

'Hayley, this is Olivia, head chef and sister-in-law,' Luke introduced.

'Hi, Hayley. I can't believe we haven't been able to meet before this. I was so excited when Luke told me you were coming here tonight. I'm a big fan of your books,' she added almost shyly.

'Oh really? I'm so pleased.'

'I've read them all. I just love them.'

She was genuinely thrilled whenever someone told her they loved her books, but she'd never quite gotten used to it. Writing was something she just did. She still found it amazing that there were people who actually bought and read what she wrote. It was humbling but a little overwhelming too. 'I'm glad you like them,' she smiled.

'Do you think it would be possible for you to sign some of my books at some stage? I can't believe I'm living next door to my favourite author,' she beamed.

'Of course. It'd be my pleasure.'

'Thank you so much,' her smile widened before she looked across at Luke and rolled her eyes at his smirk. 'Oh, be quiet, Luke.'

'What? I didn't say a thing,' he chuckled.

'He's been giving me grief ever since he found out how much I love your books,' Olivia explained.

'It's just so weird seeing the usually poised and unflappable Olivia Mason jumping up and down like a schoolkid.'

'I was not jumping up and down,' she said to Hayley, clearly mortified by her brother-in-law's teasing.

'It's okay, I didn't believe him anyway,' Hayley assured her.

'Whatever, Liv,' he dismissed.

'I've got to go, some of us have work to do tonight,' Olivia said, aiming her barb at Luke.

'Sucks to be you. Although *some of us* had to be up and working before daylight this morning.'

'Do you know what you'd like to order?' Olivia asked Hayley, ignoring Luke pointedly.

'Oh . . .' Hayley quickly grabbed the menu and scanned the list of scrumptious meals on offer before choosing the Scotch fillet.

'Make that two, thanks,' Luke said, handing over their menus with a wide smile.

'I'll get right on it,' Olivia assured Hayley before making a face at Luke and walking away.

'You know you're really famous when the *actual chef* comes out to take your order,' Luke said with a wise nod of his head.

'At least I know she isn't going to spit in my food. Not sure you can be so certain,' she said, lifting an eyebrow at him. She'd found their sibling-like banter endearing, having never had it herself. She almost felt a little envious of the relationship. It must be nice to have a close family like that.

'Nah, she loves me really,' he told her confidently. 'She really does love your books that much, though. She's been trying to get everyone to read them and that was before she even knew you'd moved out here.'

'That's really cool.'

'I do feel like a bit of an idiot for not knowing what a big deal you are,' he said with a slight wince.

'I'm not a big deal.'

'You kind of are. I googled you.'

'You did?' she asked apprehensively.

'I read some of the articles on you. It's pretty impressive.'

Hayley shifted in her seat. 'I've been lucky.'

'I'd say there's more than luck involved in having that many readers. I think it's awesome.'

'It *is* awesome. Every time I see a book of mine on a shelf, it still feels as exciting and surreal as it did the first time. I'm lucky that I get to do something I love for a job, I guess. Like you,' she added. 'You're doing what you love, right?'

'Yeah, I guess. Most days I love it,' he grinned.

'And you grow all the crops that Lochmanning uses to brew the beer right here?'

'Yep. Barley, hops, plus lucerne for feed. We also supply the restaurant with all its beef.'

'That's so cool.'

'Yeah. It's taken a bit of work, but when we went in on this venture it was so we could highlight the paddock to plate, or beer glass,' he said with a quick grin, 'model of business.' He reached forward and took his beer from the table. 'Nice change of topic, by the way,' he said with a slow smile.

❧

Luke saw the faint blush that followed his statement before she hid it behind a hurried sip of beer. He'd been serious

164

about googling her. He'd half expected to find one or two links to a book or something, but nothing like the pages and pages her name had turned up. There'd been profiles and reviews in all the city newspapers, photos of book launches and conversation pieces. Despite her attempt to downplay her status, she was a big deal. He liked that about her. Hell, he liked everything about her. Her understated beauty, her sense of humour, her down-to-earth approach. She was very different to Lucinda and her circle of arty socialites who, if truth be told, had always bored him stupid.

No matter how hard he'd tried to fit in for Lucinda's sake, he'd never quite managed it. To them he was only ever going to be *the farmer*. Eventually she'd realised that no matter how hard she tried to change him—mould him into a copy of her cultured city mates— there was just no getting rid of his country core. In the beginning Lucinda had been happy to share his lifestyle, and she'd dropped her airs and graces. That was the Lucinda he'd fallen in love with. But then she'd grown bored with country life.

A dinner party with some of her old university friends had been the last straw for their floundering relationship. Maybe he'd just been overtired after a long week and should have said no to *another* weekend in the city. Or maybe he'd finally had a gutful of the pretentious arsehole who'd been talking over everyone for most of the night. When said arsehole had learned that Luke was a farmer, he'd started going on about the farming industry being the ultimate in animal cruelty, and Luke had lost it.

He'd tried to bite his tongue, he really had. He'd sat and listened to the guy rave on and on about the enslavement and abuse of livestock, about the farming industry needing to be eliminated. Eventually Luke hadn't been able to stand the ignorance any longer.

'A farmer's animals aren't just his livelihood, they're his passion,' he'd told him. 'You don't spend years breeding and raising animals just to abuse them. That doesn't even make sense. Why would someone mistreat their livestock when it takes so much work to keep them healthy? I've been around farming all my life and I can tell you I have never met a farmer who has ever done anything to deliberately harm his animals.'

It hadn't stopped the man, he'd continued to rave on and on about how farmers had cleared the land for grazing, effectively ruining it, and it was time to phase farming out entirely, freeing all animals from captivity.

'And where exactly do you propose all these freed farm animals will actually *live*? I can guarantee a million sheep and cattle released to roam free will pretty much bring about the end to all your big plans for land rejuvenation. Do you think maybe the fact farmers *contain* their animals and manage their property for the use of livestock might actually be *saving* the rest of the environment? Farmers have been managing soil and water for generations—even before it became trendy for tossers like you to suddenly become experts on it.'

'Luke!' Lucinda had exclaimed.

'I'm not listening to any more of this shit. You people aren't even living in the real world.' Luke shook his head slowly. 'You better enjoy that pinot noir and those lattes because when you eliminate farming there won't be anyone to grow grapes or coffee beans,' he said, then excused himself from the table.

Two days later Lucinda had arrived back at Lochmanning, informed him she was collecting her belongings and left without a backward glance.

Their meal arrived, bringing Luke back from his depressing trip down memory lane, and for the next few minutes they were both too busy eating to talk. Luke watched Hayley enjoying the food with abandon, savouring the flavours and giving a small moan of appreciation that stirred him in a way that was not appropriate in a public place.

'This is so good,' she said, looking up at him.

'I'm glad you're enjoying it.'

'I haven't had a decent steak in I don't know how long.'

'There weren't any restaurants that served steak in the city?' he asked with a wry smile.

'I'm sure there were,' Hayley said. 'I just didn't really go out much. I *don't* go out much,' she corrected.

'I guess you won't have an excuse not to go out for dinner now, considering we're right next door.'

'This is true. I think I could even manage to drag myself out of tracksuit pants for a meal like this.'

'I'm sure Olivia wouldn't care if you turned up in tracksuit pants.'

'Don't tempt me. The struggle is real. I'm quite happy not to get dressed or to leave the house if I don't have to.'

'I'm glad you decided to come out tonight,' he said.

'Me too,' Hayley smiled before picking up her knife and fork again. 'So, you work in here too?'

'Sometimes, if we're having a busy night. Eventually we'd like to hold a music festival on the grounds. Grant's a big blues fan and he's got contacts in the industry.' Although the latest biosecurity regulations were going to cause a few more headaches as they figured out how they were going to organise a festival.

They discussed music and swapped concert stories all the way through the rest of the meal and on to dessert, and Luke was surprised when he looked around to find they were one of the last couples left in the restaurant.

'I guess I should let you get to bed. You probably have an early start in the morning,' Hayley said, and his spirits lifted a little at the note of regret in her voice, even if he did get momentarily distracted by the thought of bed.

'It's okay, sleep's overrated anyway.' And if it meant spending more time alone with Hayley Stevens, he was fairly sure he wouldn't care if he didn't sleep all night.

Eighteen

There was a crispness to the air and it stung Hayley's cheeks as she walked outside. She couldn't remember the last time she'd had such a lovely night out—at least not in the last eighteen or so months anyway. It was nice to smile and have a conversation, *a real* conversation that involved an actual person and not a character in her head.

'Did you have a good time?' Luke asked, almost as though reading her mind.

'Yes,' she said. 'I did.'

'You sound surprised. Were you thinking you wouldn't?'

'I guess I wasn't really expecting anything. But I really did have a lovely night. Good food, good company, good beer—what more could I ask for?'

'Well, we aim to please.'

The crunch of gravel beneath their feet was the only noise as they walked away from the brewery and headed towards Luke's house further down the property. Away from the public grounds, the path took on a more relaxed form. Wattle and bottlebrush and other natives were scattered along a narrow dirt pathway used by the family to access the main house and other residences.

'This is me,' he said as they approached a tidy cottage with a wraparound verandah. 'Do you need to hurry home or would you like a coffee before you go?'

Hayley was surprised to realise she didn't want the night to end. She waited for a rush of guilt to flood her, but strangely it didn't come. 'Coffee would be great,' she said with a small smile.

She looked around the cottage with interest and noted that it was very tidy. While it had clearly been renovated recently with new carpet and kitchen, the original tongue and groove boards had been retained, as well as what looked like the original leadlight glass in the high hallway inserts.

Where the main house was full of antiques and expensive artwork, Luke's cottage was a homey bachelor pad. He had a functional two-seater lounge, no scatter cushions or photos sitting on the mantelpiece and nothing hanging on the walls. A pile of farming magazines was stacked neatly on the polished timber floorboards next to a recliner. It looked as though a wall had been taken out at some point, because the lounge room was spacious and opened out into the kitchen.

'This is really nice,' she said, looking around the timber kitchen.

'Thanks. Yeah, it's kinda small, but I like it. It serves its purpose—it's not like I spend much time inside anyway.'

'Nice coffee machine,' she said, eyeing the gleaming stainless-steel machine on the benchtop.

'Well, not to brag or anything, but I do believe mine's bigger than yours.'

'Size isn't everything, you know,' she told him haughtily.

'You better hold off judgement until you've tried the coffee,' he warned her. Luke carried the cups back across to the lounge room and set them down on a small coffee table.

'Oh. Before I forget,' he said suddenly, turning to leave the room, only to return a few moments later carrying a folder. 'Gran gave me this to give you to read.'

'What is it?' Hayley asked, reaching to take the folder from him.

'Gran put together a bit of a family history years ago. She said you might find something on Edward in there.'

A tickle of awareness ran up her backbone as she stared down at the folder and she quickly put it down beside her handbag on the floor. 'Thank your gran for me, that was very kind of her.'

'I suspect she thinks she's found a kindred spirit in you,' he nodded at the folder. 'She's finally found someone interested in family history.'

'You're not interested in it?' she asked curiously.

'I used to be. I think it hurt Gran's feelings when I stopped asking to hear the stories.'

'Why did you stop?'

He gave a small shrug before taking a sip of his coffee. 'I guess I grew up. Family folklore lost its shine once I figured out the real story.'

'The real story?'

'The way it's always told is that Wilfred Mason cleared the land and managed to grow more crops and livestock than anyone else in the district, thereby keeping the colony in food and prospering beyond anyone's wildest dreams.'

'And you don't think he did?'

'No, he did it all right. They just don't tell you at what cost. This is fertile land. It bordered one of the best parts of the river—river land that used to be a major food source for the local Aborigines. Who more or less vanished from the face of the earth.'

'Vanished?'

'Wiped out.'

Hayley stared at him as a strange feeling overcame her. '*I know what he's planning. He's going to kill them all. All of them! Men, women and children. How can I just stand by and let him do that?*'

'Hayley?'

She blinked to find Luke watching her curiously.

'You okay?'

'Yes, sorry,' she said hastily.

He looked like he wanted to ask her something, but thankfully he didn't.

Hayley suddenly noticed the heat radiating from where his leg touched hers. There was a current in the air, like a summer storm brewing on a hot afternoon. She could feel the weight of his gaze on her, and she absently chewed her lip between her teeth. Slowly his hand lifted and she closed her eyes briefly at the touch of his finger as he ran it gently along her jawline. She couldn't help the small tremor that ran through her. Slowly she opened her eyes and lifted her face to meet his steady look.

It felt . . . right. Why did it feel so natural to be leaning in to meet his lips like this? How was it that she already knew exactly what his kiss was going to feel like?

As his lips moved across her own, a small sigh, almost like relief, escaped from her as her body melted into his.

Luke felt her sigh against his lips and couldn't have agreed more. Finally. He'd been thinking about doing this ever since he'd first laid eyes on her, and while it hadn't been an unreasonably long time since they'd first met, it was as though something inside him was saying, *Finally!* As though he'd been dithering for years about making a move on the woman. He dismissed the feeling. Right now, he had a willing woman on his lounge kissing him back and he wasn't about to get distracted. He angled his head slightly to get better access to her mouth and felt a small quiver run through her, intensifying the longing he was already feeling. Their kiss deepened and he felt like a starving man eating for the first time in years. He couldn't get enough of her. *God, it had been so long since he'd felt her against him like this.*

She gave a small moan against his mouth and a powerful surge of lust swept through him. He gently urged her back until she was lying half beneath him, her hands snaked around his neck, pulling him closer. He could feel the sun on his back, beads of sweat rolling down his spine, and beneath him her soft curves welded against him until he could no longer distinguish where he stopped and she started. His senses filled with the scent of grass, sweat and woman as his gaze wandered across the familiar face, the little scar on her lip and those wide beautiful brown eyes. Luke's eyes shot opened and he pulled back to see Hayley open her eyes, confusion and alarm flashing in her *blue*, eyes. *What the hell?*

'What is it?' she asked, and he hated that her voice sounded so unsure.

Taking a calming breath, he tried for a smile. 'Nothing.'

She searched his gaze, clearly unconvinced.

Luke gave a small groan before lifting away from her and rubbing his hands across his face. What the hell was happening to him? From the corner of his eye he saw her hastily sit up and straighten her shirt. 'I thought I . . . heard something, that's all,' he said, not wanting to tell her about the strange other woman he'd momentarily thought was making love to. He was smart enough to know that telling the woman you were kissing that you were thinking about someone else was not going to end well.

'It's getting late, I probably should be going.'

'I'll grab the keys.' He jumped to his feet quickly. 'I'll be right back,' he said, needing to compose himself. What kind of idiot ruined a perfectly delightful make-out session with a woman like that? He did, that's who. *Moron.*

He didn't even know *why* he'd be thinking of someone else. He sure as hell hadn't meant to. It had never happened to him before. He frowned at the memory of the scene in his head. It had been so real. He could hear the birds and still smell the grass. He'd never made love out in a paddock in his entire life—he'd made out in the back of his ute a few times, but not in a paddock and not in recent years. So what the hell was that?

Get a grip. He snatched up the keys from the kitchen bench and turned back. Hayley was gathering her handbag and the folder, making an effort not to look in his direction. Who could blame her? She probably thought he was . . . Who knew what she thought. Jesus, what a mess. How was he supposed to explain it to her?

'Ready?' he asked, catching her eye briefly, feeling like a jerk as she looked away. He held the front door open for her and closed it behind them, following her across to his ute. This was not the ending to the night he'd been hoping for.

✑

Hayley wished she'd argued a little harder to drive herself home. Sitting next to the guy who had suddenly decided he was repelled by her whilst they were making out was one of the most humiliating experiences she'd endured in living history.

What had she done? She'd been raking her mind, in between bouts of mortification, to try to figure it out. She discreetly sniffed under her arms, but she smelled fine. She'd been so lost in the moment she would have been hard-pressed to recall her name, let alone sense anything was wrong. His touch had sent her into a spin. She swallowed hard as the sensation swamped her once again. What had happened?

They might be neighbours but the drive home, in heavy silence, was agonisingly long.

She caught sight of her little house welcoming her with the warm glow of light spilling from the front windows and she thought she'd never been so happy to see the place.

'Don't worry about getting out,' she said quickly once the car came to a stop and Luke made to reach for his door handle.

'I'm not letting you walk inside alone.'

'I'm fine.'

'Hayley, I need to explain.'

'No, no. It's all good. I'm really tired. Thanks for dinner.' She had the door open and was already halfway out of the car before she'd finished speaking.

'Hayley,' he said louder. 'Just let me explain. Please.'

Hayley let out a resigned sigh. *Just let him say whatever it is and get it over with.* She glanced across at him when he didn't immediately launch into an explanation and saw him run a hand through his short hair and around the back of his neck agitatedly. *Clearly it wasn't going to be a good explanation if he had to summon the courage to tell her.*

'The thing is,' he started, staring out the front window.

'You have a girlfriend?' she supplied dryly.

176

'What? No,' he said, his gaze snapping onto hers.

'A wife?'

'A wif— What are you talking about?'

'I don't know,' she shot back helplessly, 'I'm trying to work out why you're having such trouble spitting out whatever it is you wanted to tell me.'

He swore under his breath and closed his eyes briefly. 'I know you must be confused by what happened. I don't blame you. The thing is,' he said, stopping to shake his head, 'it sounds stupid and I wouldn't blame you if you thought I was nuts, but as we were . . . you know,' he said, unexpectedly shy, 'I had this weird sensation. I can't quite explain it. It's going to sound really stupid,' he said, as though resigned to the fact he was making a fool of himself. 'Look, it was nothing to do with you and what was going on. I was really into that,' he said urgently, trying to reassure her. 'I'm just making it worse, aren't I?'

Hayley was still trying to make sense of everything he wasn't saying. 'You said you felt something strange?' she asked slowly. 'What happened?'

'I don't know,' he sighed. 'Saying it out loud only makes me sound like a bigger idiot.'

'Tell me,' she said, fearing what he was going to say but at the same time hoping she wasn't the only one having crazy experiences.

'One minute I was kissing you, and the next it was like . . . I was somewhere else and I wasn't kissing *you*. Only it *was* you, but . . . it *wasn't* you,' he said, his words drifting off as he looked at her weakly.

For a long moment Hayley could only stare at him.

'I know I sound crazy. I don't know what it was, but it freaked me out and I'm not easy to freak out.'

'It's not crazy,' she said.

He did a double-take. 'What do you mean?'

It was Hayley's turn to feel uncomfortable and she twisted her fingers together in her lap as she considered telling him about the weird things she's been going through. He was right: it was one thing to try to explain it all away to yourself, but when you had to say it out loud to someone else, it *did* sound crazy.

'You better come inside,' she said, making the decision to show him the research she'd uncovered. At least if he felt like he was losing his mind he wouldn't be so quick to judge her for losing hers. Hayley unlocked the front door and walked into the kitchen where her research was spread across the table as she'd left it.

'You need to have an open mind,' she warned him.

'Okay,' he said slowly.

'A few weeks ago I went for a walk out to the back paddock to have a look around. There's a bit of a rise and then it goes down onto a flat.'

'Yeah, I know the place,' he said, watching her with more interest than wariness.

'While I was out there I saw something,' she said, swallowing. *Just say it.* 'I saw two people, a man and a woman. She was really upset—scared; he was trying to calm her down. Then these men rode up to the top of the rise.' She couldn't look at him. 'I saw them shoot the couple. I saw them die.'

When he didn't reply straightaway, she risked a quick glance and felt her shoulders sag. She couldn't blame him for looking at her in that odd way, like he was waiting for her to tell him the punchline of a joke. 'The thing is, I felt as though I was there, but I wasn't. It was like watching a movie playing out. It was something that happened a long time ago. They dressed like they came from another era. I thought I'd had sunstroke or something, and believe me, I tried to forget it . . . only, once I met your gran and she showed me the paintings hanging up on the walls of your parents' house . . . It was him.'

'It was who?'

'The man from the dream . . . or whatever it was. The one comforting the woman. It was Edward Mason.'

'Edward Mason,' he said in a deadpan tone.

'I know how this sounds,' she said, holding up her hand, 'but I hadn't heard any of the stories about your family when I saw him. I can't explain how I saw a vision of Edward being shot when I hadn't even heard about him, let alone how he was killed.'

'Maybe you'd heard the story a long time ago and forgotten about it?'

'I don't think so. Also, I believe the woman he was with was Jane Carney. I can't actually verify that because I can't find a photo of her, just a vague description of her from her convict records, but I feel sure it was her.' She dug through the papers on the table and pulled out a sheet she'd printed from the internet. 'Five feet three inches, oval face, small chin, brown eyes, fair complexion. Long brown hair, small scar at corner of mouth,' Hayley read, stopping as she caught sight of the expression on Luke's face. 'What?'

'I don't know,' he said, pulling out the chair he'd been resting his hands on and sitting down. 'The scar. The description.' He reached for the paper she was holding and read it with a furrowed brow.

'The face you saw tonight, it was her, wasn't it?' Hayley said.

'It can't be, can it?' He put the page down and crossed his arms across his wide chest as he leaned back in his chair. 'That would be . . .'

'Insane?' she finished blandly. 'And now you know how I've been feeling for the last few weeks.'

'Just so I've got this clear. You think that we've both been seeing . . . people who've been dead for over two hundred years?'

'Trust me, I've worked through the stages of denial and searched for logical reasons to explain it, and maybe if I'd only had it happen once, I could almost believe I was suffering from not enough sleep or, I don't know, some kind of heat-induced hallucination. But there's been other weird stuff,' she said, hesitating briefly. 'I sat down to write my new book and, instead, Jane and Edward's story came out . . . before I even had any idea who they were. I wrote about everything, Luke—stuff I have no idea how I knew about, details I didn't even have to research—and now with your experience . . . I don't know, I just feel like there's a reason you're having them too. That somehow you and I are involved in this.'

'Involved in the lives of two people from the 1800s?'

Okay, yes, said like that it sounded really stupid. 'Well, I know what I saw. I don't know why I saw it, but I know that your family history is wrong.'

'What do you mean?'

'Your gran said that Edward was murdered by Jane Carney. That's not true. The men on the horses shot him.'

Luke was looking at her doubtfully and Hayley wished they could just rewind the night and start again. 'Based on your vision.'

'Based on whatever I saw out there, yes. Maybe Jane wants the record set straight.'

'So she's a ghost now?'

'Forget it,' Hayley said, pushing away from the table. 'You're right, it's stupid. Let's just forget tonight happened.'

Luke stood up and took a step towards her. 'Look, I agree things kind of got off track, but I don't want to forget everything about tonight. I've really enjoyed spending time with you. I want to do it again.'

'This is the part where you get to grab the escape I just gave you and run as fast as you can from the crazy woman,' she said softly as he took another step closer.

'I never was the brightest spark,' he shrugged and the corner of his mouth tugged up in a smile. 'Besides, crazy isn't the worst thing a person can be. I should know. I come from a long line of crazy.'

'Oh yeah, your family are all fruit loops,' Hayley scoffed, recalling the elegant furniture, classily dressed ancestors and antiques in the Mason family home.

'My gran reads palms and tarot cards.'

'That doesn't mean she's crazy.'

'She thinks the cat is her uncle from a past life.'

'Oh. Wait, *what*? She does?'

'Mum says it's her medication, but I don't know . . . when it comes to Gran, nothing surprises me.'

'Then why do you find it so easy to dismiss this thing with Jane?'

'I'm not dismissing it, I'm just waiting until I can think of a logical explanation. Besides, I said my family were crazy, I didn't say I was,' he grinned.

'Let me know when you find that logical explanation,' she said dryly.

'There is one, Hayley, I'm sure of it.'

Hayley searched his gaze earnestly. She hoped he was right, she really would love him to find something rational that could explain everything that had been happening to her, but she wasn't so sure he could. She nodded and gave him a hopeful smile. What else could she do?

'I guess I should let you get to bed. It's getting late,' he said finally.

'Thank you for tonight, I really enjoyed it . . . well most of it,' she added.

He flashed her another of those smiles that did strange things to her insides. 'I had a good time too.'

Hayley bit the inside of her lip nervously as he leaned close and touched his mouth against hers lightly. She stopped herself from swooning as he pulled away and fought not to hold on to his shirt and beg him to stay. Mentally, she was pretty sure she was not ready to fall into bed with anyone at the moment, and yet her body was protesting that she was. It was touch and go for a while, until thankfully Luke took a step back and she was able to regain a measure of decorum. She walked him to the front door and waved goodnight as he climbed into his ute and drove off.

Hayley closed the front door and leaned against it as the sound of the engine died away. The burden she'd been carrying should have felt lighter after sharing it with Luke, but somehow it only felt heavier. There were even more questions now, and Luke seemed to be an even bigger sceptic than she was. He should be running. Only he wasn't. But he clearly thought she was crazy if she believed that Jane was reaching out to her in some way. Maybe she was. Only that was the thing—she *did* realise how unhinged she sounded. Surely a crazy person wouldn't think they sounded delusional?

Hayley switched off the lights and headed to her bedroom. She was too tired to think anymore. Her brain was struggling to come to terms with everything that had happened. Her lips still felt slightly tingly after Luke's second kiss, and she went to sleep with a tiny smile.

Nineteen

Luke pulled up and waited as Hayley ran lightly down her front path towards him. His spontaneous decision to look at cattle had come after he'd spent the morning unable to stop thinking about her. He'd been trying not to dwell on the whole fiasco of the other night, yet questions had been swimming around in his head.

Was it possible two people could be caught up in the same delusion? There was the case of the family who'd all been caught up in the paranoid belief their parents were being chased by someone who wanted to kill them. It had made national headlines. So maybe it wasn't impossible that was what was happening here. Only he hadn't been aware that Hayley had been having visions, so how could he have been influenced by her beliefs? Something niggled in the back of his mind. It had been there since that kiss. It was like trying to think of a name or a word but coming up blank. Something important was beckoning him, but he just couldn't see what it was.

He leaned over to unlock the passenger door, feeling a little giddy when she opened it. Her hair was pulled back into a messy bun and secured with a large clip. She was dressed in a pair of jeans, fancy button-up blouse and a pair of the brightest gumboots he'd ever seen. He wanted to pull her into his arms and kiss her, but he restrained himself. What if he had another weird experience and ruined everything again?

'Are you ready?' he said instead.

'Yep,' she said and pulled the door shut behind her.

Hayley wasn't sure how they were going to proceed after their previous encounter. Although their greeting was a little stilted, it wasn't too uncomfortable. She'd been caught off guard by Luke's call only a few minutes earlier to ask if she had time to go look at the Galloways, and she was a flustered mess.

Of course, if she'd simply stayed in the same outfit she'd had on, she wouldn't have been madly dashing around before he arrived, but she hadn't. Instead she'd tried on four outfits and two lots of shoes before she heard the car and had to quickly wriggle into her jeans. She'd still been fumbling with the buttons on her blouse as she ran out the front door.

'I didn't mean to interrupt whatever you were doing,' Luke said, giving her a sideways glance.

'Oh no, I wasn't doing anything important,' she assured him, smoothing her hair into place. Oh God, her hair . . . she hadn't even looked at that.

'I just had some time this morning and figured it might be our best chance.'

'No, it's fine. I really appreciate it.'

They chatted about cattle for a few minutes, or rather, Luke chatted and Hayley nodded and hoped she looked like she knew what he was talking about. They pulled into a newly fenced property, the posts painted a gleaming white, with landscaped gardens in front of two impressive stone-walled gates. Everything about this placed screamed money. 'Wow,' Hayley breathed.

'Yeah,' Luke said dryly.

'You don't approve?'

He glanced sideways, seemingly surprised. 'Approve?'

'Of city people coming here and buying farms?'

He gave a shrug. 'I've got nothing against city people coming out here.'

'But these people annoy you?'

'I guess it's the fact that they seem to have more money than sense that annoys me.'

'How so?'

'Well, they bought this place and jumped straight into alpacas. It was the new thing in farming. So they bought all these animals, started breeding them, but for whatever reason they didn't sell many, so they got rid of alpacas and got into miniature Galloways. Low and behold, after only a couple of years, they've clearly gotten sick of them too, and so they're now selling them off and God only knows what the next trend is going to be.'

'But they're not hurting anyone by doing it,' Hayley said.

'Nope, and like said, I don't really have a problem with them, it's more of an annoyance that they clearly don't do their research before diving into one project after another. Most people can't afford to cut such big losses and keep forking out money for something new. I don't know, maybe it's jealousy. I'd love not to have to worry that something I invested a stack of money into might fail. Every venture we take on at Lochmanning has to be researched and run past Dad, and then he plays out every possible scenario of what might go wrong. We can't afford to sink a crapload of capital into something and have it fail.'

The Masons didn't seem to be struggling, but you never really knew what was going on behind the scenes—for all she knew they could be mortgaged to the hilt. There was always going to be someone richer strutting around and making everything you struggled with seem like no big deal. She'd learned to keep her head down, do her own thing and not worry about anyone else.

As they parked the car, Luke got out and approached a man who'd come out of one of the nearby sheds, extending his hand in a hearty shake before introducing Hayley.

'Hayley, this is Dudley, he manages the property.' He looked a little younger than Luke but clearly the men knew each other well. He was stocky with a slightly chubby build, his stomach folding over the waist of his jeans.

'So you're looking for some cattle, Luke tells me?'

'Yes. I'm not really a farmer, I'm just after some lawn-mowers really,' she felt compelled to explain, although she was fairly sure he'd already reached the conclusion she wasn't a farmer. A real farmer most likely would not have worn bright pink polka-dot gumboots to buy cattle.

'How many you after?'

Hayley glanced across at Luke.

'Depends on price and what you've got available. We mainly want heifers and cows. Not really interested in steers.'

'Steers have been gettin' some pretty decent returns at market,' Dudley said, tipping his hat back off his forehead.

'Yeah, not interested in the whole market thing,' Luke said, and Hayley had a feeling he was trying to politely explain Hayley's aversion to raising cattle for meat.

'Ah. Okay.' There was a nod of mutual understanding. 'Well, the heifers are a bit more expensive than the steers. Come and take a look and see what you think.'

The cattle were being held in a large yard and Hayley instantly fell in love with the woolly little creatures. The tallest of the cattle stood about chest height, but the rest were lucky to reach her hip. There were about fifty in total, all different colours and shades, but most with the distinctive stripe across their middle.

Luke asked questions and climbed the fence, inspecting a few of the animals. Hayley was impressed with the confident way he handled them. When he finished talking to Dudley, he came back over to her and climbed the fence to drop lightly at her side.

'I reckon there's more than a few good head in there. Some are already in calf, some have calves at foot. And there's a bloody good bull Dudley reckons we could get for a steal.'

'But won't a bull . . . you know . . . breed?'

'That's the general idea of having a bull, yeah,' he said with a crooked grin.

'But what if we end up with a heap of boy cows?' she said, feeling anxious as she looked over at the cattle. 'I really don't think I can do the whole meat thing.'

'I was thinking about that. What if I went in partnership with you? I'll put in some cash for the initial purchase and handle all the marking, drenching and anything else that needs doing, in exchange for any steers. You won't have to do anything but keep them on your property, and I'll give you a cut of whatever the steers sell for.'

'It's that good a deal?'

'After talking with Dudley, it's a bloody good deal. There's more here than you were initially thinking of getting, but it really is too good a bargain to pass up. I can't put any on our place at the moment because we've allotted all spare grazing land for crops, which is why I'm offering to go in partnership rather than buying up the extra myself.'

Hayley looked across at the cattle again and bit the inside of her lip. She really did love the look of them. 'You think I'll have enough room for them on my place?'

'Plenty of room. It'll only be a few months till we can wean, then we can get rid of the steers, which will cut your numbers back a bit. We'll make sure we keep a check on how many we keep at a time.'

It was kind of exciting to think about. She'd have a real farm with real animals, not including Errol, Flynn and the chooks of course, she amended. They discussed prices and Hayley did a quick calculation in her head of the amount she'd be putting in added with Luke's contribution. It was only a little more than she'd been planning to spend, so she felt confident it wouldn't be breaking the bank. 'Okay. I trust your judgement,' she said, agreeing to the deal.

'We can think about it if you want some more time. I know I've put you on the spot.'

'No,' she said slowly. She knew it was always a risk to go into partnership with someone, especially with someone she hardly knew, but it felt right. 'I think it sounds like a good deal.'

Luke held out his hand and took her smaller one in his. It felt warm and safe. 'Congratulations, partner, you just became a farmer.'

Hayley was doubtful she'd be contributing anything more than money and land in this endeavour, Luke was the one ending up with all the hard work, but it still felt exciting to find herself involved in a business venture. She vowed to make sure she learned as much about the whole process as possible. Luke might be taking on the physical aspects of owning the cattle, but that didn't mean she intended to sit at home and twiddle her thumbs. She fully intended to learn as much about these cattle as she could.

The future was taking a very interesting turn indeed.

∽

Luke gave a small chuckle as he drove home after dropping Hayley back at her place. He was losing his mind. He had to be. He'd just given Hayley a big lecture about city folk jumping into farming ventures without doing their research, and five minutes later there he was proposing a joint venture with the woman. Okay, so he wasn't exactly a novice at the whole cattle game, but talking to Dudley had opened his eyes to a potentially lucrative side deal. Hayley was actually on to something with her miniature Galloways. She'd wanted something small and manageable and these cattle fit the bill perfectly. He'd done a bit of reading on the breed and been quietly impressed. As non-selective grazers, they had the ability to forage in less than ideal conditions, yet also perform outstandingly on high-grade pasture. They were used to improve marginal lands, keeping poorer quality feed under control while encouraging the quality grass to grow, which would work perfectly on Hayley's land that had been sitting unimproved and unused for a number of years.

When it came to calving, the Galloways were an exceptionally fertile breed, regularly producing vigorous calves with ease and an abundant supply of milk. Meat-wise, Galloways were excellent quality with high yields. The fat covering and heavy muscle that was vital for gaining the best prices made them an attractive breed for feedlots getting a higher yield and profit per animal. His father was a Hereford man through and through, but maybe this was Luke's chance to prove what he'd been saying for years, that they needed to branch out and try something new.

When Dudley had told him the price and how quickly his boss wanted the stock gone, the opportunity seemed to fall into his lap. He hadn't even considered buying any of the animals for himself—his father would have laughed him out of the room had he mentioned it to him—but he was a businessman as well as a farmer and he knew a good deal when he saw one. It seemed like the perfect arrangement. Hayley wanted cattle to keep her pasture under control, and he had the cattle knowledge. He could get back his initial outlay by selling off the steers, and they'd both have a reliable, if small income on the side.

It also didn't hurt that he'd have a genuine reason to be in contact with her now; they were business partners. All in all, he was pretty pleased with the day's work.

He hadn't completely forgotten their conversation on Saturday night, try as he had to forget it. He was still unsettled by his experience of kissing another woman. He fought the hollow feeling that came with the memory.

As a kid, his gran had told him he was sensitive to things, like her. He hadn't been sure what that meant at the time—he didn't see ghosts or hear voices or anything else he'd heard his father saying about Gran. While part of him had been fascinated by the stories she had told him, as he grew older Grant had teased him about believing Gran's rubbish, and he had found himself distancing himself from her. Part of him had known he'd hurt her feelings by no longer wanting to listen to her stories or spend time together the way he used to. He'd hated that too—hated that he was sensitive or whatever the hell he was supposed to be. He hadn't wanted to be teased by the rest of his family. He'd wanted his father to be proud of him; he'd just wanted to be a farmer. For a long time, he'd resented his gran, and now looking back, he felt bad for the way he acted. He'd tried to make it up to her over the years and she'd told him more than once that she'd understood, but there was a lingering sadness in her eyes whenever they mentioned it. Sometimes he found her watching him, studying him almost, and he'd have to fight the irritation it triggered. He didn't believe in her mumbo jumbo. Maybe as a gullible kid he had, but not anymore. Whatever he'd seen the other night when he'd kissed Hayley had unsettled him more than he cared to admit. *But, no. It didn't mean anything.*

By the time he arrived home his earlier buoyant mood had been replaced with frustration.

Twenty

A few days later Luke turned up early in the morning to put up the temporary stockyards for the arrival of the cattle later in the day. There was apparently a lot to do with them before they could be released into the paddock and Hayley was getting her first lesson in cattle handling, ready or not. She wiped the sweat from her forehead as she held another panel for Luke to drop a pin into.

Luke had brought along a helper, Barry, a man she'd seen in the feed store once or twice. Luke had insisted she didn't need to be there, but she'd informed him that she was there to learn and so she'd willingly jumped in to lend a hand putting up the yards.

The sound of a slow-moving, heavy vehicle announced the arrival of the cattle. Hayley stood back and watched as the driver manoeuvred the vehicle into position. What the Galloways lacked in size, they more than made up for in noise. The driver disappeared inside the belly of the vehicle, and Hayley glanced across at Luke as the sound of loud banging against the side of the truck walls and a colourful procession of swearing ensued. When he didn't seem overly concerned, Hayley turned her attention back to the truck as there was a clatter of hooves down the ramp and cattle began to pour forth in a constant stream of small, boisterous, fluffy bodies.

Barry and Luke worked like a well-oiled machine, sorting, drenching and tagging the protesting cattle. Hayley tried not to flinch at the constant click of the ear-tag gun as it placed a brightly coloured tag in each animal, replacing the old one from the previous owner. Hayley's job was to record numbers. Luke called out how many calves they had, how many steers and how many heifers and Hayley kept a running tally. As well as that, she was the gate opener and closer when the men needed to move and separate the cattle. It kept her busy and she'd soon worked up a sweat.

Later that afternoon as the last of the cattle were tagged, Hayley brought out a sixpack of cold beer from the kitchen and passed them around.

'You did really well today. Not bad for a city chick,' Luke said, looking at her after he'd taken a long swig of his beer.

Hayley was absurdly pleased with herself over his compliment, and the lingering look he sent her made her hot and flustered—and not in a working-all-day-in-the-sun kind of way.

'Yeah, well, I better get going,' Barry said, clearing his throat, and Hayley felt her face heat up even more when she realised he'd obviously picked up on the vibe between them.

Luke thanked him and Hayley said goodbye, feeling awkward in the silence that followed his departure.

'I meant it, you know,' Luke said, breaking the quiet. Hayley glanced up at him. 'You did a great job today.'

'I didn't do that much. You guys did all the hard work.'

'Don't sell yourself short. I reckon we'll make a cattle-woman out of you yet.'

'Considering I was only thinking of a few cows I could feed over the fence,' she added dryly.

'Yeah, well, sometimes we have opportunity thrust upon us.'

'I think you're mixing up your quotes.'

Luke shrugged and Hayley found herself tracing the outline of his broad shoulders, until she realised he was watching her and she glanced away, embarrassed. He tipped the last of his beer down his throat and Hayley dragged her eyes from the hypnotising action of his tanned neck moving up and down with each swallow. *There is something very wrong with you, Stevens. Stop ogling the poor guy like he's some . . . sex god . . . Sweet baby Jesus.* Her gaze fell lower. Even though his jeans were covered in dirt and dust, they still looked so good the way they lovingly traced his muscular thighs and . . . *Oh God!* He'd caught her staring at his groin. Hayley dragged her eyes away from him so fast it almost gave her whiplash. She jumped to her feet and threw her empty can into the plastic bag she'd brought them out in and looked out over the cattle yards.

'So, how long until we can let them out into the paddock?' she asked, ignoring the smug smile he was wearing as he got to his feet. Clearly her attempt at covering up her lustful staring hadn't fooled anyone.

'I'll come over tomorrow and they should be right to let out. Usually we'd keep them segregated for a week or more before letting them out onto the rest of the place, but you don't have any other stock at risk of contamination, so it won't be a problem here.'

'Great. Okay.'

'They'll be a bit unsettled tonight. Don't worry about it, that's normal.'

'Okay,' she nodded, noticing he was moving toward her. With her back against the cattle yards, there was nowhere for her to go, and as he leaned towards her, Hayley could feel the warmth of his body, smell the tangy scent of male, a mix of sweat and deodorant, cow and dust. It should have been offensive but it wasn't. Her eyes drifted shut of their own accord, waiting for the touch of his lips . . . that never came. Her eyes shot open in an instant and she found him leaning down to put his empty can in the bag at her feet. *Could today get any more humiliating?*

She prayed he hadn't noticed her bizarre behaviour, sidestepping away from him and muttering silently to herself.

'Hayley?' he said softly, and she paused, turning back to look at him reluctantly.

His hand settled on her hip, so hot that it could have been a branding iron against her skin. This time when he leaned close, she didn't have time to close her eyes, his lips were on hers firmly, and the kiss they shared was anything but feather light. It melted her down to the bone.

Luke couldn't remember a time he'd enjoyed watching a woman more than he had today. Hayley might have been a novice around a cattle yard but damned if he hadn't gotten a little hard watching her swing her leg up and over the rails, her tight jeans moulding her backside in glorious detail with each movement. He'd cursed more than once when he'd found himself distracted and almost had his foot trodden on. If he didn't watch himself he'd end up with some ribs cracked or worse. The miniature Galloways might be smaller than the cattle he was used to handling but they still outweighed him and could do some nasty damage if he didn't keep his mind on the job.

He wasn't ashamed to say he got a kick out of catching her checking him out earlier. He was pleased to see she was affected by him as much as he was affected by her. He probably could have hidden the fact he'd seen her but she looked even cuter when she turned bright red. She did have the last laugh, though, when he'd caught her staring at his junk. Her gaze had felt as hot as a touch and he was sure the effect was visible. He wanted her. There was no point denying it. He'd wanted her for weeks now. He couldn't stop thinking about her and there was no denying she felt something for him too. The only thing stopping him from acting on his impulse earlier had been the memory of what happened last time they'd kissed. But one touch of her skin now and none of that mattered. He needed to kiss her. He needed to feel her against him and he didn't give a toss about what might happen if he acted on it.

As her lips moved under his, he could taste malt from the beer they'd just drunk, and something else sweet, something undeniably Hayley. His chest felt like it was ready to explode, along with another part of his anatomy as the kiss deepened. He pushed against her, yearning to be closer, needing to feel her against him, but when she gave a small groan that somehow registered in his brain as more pain than pleasure, he swiftly turned them so *his* back was up against the rails, lifting her so she could wrap her legs around his waist. He could feel the heat of her against his bare stomach where his shirt had ridden up, and a low guttural curse ripped from his chest as a wave of pure need washed over him.

He couldn't remember a time when he'd felt so out of control. But she deserved better than a quick shag against the stockyards. It took everything he had to pull back from her and catch his breath, but the dazed look in her eyes was almost his undoing. 'This is probably the dumbest thing I've ever said in my entire life, but I think we should stop. I seriously stink, and I'm pretty sure you're not going to appreciate getting cow manure and hay in your hair, so maybe this isn't the best time to . . .'

Her initial confusion slowly transformed into a shy grin, stopping his attempt at chivalry in its tracks.

'I can solve both problems,' she said quietly, taking his hand and leading him wordlessly through the paddock and back towards the house.

Maybe he hadn't completely ruined his chances after all. He kept his mouth shut in case he said something to spoil the moment.

∽

Inside Hayley was shaking as she led Luke to the house. Was she really doing this? *Hell yes, you are*, a little voice said defiantly. There was something explosive between them, it was undeniable. In fact she was so immersed in lust that she was prepared to get down and dirty—literally—in the middle of a paddock in full view of a herd of cattle.

Thank goodness one of them had the sense to put a halt to it before things went too far and yet . . . She couldn't recall a time she'd ever felt that reckless. She hadn't cared about anything other than Luke. Sure, afterwards she'd probably have been horrified by her actions, but she was pretty sure if Luke hadn't stopped, she would have happily continued. Somewhere along the line she'd made a decision she was going to see where this thing between them led. She hadn't gone looking for it, but now that she'd found it, she was ready to see where things went.

Hayley stepped into the bathroom and swallowed nervously before turning to face him. 'There are clean towels in the cupboard over there,' she said, clearing her throat when her voice came out sounding like a squeak. 'I'll leave you to it then,' she said, moving away.

He reached out and took her hand. 'You know, in the country you have to be careful how much water you use. There's this thing we do to save it,' he said, his low voice close to her ear.

'Really?' she said, feeling her breath quicken as he leaned closer.

'If we get in together, we'll use less water.'

'Oh. Well, maybe we should do that,' she agreed, surprising herself by making the first move and pulling her T-shirt up and over her head.

She took a moment to appreciate the darkening surge of need she could see in Luke's eyes as his gaze swept across her torso. He made quick work of the buttons down the front of his filthy shirt and tossed it on the floor, before closing the gap between them and pulling her against him.

The flame was instantaneous. It licked at her insides, igniting her desire into an inferno. His mouth found hers and she was swept away by the intensity of it. The touch of his skin against her own sent a quiver of longing through her as he ran his hands up along her sides to lightly brush her covered breasts. Leaning away, she swiftly unhooked her bra and let it fall away. She smiled a little at his whispered oath, moments before he rid himself of the rest of his clothing then helped divest her of her own.

Luke pulled away and she heard him mutter beneath his breath. She opened her eyes to see he'd reached back to turn on the water but nothing was happening. Hayley opened her mouth to warn him but it was too late, the water suddenly gushed forth in a spluttering torrent of icy-cold needles, catching Luke full force and dragging out a rather unmanly squeal that momentarily distracted her from her own shock at having ice-cold water splashed over her.

'Holy fu—'

'You have to give the water a minute to warm up . . .' she told him too late. 'I've been meaning to get it fixed. Here, let me,' she leaned past him to adjust the water temperature, but her foot slipped on the wet tiles and she fell heavily against Luke's chest, knocking him off balance and pressing his back against the freezing wall tiles, tearing another yelp from him.

'Sorry,' she winced, finally adjusting the temperature of the water. 'There, that's better,' she said, trying for a calm smile, but distracted by the feel of solid chest beneath her hand. 'Are you okay?'

'Apart from my testicles lodging somewhere up around my throat . . . I'm fine,' he said with a wince, which turned to a sigh of relief as he angled his back under the now warm stream of water.

'Here, let me help. Turn around,' Hayley said, taking a bottle of shower gel and a fluffy sponge and starting to lather his wide back. He let his head drop and sighed as she worked the muscles of his shoulders and neck. Her gaze wandered lower and she found herself contemplating his buttocks and legs, white against the tanned skin of his arms. She followed the soap suds as they trailed down over his firm backside. *Sweet baby cheeses, that butt's firm enough to . . .*

'What?'

'What!' Hayley gasped. Oh, my God, she *did not* just say that out loud . . . did she?

'I thought you said something,' he said, looking over his shoulder at her.

'Nope. I didn't say a word.'

'Here, I think I'm clean enough now, but you, young lady, are filthy,' he said, and his voice dropped so low that it gave her goosebumps as he turned and took the sponge from her loose grip.

Oh, she was filthy, all right. Her mind had never had this many lurid thoughts running through it in her entire life. And now she understood why he'd sighed—she'd forgotten how wonderful it was having your shoulders rubbed, especially after a long day outside working cattle. *Look at me saying working cattle like a real farm worker person.* Oh yeah, she could get used to this, she thought as the soapy sponge ran in circles over her back. Her eyes widened. Okay that was *not* her back and she was fairly certain that had *not* been exposed to dirt and dust throughout the day either. Hayley swallowed hard as she fought to keep from panting out loud. The man sure knew how to clean, but she wasn't sure she could remain standing for too much longer. As a ripple of longing passed through her, Hayley arched and tipped her head back. Unfortunately, at that exact moment Luke had been about to kiss her neck and she cracked her head against the bridge of his nose with an eye-watering whack.

'Ouch.' Hayley's hands went to the back of her head as she turned, only to find Luke clutching his nose, blood spurting out through his fingers.

'Oh shit,' Hayley gasped, forgetting her own pain to exit the shower stall and grab a wash cloth. 'Here, put this on it,' she said, coming back to the shower.

'This is not how I was expecting the afternoon to end,' Luke said, his voice muted behind the cloth.

'I'm so sorry,' Hayley apologised, feeling terrible and reaching out for a towel to wrap around herself.

'It's okay,' he said, turning the tap off with one hand as he stepped from the stall.

'I think the universe is trying to tell us something here.'

'Yeah,' he agreed caustically, 'like maybe next time I should keep my mouth shut about a bit of cow shit and sweat.'

'In all fairness, I'm willing to bet something even worse could have happened out there.'

'I don't know . . . this was pretty damn spectacular.'

Hayley left him to take care of his nose while she headed to her bedroom to find some clean clothes. When Luke was dressed, Hayley made him sit at the dining table and tip his head back and placed a pack of frozen peas over the red, swollen nose.

'I'd offer you a coffee but I'm pretty sure having something hot isn't good for a nosebleed.'

'Thanks anyway, but I better be getting home. I still have some things to finish up.'

Hayley wrung her hands together. 'I feel really bad about this, Luke.'

He gave a strangled-sounding chuckle and took the peas off his face. 'I'm sure we'll look back on this and laugh someday. Someday, but not today,' he added.

They walked towards the door together and Hayley tried to summon a smile as he turned to look down at her.

'Seriously, Hayley, despite everything, I'm glad we took things to the next level. It would have better if it hadn't involved a bloody nose, but I still prefer what we had today over nothing.'

'Me too,' she whispered.

He leaned down towards her and Hayley moved to meet him, but he pulled back and gently placed his hands either side of her head, holding her steady. 'No offence, but I'm not taking any more chances,' he murmured before touching his lips gently to her forehead. 'How about I take you somewhere for lunch tomorrow?'

Lunch sounded safe—safer than being alone together here at least. 'Okay.'

'Great. I'll drop by and let the cattle out before we go,' he said, turning away.

As she watched him drive away her heart was beating out of kilter. She thought back over the things they'd done earlier and a small smile touched her lips. It hadn't been a complete disaster.

Twenty-one

Music filled the space between them for a few kilometres before Hayley relaxed into her seat. 'So, where are we going for lunch?' She tried to keep her thoughts from images of Luke naked in the shower.

'I thought we'd just drive and see where we end up,' he said with a grin. His nose seemed better today; there was no sign of the hit it had taken yesterday.

As they drove, Luke pointed out places of interest and told her entertaining stories of his childhood and growing up in the area. Neither of them mentioned their disastrous attempt at foreplay and she was more than happy to leave it that way. She didn't want to spoil the easy conversation and relaxed banter between them.

The winding road brought them to a small village, one of many along the river. There was an antique store and a shop called Fuss Pots that sold specialty teas and housed a museum dedicated to teapots. Across the road was a building clad in rough-sawn timber logs, with gingham curtains in the window and tables and chairs out the front under umbrellas. A sign rocked gently in the slight breeze indicating this was the Do Drop In Café.

A young woman greeted them, showing them to a table near the window.

Hayley looked at the menu and felt suddenly ravenous. 'Pancakes. I'm all set,' she said, smiling.

'You can have something a little fancier if you want.'

'What's wrong with pancakes?' She arched an eyebrow. 'I'm seriously not that complicated. Give me pancakes and coffee and I'm happy.'

Luke smiled and Hayley took a moment to appreciate the way the small crinkles that appeared around his eyes softened his otherwise stern good looks. His jaw was defined and angular; the rough stubble was sprinkled with a mix of the dark and lighter caramel colour of his hair and only helped define the rugged jawline even more. It was almost a shame when their order came and she had to concentrate on eating rather than admiring the man across from her.

After their brunch stop, they drove further, the road turning to dirt as they wove their way along the river. As they rounded a bend, Hayley spotted a curious fenced area beside the road. 'Stop,' she said, leaning forward in her seat to get a better look. 'Is that a graveyard?' she asked, squinting to read the sign.

'Yeah. An old one. It's not used anymore,' Luke said, pulling off the road.

'Can we have a look through it?'

'If you like,' he said, looking across at her curiously. 'It's a bit rundown.'

'That's okay, I don't mind. I guess a graveyard tour wasn't on your list of things to do today,' she said lightly, opening her door.

'Not exactly, but at least you're easily pleased,' he grinned.

'I did try to tell you.'

She opened the wooden gate and walked through, taking in the small cluster of old headstones scattered at odd angles as though tossed into the air to fall where they may. Some fallen and broken, others leaning precariously but still upright. The stones were stained by age and moss, having weathered the last two hundred years beneath the giant gum trees in this secluded little grove.

Hayley ran her hand along the top of a nearby headstone and read the inscription, silently greeting the person buried below. She didn't know who Charlotte was but she'd been someone's daughter, wife and grandmother and it was nice to think of her as the person she once was before all that remained of her was a name on a headstone. As Hayley moved through the grounds, she noticed memorial plaques had been placed on some of the headstones commemorating First Fleet arrivals. The significance of the history hit Hayley square in the face. Yes, Sydney was technically older than this area, but you didn't think about it, living in the city, the way you did when you were confronted with the graves of people who had arrived on the First Fleet.

'This place is so old,' she said quietly when Luke came to stand beside her.

'Yeah, it is.'

'Have you been here before?' she asked him, looking up.

'A few times. Actually, Gran and Granddad donated some of the money to restore the place. It was more or less forgotten about for a long time.'

Hayley noticed something in the uncleared undergrowth nearby and moved towards it. A tiny headstone poked up through the dead leaves and vines, its faded stone almost blending in with the vegetation. 'There's more graves through there.'

'Yeah, they managed to uncover the best of them. There's a whole bunch that were too far gone to save, so they left them uncleared.'

'That's sad,' she said, feeling sorry for the unknown person buried below.

'I guess for a long time people in these parts had more important things to worry about than maintaining a grave-yard. It was a pretty hard life in those early years. This area was remote and dangerous for a long time.'

'Yes, I suppose so.' Hayley gave the little stone one more glance before moving away towards a group of tall monuments. She gasped. 'Are these your relatives?' She looked at the name on the nearest one: Thomas Mason, died 1838.

'Yeah. Some of them. That's Wilfred Mason's son and his wife and baby daughter. They died in a fire.'

'How tragic.' Pearl hadn't gotten any further than Edward when she'd given Hayley the tour of the earliest of the Mason lineage. 'So are Wilfred and Henrietta buried here too?' Hayley asked.

'No, they're buried up at the old church. At least it used to be a church, now it's a function centre. They'd helped build it and it became the preferred place of burial for most of the wealthy locals. But this one over here might interest you,' he said, heading to the far end of the row and waiting for her to catch up.

Hayley could feel her fingers go cold and numb as they hung by her side as she read the name on the stone. Edward Mason.

She saw gentle eyes and a beautiful smile and a deep sadness began to fill her. She stepped closer, almost without thought, and placed her hand on top of the cold stone. Tears welled in her eyes, spilling down her cheeks.

'Hey,' Luke said, stepping closer. 'It's all right. It happened a long time ago.'

He doesn't understand. The thought came to her from nowhere and made her even sadder. Hayley knew on some level it was stupid to be upset about a man she hadn't known and who had died over two hundred years ago, but she couldn't help it. It was like she had no control over her emotions. Seeing the name like that filled her with an aching loss. It didn't make sense, but she felt it as real as the blister that had been forming on her heel where her shoes were rubbing.

She'd once loved the man who was buried here.

The moment she identified the thought, Hayley pulled her hand away and stepped back. *No. That was insane.*

'Hayley?' Luke approached her cautiously, concern written across his face. 'What's wrong? Did you get bitten by something?' He scanned the immediate area, looking for any sign of what could be causing her distress.

'No,' she managed to get out, desperately trying to compose herself. 'I'm sorry.'

'Don't be sorry. Just tell me what's wrong.'

'I can't,' she said, shaking her head helplessly. How could she? How could she tell him she was mourning the loss of a man she'd loved from two centuries ago?

'Here, come and sit down for a minute,' he said, steering her towards a bench erected by the descendants of the pioneers buried here.

She needed to pull herself together, this was ridiculous. 'I'm sorry. I . . . I don't really know what came over me,' she said.

Slowly the stillness of the little cemetery helped calm her. A soft breeze played with the leaves high in the canopy of the giant trees that stood as silent guardians. Birds fluttered about and the quiet felt peaceful.

'This has to do with what we talked about the other night, doesn't it?' he said quietly after a few moments.

Hayley closed her eyes. 'It doesn't matter.'

'It does.'

She felt his warm hand close over hers on the bench between them and opened her eyes. Things had been going so well between them and now this was going to spoil everything. 'I know it seems hard to believe after everything I told you the other night, but I've always been completely normal. Like, I'm talking *boringly* normal. I've never done drugs of *any* kind, I've never been into psychics or tarot readings . . . I don't even read my stars in the paper.' She gave a firm shake of her head. 'I just don't understand why I'm suddenly feeling these things and seeing . . . whatever the hell it is I'm seeing. This kind of stuff just doesn't happen to people like me. I'm a sceptic.'

He gave a twist of his lips, looking over towards the headstones where his ancestors lay. 'I have to admit the stuff that happened the other night shook me up a bit, and I can guarantee I'm a bigger sceptic than you are.'

'Then what's happening? Why did we both see things?'

'I don't know.'

'Well, what should we do about it?'

'Nothing,' he said simply. 'I mean, what can we do? Put it down to some weird experience and move on.'

'But don't you want to know why it's been happening? I mean, what if it doesn't stop? What if you keep seeing faces and what if I keep . . .'

'Keep what?'

'Keep feeling like I'm somehow connected to Jane and Edward's story.'

'Look, I can't explain the things that have happened,' he said, turning to her. 'And the truth is, I don't want to.

If I look into it any further, I'm not sure I'll be willing to accept what I find, so there's no point thinking about it.'

Maybe he had a point. To certain degree, Hayley was still sceptical, but it was becoming harder to ignore the evidence that this was indeed *something*. She didn't know what exactly, but she knew she couldn't just push it to the back of her mind and ignore it like Luke. She needed to figure out what was going on and she wouldn't be able to rest easy until she did. But she also knew Luke didn't feel comfortable talking about it and she felt a wedge driving itself between them. If there was going to be anything between them she knew it would only happen if this Edward business stopped. But in order to make it stop she had to find out what it was. She needed answers, and it seemed she'd have to find them on her own.

'Okay,' she finally said. 'Let's agree not to talk about it again.'

Luke sat, arms braced on his thighs and hands clasped loosely, staring down at the dirt beneath his boots. At first she thought he hadn't heard her, but after a little while he sat upright and nodded. 'I think that would be best.'

Her heart felt heavy as they rose from the seat and headed back to the car.

'Are you all right?' he asked gently as she opened the passenger door.

Hayley glanced back briefly at the tall headstone and forced a smile to her face. 'Yeah, I'm okay.'

For a moment Luke looked as though he wanted to say more, but a flash of irritation crossed his face and his mouth drew back into a straight line and instead he opened his door and climbed in.

The little cemetery was a sad place, but she felt a strange connection to it just the same. She knew she'd be coming back here again. There had to be answers somewhere. She just had to find them.

⟳

Luke let out a long, shaky breath as he drove away from Hayley's house. She'd asked if he'd wanted to come inside, but he'd declined. He'd been trying to hold himself together ever since the episode in the cemetery, but there was no way he could keep up the front much longer. He needed to get away. Now.

He pulled over once he reached Lochmanning, tipped his head back against the headrest and closed his eyes. What the hell was happening?

Everything had been fine until they'd reached that damn headstone. *He'd* been fine. Hayley had started falling apart and he'd reached for her, alarmed by her distress, and then it had happened. It was like getting zapped with static electricity when he touched her, only it didn't give him an electric shock—it gave him a memory.

No, he thought irritably, it wasn't a memory. It was Hayley talking about Edward Mason all the bloody time. Only, it hadn't been a memory that had anything to do with all the grief Hayley had been talking about. This had been different. He'd been holding a woman, looking into her eyes . . . brown eyes. He could see a reflection shining back in her eyes and he felt the sweat beads breaking out across his forehead as he remembered. The image he'd seen hadn't been his reflection. It had been someone else's.

In his mind he heard his gran's voice, soothing, calm and gentle—in a way he'd forgotten since he'd grown up. 'Don't be afraid,' she said, 'the past can't hurt you.'

He opened his eyes and pushed open the door. He leaned against the bull bar and stared out across the paddocks. There was an uneasy feeling hovering inside him again, and the constant frustration of trying to grasp something that danced just out of reach. The only thing he knew for certain was that somehow it all connected back to Hayley.

Twenty-two

As Hayley headed out to feed the chooks she was still excited about the new pen. It was everything she'd hoped for. The orchard was the perfect spot for the birds: they could scratch around the base of the fruit trees and keep the weeds at bay and have plenty of room to explore. Jason had moved on to the fencing and soon Errol and Flynn would have their new, bigger paddock to live in.

Each day she crossed her fingers, eagerly awaiting the discovery of an egg. Going from the seller, it should be any day that they started laying. This morning as she let the girls out of their coop, she discovered one of them still sitting inside. 'What's the matter with you? Don't you want to eat breakfast?' Hayley asked, watching the chook as it made irritable noises at her. 'Well, fine. Stay there then,' she said, giving up trying to coax the bird outside to eat with the others. She made a point of coming back an hour later to check on her and, to her great surprise, found an egg in the hay she'd laid out for them. 'So, that's what you were doing?' she said, feeling slightly stupid for not realising. She carefully picked up the smooth white egg and grinned. It was still warm. Her very first egg. She couldn't have been prouder if she'd laid the thing herself.

She'd already had breakfast, but she went straight into the kitchen, filled a saucepan with water and dropped in the egg, then stood over the stove to watch it boil.

A little while later, she was seated at the kitchen bench savouring the best-tasting egg she'd ever had in her life. She may have been a tad biased, but it was definitely the best-tasting egg she'd ever *hand-grown* . . . or whatever the raiser of hens officially did.

Puss came strolling out of the laundry, three balls of fluff tumbling and tripping along behind her. The kittens were growing fast.

'Hello, coming out for your morning visit, are you?' Hayley scooped the three kittens into her arms, their tiny meows now a familiar sound in the house. Puss no longer hovered when Hailey played with them, in fact lately she'd been using the time to disappear, presumably for a few minutes' peace and quiet. 'I don't know how I ended up as the babysitter,' Hayley said to the kittens as she snuggled them against her. They really were too cute for words. They were also incredible time wasters and Hayley reluctantly put them down, calling out for their mother, who reappeared a few minutes later and patiently took them back into their bed in the laundry.

She'd tossed and turned most of the night after trying unsuccessfully not to think about everything that had happened that day. The drive home had been quiet, both of them preoccupied with their own thoughts. When they'd arrived at Abby Cottage, she'd followed Luke out to check on the cattle and invited him to stay for a while, but he'd declined, saying he needed to get home and finish a few jobs before dark. Although she knew he probably did have work to do, she suspected his sudden desire to get away from her had more to do with that what had happened at the cemetery.

Somehow she'd thought Luke of all people, having lived around his gran, would be a little more open-minded. Apparently in Luke's case it did the complete opposite. She'd freaked him out. Big time.

Hayley pulled up outside the main house at Lochmanning and tried to shake the slightly guilty sensation she had. She wasn't sure why she felt guilty; maybe it had to do with implying to Luke the other day that she wouldn't talk about it anymore. *With him,* was what she'd meant. She didn't say she wasn't going to talk about it with anyone else. Pearl hadn't seemed particularly surprised by her call, and Hayley wasn't sure if that was a good thing or not.

When they were seated together on the lounge in the drawing room, its big windows allowing the morning sunshine to stream in, Pearl reached over and patted her hand. 'What is it you wanted to talk about, dear?' she asked, getting straight to the point.

'I'm not sure where to start,' Hayley said, feeling nervous. 'This might sound a little . . . strange.'

'I've seen and heard a lot in my years, dear. Things only seem strange when we don't understand them.'

'Well, I don't understand anything that's been happening lately.'

Pearl gave a kindly smile and waited patiently for her to continue.

'It started a few days before I came here for the first visit. I was out in the paddock and I saw something. It was like a vision.'

'Tell me about it. What did you see?' Pearl asked curiously.

'I don't actually know if that's what it was. I've never had one before.'

'Maybe you just haven't been allowing yourself to be open to them. When I read your palm the other day, I saw very strong lines in your Mercury mound. That means you have a strong psychic ability and a connection to spirituality.'

Well, that wasn't comforting in the least. Was she going to have more of the damn visions? God, she hoped not; she really hadn't enjoyed the last one particularly.

'What was it that you saw?'

'It was Jane and Edward,' Hayley said with a slight grimace. 'I didn't know it was them until I saw that sketch of Edward hanging in the hallway,' she added quickly, 'and

I haven't seen a picture of Jane, but I did find a description in the archive on her indentured records.'

'That's why you looked so shocked that day.' Pearl nodded as though everything was falling into place somehow.

'The thing is, I don't think Jane killed Edward as it was reported. I saw them being shot by a group of men on horses. Also,' she went on, 'a few days later I found myself writing a scene that had nothing to do with my current book. It was like I wasn't even writing it. I think it was about what happened to Jane the day she killed Gilbert Mears. She killed him in self-defence.'

'Well, that is interesting,' the old woman pondered.

'Why would I have seen that? What does it mean?'

'It could mean a few different things. Maybe the place where you saw it still has a tremendous amount of tragedy attached to it and anyone who has the ability to pick up on this energy may be able to see a glimpse of what happened there.'

'Like ghosts?' she said doubtfully. Pearl's silence was a little disconcerting. 'You said it could mean a few things, what are some of the other possibilities?'

Pearl tilted her head and studied her thoughtfully for a moment. 'It could be a memory.'

'How could it be a memory when it was something that happened two hundred years ago?'

Pearl continued to simply look at her calmly, until the realisation of what she was saying began to sink in. 'You're not seriously suggesting . . . *I* have some kind of memory of this . . . that it somehow happened to . . .' She couldn't even finish the sentence, it was too ridiculous. And yet . . .

'You?' Pearl smiled gently. 'Maybe. Maybe not. Though tell me, have you ever experienced déjà vu?'

'Well, yes, I suppose, but everyone has at one time or another . . . right?'

'No, not everyone. Some people aren't open enough to recognise that it's a moment they've had before. I'm not saying that's what this is, but I'd be curious to know how you saw what you did if everything in the history books, so to speak, tells it differently.'

'I don't understand.' Actually, if she were being honest, she was worried she *did* understand and that scared her even more. 'Are you suggesting I saw what I did because I was somehow there . . . back then?'

'Yes. But I suspect you weren't there as a bystander. I believe what you were seeing was what happened to you. To Jane.'

'You think I was Jane. In a past life?' she said drolly.

'It's not as strange as it seems, dear.'

Oh, I don't know, Pearl. Right about now it's feeling pretty bloody strange.

'Just keep an open mind. How many times have you met someone—anyone, a co-worker or a new friend or a complete stranger—and within a few minutes of talking, you feel like you've known that person forever?'

'And because you find some common interests with that person, that means you've known each other in a past life?'

221

'Yes,' she said simply and Hayley couldn't hold back the small disbelieving laugh that escaped.

'We're attracted to those people we've known before. Good or bad. They always come back into your life. Think back to people you just can't stand—you can't explain why they annoy you so much, but they do.'

'Pearl,' Hayley started but was cut off.

'Yes, I know how it sounds. The old lady is losing her marbles,' she said with a chuckle, and instantly Hayley felt bad, mainly because that's exactly what she'd been thinking. 'I'm used to people thinking that. My own family have been thinking it for years. But I know what I know,' she said, holding Hayley's gaze.

'I don't even look like Jane.' Hayley knew she was grasping at straws here, but she really was struggling.

'The body is never the same, only the thing that counts— the soul.'

She couldn't seriously be considering this? *No,* she told herself. *This was too outlandish.* She was not the reincarnation of a convict named Jane Carney. 'You know, I think I'm happy to say I saw ghosts and leave it at that.'

Pearl eased back in the chair and watched Hayley thoughtfully. 'Why is believing in visions and ghosts any easier to accept than the possibility we all live many lives?'

She had a point but still . . . No, it was freaking her out too much. 'I'm sorry, Pearl,' she said, getting to her feet. 'I need to get going.'

'It's all right, dear, it's a lot to fathom. Before you go, bring me the book over there on the desk, the black leather one,' she said, directing Hayley to the back of the large room to where an elaborate desk dominated the far wall. She found a black organiser, about the size of a small novel, fastened with a silver clasp, and held it up.

'That's the one. Bring it over here.'

Hayley watched as Pearl opened it and flicked through, searching for something before sliding out the pen from its holder and scribbling down something. The sound of paper ripping seemed loud in the quiet room. 'This is for you. If you decide you want to find out more.'

Hayley glanced down at the paper and saw Pearl had written a name and a phone number. 'Thanks. Although we might have to agree to disagree on the reincarnation thing.'

'That's all right, dear. Live and let live is what I say,' she said, closing the book with a snap. 'You were just as hard-headed about it all during the signing of the Magna Carta and again during the fourteenth century. It's just your way,' she said with a patient smile.

Hayley paused, eyeing the old woman who looked back at her as calm and reasonable as though they'd just been discussing something as mundane as the current stock prices. *She honestly believes she isn't crazy.* 'Thank you for the cup of tea, Pearl.'

'Any time, dear.'

Hayley's smile dropped as she almost ran into Del as she stepped through the front door.

'Hayley? Is everything okay?' Del asked, taking in Hayley's worried frown.

'Yes, everything's fine,' she said, summoning a smile. 'I was just visiting with Pearl.'

'Oh. I see,' the woman noticeably relaxed. 'That explains it.'

Hayley's eyes widened at Del's knowing look. 'Has Pearl ever mentioned . . . reincarnation to you?' she asked a little reluctantly. She didn't want to think Pearl was crazy, but if that were the case, maybe it would be easier to dismiss her outlandish theories.

'I thought that might be what was going on,' she said with a crooked grin. 'She's been talking about it a bit lately. I remember the first time I met her, she was younger of course and maybe a little less eccentric, but even then I wondered what kind of family I was marrying into.' Del paused and eyed Hayley thoughtfully. 'You know, I don't necessarily believe everything Pearl believes in, but there have been things she's said that I can't explain. I refuse to let her read my cards now—but there are people who swear by her ability.'

'You said you don't have cards read anymore . . . why did you stop?'

A flash of emotion crossed Del's face. 'Not long after Luke was born, I fell pregnant again,' she said quietly. 'Pearl did a reading for me and saw something. She didn't tell me what it was, but I knew it was something bad. Two days later I miscarried and for a long time I blamed Pearl, like she'd somehow jinxed me. I knew it was silly,' she hurried to explain, 'but after that, I don't know . . . I guess I have a wary respect for her ability. It scares me, if you want to know the truth . . . I think that's why I try to play it down.

I don't understand what it is and I don't want to. It's part of her and I can't change that, but I don't have to partake in it or encourage it. If she's said something to upset you, I can have a talk to her.'

'Oh no,' Hayley quickly assured her. 'I think Pearl's wonderful. It just took me by surprise, that's all.'

'That's our Pearl, she doesn't mince her words. She means well though. Actually, Hayley, now that I've got you here, there's something I've been thinking about lately and I wanted to run it past you,' Del said, indicating a white settee outside and taking a seat. 'When Abby Cottage came up on the market, I was giving serious thought to buying it,' she said, without preamble.

Hayley's eyes widened. 'You were?'

'Yes, but before I could even get myself organised, you slipped in and snatched it up,' Del grinned as Hayley cringed. 'It's all right, I really didn't need the extra stress anyway,' she assured her. 'The thing is, accommodation is the one thing Lochmanning's missing. Patrick and the boys don't particularly want to go down that track, and quite frankly we've got more than enough on our plate with the bar and restaurant and the reception centre. Not to mention all this fuss over biosecurity,' she added gravely. 'And yet being able to provide accommodation for our customers would make a lot of sense.' She paused, studying Hayley silently for a moment. 'Have you thought about re-establishing the B&B side of things at your place?'

Hayley was surprised by the question. 'Well, I've thought about it . . . as something I could do down the track. But

I wouldn't use the cottage itself, so that really only leaves the caretaker's cottage.' The previous owners had let out the spare room in the main cottage, but Hayley valued her privacy too much to consider sharing her house in that way.

'Look, this is just me thinking out loud, nothing more, but if you were to open again, we could look at using the cabin as part of a bridal package, providing accommodation close to the venue. It would be ideal.'

'I wouldn't even know where to start,' Hayley admitted.

'I'm happy to help out wherever I can. Anyway, have a think about it. Maybe we can both come up with some ideas.'

Hayley nodded, 'I'll definitely think about it,' she promised. The extra income would be welcome, and her mind was already mulling things over as she took her leave and headed home. She'd gone over to Lochmanning with one problem and was returning home with no sensible answers and a new business venture. Life was certainly never dull around here.

Twenty-three

'All done,' Jason said, making Hayley jump.

'How do you do that?' she asked when her pulse had slowed back down again.

'Do what?'

'Sneak up on people.'

A muscle in his jaw twitched slightly. 'Habit, I guess.'

'You make a habit of sneaking up on people?'

He jammed his hands in his pockets and looked down at the ground. 'Used to.'

'In the army?' Hayley asked, then regretted it as his face hardened slightly.

'So you've heard the gossip.'

'Just the abridged version,' she said, putting her computer aside. 'Do you want a cuppa? I'm ready for one.' She didn't wait around for him to decline and as she headed for the back door she heard him mutter, 'Yeah, sure, I guess,' and smiled to herself.

'I'll just pack away my gear,' he called out as she walked into the kitchen.

A tiny voice reminded her about Luke's warning, but she pushed it away. She'd seen nothing that supported his theory that Jason was unstable. He was a hard worker and she barely saw him for more than a few minutes each morning when he arrived.

She put the coffee cups on a tray and added a few Anzacs biscuits, then headed back out to the table beneath the tree. She was just putting it down when he walked across to meet her.

She took a seat and reached for her cup, watching as he did the same after only a brief hesitation.

While he busied himself adding sugar to his coffee, Hayley studied him. She'd gotten a shock when she'd seen him this morning—he'd shaved off his stubble and had a haircut and he looked younger.

'Let me guess,' he said, breaking the silence. 'You heard I was a nutcase?'

'I wouldn't use that term exactly,' Hayley said, but didn't bother to deny it.

'What term would you use?' he asked, eyeing her over his cup.

'I wouldn't use any term. I choose to make up my own mind about people.'

'Then you *really* don't fit in around here.'

'I guess not. But if that's what it takes to fit in, I don't know that I want to.'

'Give it time. Pretty soon you'll be as eager to hear gossip as everyone else around here. There's nothing else to do.'

'Why did you move back here if you don't like it?'

'Where else would I go? I didn't have a job.'

'You seem to be doing okay with your business.'

'Business?' he gave a harsh laugh. 'I'd hardly call two jobs a business. There's not too much work for a guy everyone thinks is going to lose his shit at the drop of a hat.'

'Are you?' Hayley asked bluntly and saw him do a double-take.

'I don't know. I used to. I had a lot of problems when I first came back.'

'Because of what happened to you?' she asked a little more hesitantly this time.

'That and . . . other things.'

'From your time in the army?'

'Yeah. I've seen some pretty heavy shit. But it goes with the territory,' he shrugged, taking a sip of his coffee and avoiding looking at her.

'How long ago did you lose your leg?'

'You don't pussyfoot around a subject, do you?'

'You can tell me to mind my own business,' she said, leaning across to take a biscuit. 'I guess that's what happens when you don't listen to gossip—you have to find out the real story directly from the person involved.'

His chuckle surprised her, and maybe himself a little, judging by the abrupt way he stopped. She wondered how long it'd been since he'd last found anything funny. 'I guess you got me there, huh?'

'You really don't have to talk about it,' she said gently.

'It's no big deal, just no one's really ever asked me upfront about it before. When I came back it was like everyone did their best to avoid it. They all tried to act as though they couldn't see it, you know?'

She didn't, but she could understand people trying to make him feel less awkward about his injury. 'Maybe they were just trying to help?'

'Yeah, maybe.' He gave a long sigh and stared down into his cup. 'I never could stand people feelin' sorry for themselves. Never had time for it. If something's wrong, you find a solution and fix it. Complaining about how hard something is isn't going to change your situation, you know?' Hayley nodded. 'But after I came home, I became the kind of person I'd always despised. I guess I didn't make things easy for anyone tryin' to help me.' He leaned over and snagged a biscuit but didn't take a bite, just turned it over in his hands a few times. 'Pretty soon people started avoiding me, averting their eyes whenever I came into a store, that kind of thing. I'd already been havin' trouble holding my shit together. I was drinking too much, getting into fights. I lost a good friend through it all, and I still feel pretty bad about that.'

'What happened?'

'He was one of the people tryin' to help,' he said with a wry twist of his lips. 'He dragged me home from the pub more times than I can remember. Tried to step in and repair all the damage I was doin'. But one night I guess I snapped and I hit him. We got into a hell of a fight . . .' He stopped talking and the silence spoke volumes about the effect that night had had on him.

'I'd gone from wallowin' in pity to just plain angry. I couldn't do what I was trained to do anymore. I'd lost my old life and I was tryin' to deal with losin' my damn leg on top of everything . . .'

Hayley remained silent, unsure what to say but feeling as though he probably needed to get it out.

'Mum tried her best to help too,' he said after a while. 'But then she got sick and she's been livin' down in the city with her sister so she could be closer to the hospital. I kinda stopped tryin' after she left. I had a lot of baggage I needed to sort through, I guess. And the drinking didn't help matters.'

'So what happened to turn it around?'

'I heard one of my mates from the army had killed himself,' he said, shaking his head and looking across the garden. 'He had a wife and kids . . . *both his own legs*,' he added dryly. 'I just remember thinking what a fuckin' waste. Sorry,' he said quickly. 'I guess it was the kick up the bum I needed to ditch the self-pity. Everyone has problems, we're all dealin' with our own stuff. I could either sit there and keep feelin' sorry for myself or get off my arse and get myself together.'

Hayley saw his flicker of a smile and gave one of her own. She could only imagine how difficult that time of adjustment must have been.

'Ernie at the feed store was a mate of my old man's before he died. I worked for Dad when I first left school, finished my apprenticeship, then decided I didn't want to be a builder and joined the army. Anyway, Ernie had been tryin' to throw some odd jobs my way ever since I got back, so I finally took him up on it.'

'I knew that man had a heart deep down inside,' Hayley said triumphantly.

Jason chuckled again. 'Don't say that to his face though.'

'He'll come around. Give me time.'

'So, you wanna take a look at the finished product?' he asked, finishing his coffee and ending their brief moment.

'Sure.' She walked with him through to the rear of the yard where he'd been working. Hayley couldn't help but smile as she looked at the newly fenced paddocks and Errol and Flynn's new enclosure. 'It's perfect,' she said, beaming at him.

'Glad you're happy,' he said gruffly. 'Anytime you need something built or fixed, you've got my number.'

'Actually, I've been thinking of another project. I was going to ask your opinion on it.'

'Oh yeah? What are you buying now? A camel? Giraffe?'

'Funny,' she said sarcastically. 'I was thinking about turning the shed over there into accommodation, maybe even building a few cabins.' Further down the back, the big shed was currently sitting empty as Hayley didn't have any large machinery to store, which she assumed was what it had most likely been built to house.

'What for?'

'To rent out. Del Mason was telling me there's a real need for places to stay. She wants to use Abby Cottage in wedding packages, plus there's the weekend city trade. They'd probably stay overnight if there was decent accommodation.'

'Masons would know. They've always been able to make a quid.'

His abrupt tone made her curious. 'Luke said you knew each other.'

'Went to primary school together.'

His tone warned her not to push it any further. 'What do you think? Would it be possible to convert the old shed?'

'Anything's possible, but it might be a bit out of my league.'

'Could you have a look and see what you think?' she prodded.

'You're not doing this as some kind of charity thing, are you?' he asked, looking over at her steadily. 'Giving me work?'

Hayley was surprised by the question. 'No. Del's idea has merit . . . I just don't know if it's doable or not, and I don't know anyone else to ask.'

He seemed to consider her answer for a moment before giving a nod. 'Yeah, okay. I can take a look, I guess.'

Hayley pushed open the door to the old shed, stepping inside and finding the light switch. The room lit up and she shuddered as she caught sight of something scurrying away. As soon as Puss was ready, she would be having a sleepover in the shed. It would be good training for the kittens.

'So, what were you thinking? Dividing it into separate rooms?'

'Yeah, maybe two separate rooms here,' she waved her hand vaguely, in the huge void of space, 'and the end bit with the loft would make a pretty awesome studio apartment.'

He went for a walk around, kicking posts and knocking against the walls, turning in a circle as he considered her options. 'Yeah, I reckon it's doable. It'd cost a bit though, but your basic framework and structure is already there, and it's sound, so that would save you a lot.'

'Would you be interested in costing it up for me?'

'Sure. I'll come by Wednesday morning.'

'Great,' Hayley smiled.

She turned and closed the door behind her. She had a good feeling about this.

Twenty-four

Luke watched Hayley get into her car at the feed store. He knew she hadn't seen him, and he could have easily caught her before she drove away, but he held back. He didn't know why; well, he did know actually, he just found it difficult to admit it to himself. She scared the hell out of him. Not *her* exactly, more the things she brought out in him. This whole Jane and Edward scenario had rattled him more than he cared to admit.

He'd lived with his gran long enough to have worked out how to switch off from all her talk, and while they were mostly a family of sceptics, even he couldn't deny that Gran did have an uncanny record of predicting things. She'd come to accept her family was pretty much unappreciative of her particular skill set and rarely offered to read their cards anymore, but other people had no such qualms and at one time she'd had quite a successful sideline business.

But there were still times when, try as he might not to, he remembered being a kid and sitting on his gran's lap, listening to her tell him stories of people from another age who had seemed so familiar and alive to him. His arms prickled and he gave a small shiver. He worried that, with Hayley talking about some kind of connection to Edward and Jane, he was starting to lose his tight grip on his inner sceptic.

He didn't want to be a crazy person, and he sure as hell didn't want the woman he loved being one either. For a moment it didn't register what he'd just admitted. *Until it did.* He stared out the front windscreen without actually seeing anything. *The woman he loved?* He barely knew her. And yet he felt as though they'd known each other forever. They had a chemistry, and when he was with her he knew he could just be himself. She wasn't judging him or wanting him to be someone different. Hayley didn't care about impressing people or fitting into a social clique. And she'd actually *chosen* to move to the country. A memory of the shower incident made him give a low snort. *What a freakin' circus that had been.* He shook his head, but couldn't help but grin at the memory. She was funny and independent and she had a good heart—the woman was damn near perfect. Except for this whole vision thing she had going on. He sighed and tipped his head back against the headrest. He needed time to work his feelings out. Work out how to put all the freaky shit back into its box and bury it.

He saw Hayley drive away and took the keys out of the ignition before pushing his door open. Then maybe he'd be able to deal with starting a new relationship.

∽

'Morning.'

Hayley was sitting at the table under the tree, her head dropped on top of her folded arms, trying to decide if she wanted to cry or scream.

She lifted her head and watched as Jason came to a stop beside her.

'Wow, you look like crap. Rough night?' he asked.

'Gee, thanks,' Hayley said, running her hand through her hair. In her defence, she hadn't been expecting visitors, so she hadn't bothered putting on makeup or brushing her hair.

'What's going on?' Jason asked. Obviously he wasn't going to apologise for turning up unannounced.

'Nothing. Absolutely nothing is going on,' Hayley said, reaching over and closing the lid of her laptop and giving it a hard glare.

'Writing still not going well then?'

'Not going well would imply that it had at some point been actually going. I don't get it—I can write a whole book in less than a month when I'm not supposed to, but try to write a book I need to . . .' she threw up her hands. 'It's beyond ridiculous.'

'I take it this has never happened before.'

'Never. I write every day—religiously. I've never had writer's block stop me like this before.'

'Maybe it's not writer's block,' he shrugged.

Hayley glanced across at him. 'Then what is it?'

'Wouldn't have a clue, but it seems to be all in your head—so maybe its psychological.'

'Like I'm going crazy?' she said dryly.

He gave a small twitch of his lips. 'Like maybe you've got a lot on your mind.'

Well, that was true, she supposed. But then again it wasn't the first time she'd had stuff on her mind. 'I've got a deadline and I'm seriously beginning to think I'm not going to make it.'

'What's this book you wrote that you weren't supposed to?'

Hayley groaned. 'It's nothing. It's just some weird historical thing set in early colonial days . . .'

'Can't you send them that?'

'I don't think my publisher would look at a historical. I write crime and butt-kicking type stuff.'

'Butt-kicking and crime type stuff can't happen in historicals?'

'No, see, my main character is an ex-detective and . . .' Hayley stopped. What if she wrote Jane and Edward's story into the background of that new book? It certainly had crime, well, a murder at least . . . Maybe she could write a parallel story set in the past that could work alongside Chance's contemporary storyline of a murder committed by an abused woman . . . that was certainly up Chase's alley. Discovering a long-forgotten murder by a wrongly accused convict woman . . . fighting for an underdog. The more she thought about it, the more ideas began to unfold in her mind. She could then link the real story to a blog on her webpage so anyone interested could read more about the lives of Jane and Edward. The true story behind the fictional one. It was as though someone had cut a tight length of twine that had been wrapped around her inspiration and suddenly it all sprang free.

'You're a genius, Jason Weaver,' she said, feeling a grin stretch across her face as she reached for the computer. 'I've just got to jot down some ideas before I forget them. I won't be a sec,' she said, and her hands began flying across the keyboard at lightning speed.

'I don't know how I helped, but, okay, knock yourself out. I'm just here to get a few more measurements so I can make up the quote for the new accommodation.'

'Sure, fine, go for it,' Hayley said without looking up. She didn't hear him leave and she didn't see him return until he called out on his way past.

'I'll drop by later with the quote,' he said.

Hayley lifted her hand to wave in his general direction, but she dared not stop in case this flood of creativity dried up again.

When at last her hands began to cramp and her back started to ache, Hayley stretched in her seat and stared at the screen before her. She'd gone back and begun filling in between Jane's story with Chance's new storyline. It was after lunch, which would explain her cramped fingers. She was impressed with how much she'd achieved. It never ceased to amaze her how ideas went from a vague notion in her mind to something tangible on paper. It was a complicated process to get to the final product, but the hardest part of it all was cultivating the seed of an idea to start with. After that, everything usually flowed.

She went into the kitchen and grabbed something to eat, then continued working long into the early hours of the morning.

Twenty-five

The next afternoon as she had just finished making coffee, a knock at the front door surprised her. Hayley glanced out of the window and saw Jason's ute parked out the front.

'Hi,' she said, surprised to see him back so soon.

'I thought I'd bring over the quote and see if you wanted to go through it.'

'Sure.' She turned to let him through the doorway, making her way towards the kitchen. 'Do you want a coffee?' she asked him as he pulled a chair out from the kitchen table.

'No, thanks,' he said, unrolling a set of plans.

Hayley sat next to him and peered at the drawings keenly. 'Did you do these?' she asked, looking up.

'Yeah, they're not architect quality, but I was thinking about some ideas and thought if I drew them it'd give you a better idea of what I was talking about.'

She guessed that had something to do with the decidedly untechnical way she'd tried to describe the chook pen she'd wanted him to build. He probably thought he'd save himself the headache of trying to explain where walls and doors would be going on a much larger build.

'I thought, seeing as you wanted a loft-style apartment, we could actually manage to squeeze a spa into the bathroom if we built the staircase out over the bathroom area, see here?' he said, tracing his finger along the lines on the paper. 'I was looking at the loft and thinking how difficult it would be to get up into the bedroom—even with two legs,' he added dryly, 'if you kept it as it is now with just a ladder set-up, but then it occurred to me, if you made like a staircase it would be easier to get up to the bed, and let's face it, if your main clientele are newlyweds, that's probably a priority,' he grinned. 'This way you could use the staircase to divide the bottom floor of the apartment.

'This is really great,' Hayley smiled. He'd drawn in large windows and a fireplace on the bottom floor, and Hayley could imagine curling up on a comfy sofa in front of a cosy fire on a cold winter's night.

'Then these other rooms, I reckon you could get three out of the space if you didn't have kitchens in each of them.'

'I don't know about that,' she started hesitantly. 'I mean, I don't want to provide meals, and other than next door at the restaurant there's nowhere nearby where guests can duck out for dinner or takeaway. Having kitchenettes in each room would at least give them the opportunity to make their own meals if they wanted to.'

'But what if you converted this into a common-use kitchen?' he said, pointing over at the stone outbuilding at the rear of the overseer's cottage.

Hayley shivered despite herself. It was such a dark, horrible room. A sudden image of standing over Gilbert Mears's dead body flashed before her eyes and she felt herself pale. 'That's where it happened,' she murmured, staring at the plans weakly.

'Where what happened?' he asked, looking across at her and frowning at her startled face. 'Are you okay?'

No wonder the place gave her the creeps. 'Yeah, I'm fine. You're right, it's a good idea.'

'I don't think it would take much to convert it. I think at some stage someone had it as an outdoor laundry, because I noticed the other day that some plumbing had already been done.'

Hayley tried to concentrate on what Jason was saying. 'I suppose it makes sense to use it, it's not doing anything sitting there empty the way it is.'

'That would give us three double rooms and the loft.'

Hayley nodded thoughtfully as she studied the drawings. 'What do you think?'

'I think it looks awesome,' she smiled up at him, genuinely impressed. 'But I guess the next question is, how much is it going to cost?'

'Yeah that's the bit that hurts,' he winced, 'but I reckon we can keep costs down a fair bit if we use as much of the original structure and materials as we can.'

She took a deep breath as he slid a piece of paper across the table. She looked at it and then breathed out gently. 'Okay, well that's not as bad as I was expecting,' she said slowly, trying to work out sums in her head. The big question was, would she make back the outlay of costs, and if so, when? Would they get enough clientele to make investing this much money worthwhile?

'What do *you* think?' she asked Jason, seemingly catching him off guard, because he took his time answering.

'I've seen a big change in this area since I came home,' he said slowly. 'It's got a lot more, I don't know, energy about it,' he said, looking slightly uncomfortable. 'A lot of the oldies weren't too keen on the idea of new people buying up land and moving in, but farming's not the main industry anymore, it's just not feasible. Over generations the land's been subdivided down and sold off, so the farms aren't big enough to support a big agriculture trade the way it used to be when I was living here as a kid. Times are changing,' he shrugged. 'I think this new tourism trend is definitely worth trying to cash in on.'

'Del's convinced accommodation's the way to go.' Hayley sighed and looked out the window, straightening as she saw another car pull up outside. What was Luke doing here? She saw him exit his car and head towards the front door. 'Excuse me for a minute,' she said, getting out of her seat.

She opened the door before he'd even had time to knock. 'Hi,' she said curiously. 'What brings you here?' He'd been conspicuously absent over the last few days and it hadn't gone unnoticed.

'Hi. Ah, Mum wanted me to drop off this,' he said, holding out a large envelope. 'It's something about wedding accommodation packages or something.' His voice trailed off as he looked over her head and spotted Jason at the table.

'G'day,' Luke nodded stiffly.

'Luke,' Jason replied with equal abruptness.

'So you two know each other from school?' Hayley asked, trying to break the strange tension between them.

'A long time ago,' Luke said, holding the other man's level gaze. 'You *still* working on that chook pen?'

'He finished that a while ago. I've been finding him all sorts of jobs to do since then,' Hayley cut in, not liking the accusatory tone to his voice.

'You know you can ask me if there's something you need fixed,' Luke said, lowering his voice slightly.

Hayley tried not to look as awkward as she was feeling and forced a polite smile to her face. 'Thanks, but I know you're busy with your own place. Jason's been a godsend.'

'Yeah, well, I better get going,' Jason said. 'I'll leave these here with you to have a look over. Just let me know what you want to do.' He rolled the plans back up and snapped the rubber band back into place.

'Thanks, I'll call you later,' Hayley said, watching him walk to the door. When the door closed behind him, she looked across at Luke and found him watching her thoughtfully. 'What?' she asked self-consciously, then was annoyed that he was making her feel like this.

'You two seem pretty chummy.'

'He's a nice guy. He's been doing a lot of work for me.'

'Did you even hear what I said the other day about him?'

Hayley prickled at his attitude. 'Yes, I did.'

'And you chose to ignore it?'

'I chose to make up my own mind. What is it with you two anyway? And don't tell me it's because he's got problems. We've all got problems. There's something going on between you two—what is it?'

'Like I said, we knew each other once.'

'You were friends?'

'*Were*.'

'What happened?'

'When did this turn into an interrogation?' Luke shot back.

'When you decided not to answer a simple question.'

'Look, we were friends growing up. He left for the army and when he came back he wasn't the same person. That's all.'

'If you were his friend, why didn't you try to help him?'

'I did try,' he said tightly. 'He didn't want my help.'

Hayley studied Luke's stiff shoulders for a moment before it sunk in. 'You were the friend he got into a fight with,' she said slowly.

The swift glance Luke sent her confirmed it.

'He told me the other day that he'd lost a good friend. Luke, he seems upset about what happened, and he's pulling himself together. You should try to reconnect with him again.'

'I tried to *reconnect*,' he said sarcastically, 'and I got a fist in the face for my trouble, so no thanks. I won't be making that mistake again.'

'Luke—' she started.

'Look, I knew him better than anyone and I cared about him and he turned on me. That's why I warned you about him. If he can turn on his best mate, he can turn on anyone.'

'I'm grateful for your concern but I can take care of myself.'

'I was just trying to look out for you.'

'You have a funny way of looking out for people,' she said softly, her anger vying with her hurt.

'What's that supposed to mean?'

'I haven't heard from you since the other day at lunch.'

He dropped her gaze briefly and shifted his weight uneasily. 'I've been working. We're flat out at the moment, between implementing all the biosecurity requirements and trying to get everything in the ground before the rain hits.'

When he said it out loud, it made perfect sense, but something told her there was more to it than that. He'd been avoiding her since their cemetery visit, that much she knew for certain. 'You must be really busy if you can't even send a text. I'm surprised you had time to drop this off for your mum.' Hayley regretted her words the moment they came out of her mouth. She sounded like a demanding girlfriend. She had no right to expect a phone call or text—she was the guy's next-door neighbour, nothing more. 'Forget it. Thanks for this, tell your mum I'll look it over and call her for a chat.'

'Hayley,' he started, then seemed to hesitate. 'There's just a lot going on right now.'

'Yeah, there is,' she agreed.

'As soon as things settle down a bit . . .'

Hayley could have made it awkward and waited out an ending to whatever he was trying to say, but the reality was she was too damn tired to bother. 'There's nothing to work out,' she said, holding his gaze steadily. 'Thanks for dropping this off.'

She saw him frown and open his mouth to speak, but she held the door open, giving him no choice but to leave. She couldn't deal with this after everything she'd been through during the last year and a half. She'd come here to start afresh and to find a peaceful place to hide away and write, and that's what she needed to concentrate on now.

'I'll see you around,' he said, looking back at her one more time before heading over to his vehicle.

♒

Luke swore as he drove away. Why was everything where women were involved so damn complicated? Admittedly, whatever he and Hayley had been going through wasn't your typical kind of new-relationship hurdle. But still, why couldn't it be as simple as meeting your new neighbour and falling for her?

It could be that simple, said a little voice that sounded suspiciously like his gran. Maybe Hayley was right to end it before it'd even begun. His plan had basically been to stay away long enough and hope that it all somehow sorted itself out. It probably wasn't the greatest plan. *Neither was becoming the woman's business partner, idiot.*

And now it looked like his mother wanted to go into business with her too. *She's your neighbour, dipshit, it's not like you're going to be able to avoid her completely.* Damn it, he didn't *want* to avoid her. Today when she'd opened the door it had been the first time in days since he'd been close enough to see the blue of her eyes and smell that faint whiff of vanilla from the perfume she wore. He'd missed it. He'd missed her. Staying away, being *just* neighbours—their only contact being a wave as they passed each other on the road—was depressing to even think about.

Then there was Weaver. What the hell was he doing in her house? Hayley had said he was her handyman, but they seemed to have a pretty damn cosy kind of relationship for someone who was *just* her handyman. He couldn't blame the guy—why wouldn't Jason be just as interested as he was?

So do something about it, you knucklehead. The thought remained with him for the rest of the day.

Twenty-six

Hayley read over Del's proposal and was impressed by how thorough it was, not to mention how successful her reception centre was. During the spring and summer months the place was booked solid. Winter was a little quieter but autumn wasn't too far behind. People, it seemed, loved a rustic wedding.

The more she thought about it, the more Hayley was excited by the prospect of adding accommodation to the place. It would be included in any packages Del sold to her wedding clients, but it would also draw in other tourists: the daytrippers who decided to stay overnight, the city folk who were looking for a short getaway not too far from the city, for a romantic weekend perhaps, or maybe she could even advertise it as a retreat for writers.

She had enough to pay for the renovations, thanks to her latest royalty cheque and her investments, so money wasn't a real issue, but it would mean she'd be running a business as well as writing, so effectively she'd be juggling two careers.

After two days of deliberating, Hayley knew she couldn't turn the opportunity down. She called Del and invited her over for coffee and then called Jason to tell him she wanted to go ahead with the project. This was good, she thought firmly that evening as she got up from the sofa to go to bed. The busier she kept, the less time she had to dwell on anything else, and that included Luke Mason.

She'd spent the last few days moping and had had to give herself a mental shake. There was nothing to mope about—she and Luke had barely even *had* a relationship to end, and yet she here she was burying her misery in front of the television, alone with her four cats, watching sad movies and eating ice cream. *But it could have been something,* a little niggle reminded her. Maybe. But then she'd revealed her crazy attachment issues to a guy who'd been dead a couple of centuries, oh, and who also happened to be his ancestor. Not to mention she'd been an eyewitness to a double murder that history had apparently gotten wrong. Oh lord, she groaned, no wonder the guy didn't want to be around her . . . she sounded like a fruit loop.

Grabbing the remote, she switched the television off, gathered the now empty container of ice cream and sidestepped playful kitten paws reaching out for her. A relationship was the last thing she wanted right now.

She had her career to focus on and a host of exciting new business opportunities. She didn't need a man.

∽

Luke knew it was going to be a crap day when he spilled his first cup of coffee all over his kitchen table and then couldn't find one of his boots because his father's new cattle dog pup had obviously been doing the rounds again and decided to carry it off somewhere. All before six in the morning.

The main house was a flurry of chaos with the wedding of his mother's big client about to unfold, and as Luke walked inside he found Del in her usual work-focused zone. She could never think about anything else on wedding days, so there was no point even attempting a conversation with her.

'Dad, you need to do something about that pup. It's been taking off with shoes again.'

'Well put your shoes away,' he said without looking up from the newspaper at the table.

'I thought you were training it.'

'I am. He's a smart one that little fella. He's gonna be even better than his great-grandfather, Ironbark Jim,' his father boasted, and Luke tried not to groan out loud. He was in no mood to hear the legend of Ironbark Jim, the best stud cattle dog ever known to mankind.

'Yeah, well keep him locked up at night, I'm sick of buyin' new boots.'

His father opened his mouth to protest but was interrupted by the ringing of the house phone. He flicked his paper with an insulted glare and went back to reading.

'No, really, don't get up. I'll get it,' Luke muttered, stalking towards the phone on the kitchen counter, snatching it from its cradle and saying a curt, 'Lochmanning Estate.' His irritated scowl slowly transformed into something worse as he listened to the speaker on the other end of the line. 'Yeah, no worries. I'll send someone down there to let you in.'

Luke let out a short sharp curse and his father frowned as he looked up from the paper once more. 'Who was that?'

'You need to head down to the front gate and let in the auditor.'

'The what?'

'They're doing an audit drop-in. Checking that we've complied with the biosecurity regulations.'

'Tell 'em to piss off,' his father muttered.

'Yeah, that'd go down real well,' Luke said, running a hand through his hair. 'Dad, this is serious. You need to go let him in. I have to find the bio plan files and finish them before he gets up here.'

'He can wait till I've finished my cuppa.'

'Dad!' Luke yelled.

'Well, he shoulda made an appointment if he wants us to jump when he flamin' says so.'

'The whole point of a surprise audit is that they turn up unexpectedly. To make sure we're complying with the rules.'

'And we are. They wanted a lock on the entry gate. We put a lock on the entry gate. Now they can't get in till we decide to unlock it,' his father said with a smug smile. 'Let 'em wait.'

Luke didn't have time to argue with him, he still had to finish filling out the last of the report and he needed every second he could get. Eventually he heard his father's ute start up and head down the driveway as his fingers fumbled across the keyboard entering in the information required.

He'd just hit print when he heard the sound of vehicles coming towards the house. He grabbed the sheets of paper and shoved them into a folder, just as he heard heavy footsteps out on the verandah.

He walked out, a friendly smile plastered across his face, and extended a hand to the small man in a very large hat, who was looking more than a little out of sorts.

'Luke Mason, how are ya, mate.'

'Brian Morrison,' he said briskly.

'You want a cuppa?' Luke asked, wishing his mother wasn't so preoccupied—she always knew how to smooth over ruffled feathers.

'No, thank you, I'll just go about my inspection and be on my way.'

'Okay. Well, here's our biosecurity plan.'

'Right, I'll look this over. In the meantime, I'll need to have a look around, check your washing bay area and make sure stock can't access sheds, take a look at your dump site and check your chemical storage, then check it all off against your records,' he said, holding up the file Luke had just given him.

'Tell you what,' Patrick said, grabbing Luke's ute keys off the hook, 'I'll even come with you. Now that I've got one of you blokes here, face to face, there's a few things I want to discuss with you.'

'I'm not sure—' the man started, but Patrick just took his elbow and pushed him towards the door.

'There's no point wasting all that time we'd have to take washing down your vehicle, is there? You *would* be washing down your vehicle, wouldn't you?' Patrick asked pointedly.

'Well, of course,' the man stammered.

'That's what I thought,' Patrick nodded, and continued walking, 'so we may as well take the work ute. Makes much more sense, doesn't it, Brian?'

Luke was feeling just as apprehensive as poor old Brian was looking. Christ, his father alone with the bloke doing his audit—what could possibly go wrong? There was nothing he could do about it now, he thought as he headed outside to make sure everything was up to code that Brian might check.

He was heading towards the bar to find Grant and let him know about the audit but turned as he heard his mother calling, waving frantically as she ran towards him. *What now?*

'Luke, it's a disaster,' his mother started.

'Mum, calm down. What is?'

'The gate. It's locked.'

'Dad unlocked it,' Luke said, frowning.

'Then relocked it, apparently. I just had a call from the bride and her family. They're waiting to be let in. I can't find the key.'

Luke swore beneath his breath but it still earned him a look from his mother. 'Okay, I'll look for the keys.' It really *hadn't* been a challenge to the universe when he'd asked how much worse today could get.

He followed his mother back to the house and headed for the key rack, not seeing the set marked front gate hanging in its usual spot. 'There's a set in the office,' he said, leaving his mother, who had begun doing some deep breathing techniques. He pulled open the desk drawer and rummaged through the spare keys he kept there, but came up empty. 'Damn it.'

His mother gave a small whimper when she saw he'd returned empty-handed. 'Don't panic,' he soothed.

'I have *wedding guests*, Luke, waiting to come in and set up for the biggest wedding I've ever hosted,' she said, pacing the room. 'Where's your keys?'

'In the ute that Dad took,' he added pointedly.

'Well, then, where's your father's set?'

'Probably in his damn pocket. When does he ever hang them where they're supposed to be?'

'My car's in at the mechanics . . . I'll race over and get Grant's set,' Del said, turning to leave, then stopping, putting a hand to her head. 'Olivia's gone into town,' she groaned. 'My guests! What am I supposed to tell them? They barely even speak English. How am I going to explain this?'

'I'm calling Dad,' Luke said, already scrolling to his father's number. 'I'll get him to drop them back.' The call went straight to message bank and he briefly shut his eyes, opening them again in shock when he heard his mother let out a curse. This *was* serious. His mother never swore.

'I'll drive out and find Dad and get the keys off him. You head down to the front gate and let them know I'm on my way.'

'I'll take refreshments,' she said, holding her finger up as inspiration struck.

By the time Luke had located his father and retrieved the keys, the sun was already high in the sky and the temperature was soaring. As he got closer to the front gate, he lifted his sunglasses to peer at the scene before him, unsure what he was seeing.

'Luke! Thank God you're here,' his mother said, rushing towards him in a fluster.

'What the hell?' he said, climbing out of the car and staring at the scene before him in amazement.

A well-dressed woman, who he took a guess as being the mother of the bride, was straddling the top of the gate, clinging onto the top bar tightly and yelling down to her husband below in a string of Chinese that more than likely contained a great deal of abusive language if her unhappy expression was anything to go by.

'What the hell is she doing up there?' Luke asked.

'I tried to explain that you were coming with the key and we had to wait, but then the father of the bride started climbing the fence, and while I was trying to get him to stop, he called his wife over, and well . . .' Del placed her hands against her cheeks, 'something was lost in translation, apparently.'

Luke gave a harsh chuckle. *Ya think?*

'It's not funny, Luke. She's stuck. I think her dress is caught. I don't know why he won't go back up and help her, all he's doing is yelling at her and she's got herself worked into such a state. Help her, Luke,' she said, urging him forward.

Luke gave a sigh as he approached the couple, speaking slowly and calmly in an attempt to sort out the situation. 'I'm going to go up there and try to untangle your wife,' he told the older man, before finding a foothold in the gate and hoisting himself up. Of course his mother had insisted on installing the most elaborate set of iron-forged entrance gates known to mankind. 'It's all about the first impression,' he'd heard her say a hundred times in defence of the astronomical cost of having them installed. *She couldn't have a set of farm gates like everyone else in the district, could she?* Luke thought as he climbed up level with the woman.

Taking a good look, he summed up the situation. 'Yep, she's stuck,' he called down to his mother. 'I'm going to have to try to unhook your dress,' he said, but the woman made no indication that she understood. She just continued to stare at him, wide-eyed and terrified. He awkwardly reached around her to try to dislodge the material where it had been caught up on one of the steel spikes. He really hoped the guy on the ground couldn't fight—feeling around under someone's wife's dress was likely to be frowned upon in any culture. Why the hell had they tried to climb the gate in the first place?

He finally managed to unsnag the dress and slowly guided the woman down the other side. Once on the ground, he took out the key and unlocked the gate, stepping aside so the unhappy couple could hurry back to their vehicle.

His mother was in frantic talks with a distraught bride-to-be, who thankfully hadn't made the decision to go gate climbing, and after a few minutes she seemed to have calmed down, walking back to her parents and relaying whatever message his mother had given her.

'They right?' Luke asked, coming to stand beside his mother.

'I don't know. They're very upset. The father wanted to call off the wedding. I'm hoping his daughter can talk him around. What a mess,' Del sighed, before looking up at him and summoning a weak smile. 'Thank you, darling. You saved the day.'

'That's me. Farmer, son, hero,' he shrugged. 'You want me to hang around here with you?'

'No, it's all right. I better go into damage control. You go on and do what you need to do,' she said, patting his arm and walking towards the car in the driveway with a charming smile.

Later when Brian Morrison came back, Luke held his breath as he handed over a checklist with only a few minor things that would need attending to before the next inspection, then wasted no time beating a hasty retreat.

'What did you do to him?' Luke asked warily as his father came to stand beside him, watching the auditor drive away.

'We just had a bit of a chat. He explained a few things to me, I asked a few questions. He's not a bad bloke really. I think we both got something out of the experience,' Patrick said with a decisive nod.

Luke could only stare in wonder. Still, maybe there was method in his madness. If it had made the auditor want to get the inspection over with as quickly as possible then who was he to argue? 'Good work, Dad,' he said, slapping him on the shoulder as he turned away.

Now maybe he could finally start the jobs he was *supposed* to be doing. God, he hoped the rest of the day involved a little less drama. He wasn't sure he could cope with much more.

Twenty-seven

She'd give Jason one thing—the man did not waste time. It had only been three weeks since they'd agreed on the renovation plans and he'd already lodged all the council applications and, while he was waiting for those, he'd made a start on what he could.

Hayley wasn't wasting time either. She'd spent the previous three weeks writing and was excited by the result. The last few days she'd been putting together a blog for her web page on the original story. There was a certain feeling of contentment now when she worked on her project. Jane's story needed telling. History had wronged her and Hayley felt compelled to right that. Maybe it wasn't a huge deal to anyone else—she doubted anyone would even really care—but it mattered to her and somehow she felt she owed it to Jane too.

She'd be lying if she said she didn't think about all the weird things that had been happening, but she still had to function and if she spent too long trying to find a logical explanation, it would send her batty. She'd pulled out the piece of paper Pearl had given her and looked at it more than a few times over the last few days, but each time she'd put it down and walked away. She wasn't sure why; maybe it was because she was scared. After all, it'd changed Luke's mind about her. It was weird. *She* was weird. Did she really want to tell another person about what had happened to her?

She'd started going for a walk early every morning, after giving a carrot to Errol and Flynn and feeding the chooks, to inspect the group of cows who were ready to deliver any day. There were seven in total and Hayley had named them all. Luke had moved them to the paddock closest to the house, so they'd have a safe place to calve, and it felt like the excitement of Christmas morning every day she came out to the paddock to check on them.

This morning it was noticeably cooler. There was a decided nip in the air as she trudged through the early morning dew in her bright gumboots. She didn't notice anything out of the ordinary until she counted the now familiar faces of the wide little cows as they grazed cumbersomely in their paddock. Four, five, six. She paused, frowning as she scanned the paddock for number seven. She did a recount, still coming up one short, and realised it was Flossy who was missing.

A movement near a small tree caught her eye and she climbed through the fence to get a closer look. While the cattle were quite docile and calm, and usually came up to the fence to see her, they didn't let her get close enough to touch them yet—something Hayley was keen to correct in time. As she approached the tree, she saw Flossy lying on the ground and her heart gave a leap of excitement as she spotted a tiny fluffy white head pop up in the long grass. Flossy diligently went back to licking at it, then clumsily got to her feet.

Hayley grabbed her phone from her pocket and scrolled to the number she needed, barely waiting for Luke to answer. 'Flossy had the baby! Just now.'

There was a moment of silence on the end before Luke responded, clearly not expecting a call from her, and probably not one that didn't even start with hello, but he seemed to recover well. 'Did you see it delivered?'

'No, but I must have only just missed it because she was cleaning it when I arrived.'

'I'm on my way. Don't go near it. Remember, mothers are protective of their young.'

'Yeah, I know, you told me. I'm standing back. Hurry up.' She disconnected the call and went back to watching, trying to catch a glimpse of the calf again.

∽

Luke pulled up near the fence and climbed out, looking for Hayley. When he spotted her inside the paddock, he instantly panicked. He'd just told the woman not to go near the damn cow. What the hell was she doing? He vaulted the fence and skirted the nearest of the cattle, trying not to make too much noise as he approached Hayley's position.

'What are you doing?' he said in a low tone. She turned glittering blue eyes on him and he almost forgot what he was angry about . . . almost. 'I thought I told you not to go near them?'

'I didn't. I've been standing here the whole time.'

'*This* is near them,' he stressed, trying to remain calm.

'It's nowhere near them,' she argued, her eyes losing some of the sparkle and a frown creasing the centre of her brow.

'We don't know how these cattle are going to react—they're unpredictable. They're not cats. They can be dangerous.'

'So I probably shouldn't have patted her then?'

Luke's heart lurched only for a split second before he saw she was joking—at least he hoped to God she was joking. He relaxed a bit when she rolled her eyes and gave a small huff of irritation.

'I couldn't see them properly. I just wanted to make sure she was okay.'

'Yeah, well, next time wait for me. I don't want you in here with them alone, okay?'

'Yes, Dad,' she mocked, and something about her defiant tone made him want to shake her and kiss her in equal measure. He was still deciding which one he wanted to do first when he saw her eyes light up again as she pointed back towards the cow and calf. 'Look, it's already standing up,' she said, clearly trying not to squeal.

Luke followed her gaze and had to admit what he was seeing was pretty damn cute, *for a cow,* he quickly amended.

'It's so tiny.'

It was tiny—he wasn't used to calves this small—but as far as he could tell it was doing all the right things. Later he'd be able to get a closer look, once he could get them into the yards.

'Can you tell what sex is?'

'Not from this distance. We'll be able to get a better look over the next few days, once it's up and running around.'

'This is the best thing ever. I'm so glad we decided to buy them,' she said, her smile so wide and beautiful it hurt something in his chest. He couldn't help himself, he leaned down and kissed her, his arms sliding around her waist as he pulled her against him. He felt her initial surprise but was relieved when he felt her melt into him and kiss him back. It felt so right, the way their bodies aligned—as though they were carved from the one piece of wood, made to perfectly fit together.

Easing away slightly, Luke rubbed the edge of his thumb along her jawline, taking in the rosy shine of her lips. 'I can't stop thinking about you, Hayley. I know things ended . . . a bit weirdly last time I was here . . . but I can't stay away anymore.'

'No one asked you to,' she said, but without the anger he was half expecting.

'I know. I just needed to wrap my head around a few things.'

He saw her watching him intently, and knew that he'd let her down.

'Did you figure anything out?'

'Only that it sucks more without you around,' he admitted ruefully. 'All I've been able to think about is you and this,' he said, lowering his head once more to kiss her.

A long time later she pulled her mouth away from him and, breathing heavily, whispered four words that made his gut clench. 'I want you too.'

He didn't need any further encouragement, he swooped her into his arms, ignoring the yelp of surprise, and hotfooted it towards the house. She wasn't big, but he was breathing heavily before he'd even cleared the paddock fence. Maybe he should have thought through this plan a little more before acting on it. He could feel her giggling against his chest and it fuelled his determination.

'In there,' he heard her say, following her arm she pointed towards her bedroom.

Thank Christ for that. He leaned down so she could open the door and staggered inside. *Manhood intact after preforming heroic gesture, tick.* He just hoped to God he hadn't used up all his strength getting here.

Her amusement faded as he leaned towards her and lowered her back on the bed. His hand slowly edged up the T-shirt she wore, and he felt goosebumps explode beneath his touch. Her mouth softened and the kiss deepened, becoming hungry and demanding, and soon without conscious thought their clothing seemed to dissolve, being thrown in all directions in their desperate need to be closer.

Luke swore his heart was banging against the wall of his chest it was hammering so hard. He wanted her, more than anyone or anything he'd ever wanted before, and the force of that need shook him. He was like any other red-blooded male—he enjoyed sex, he'd wanted women before, but this was different. It went deeper. It was more than just an urge to bed her. He *needed* her, and the depth of that knowledge should have scared the hell out of him, but it didn't.

He brushed his hand against the underside of her breast and watched as her eyelids fluttered open, her heavy eyes holding his steadily. Her lips parted slightly as his fingers grazed her nipple and he throbbed in response, leaning down to skim his lips along the trail his fingers had just followed.

Her skin was smooth against his as she moved beneath him, silently demanding more. He was lost, consumed only with her—her scent, her soft cries of ecstasy and the ripple of desire he felt running through her body below his. Right in this moment nothing else mattered except her. He couldn't take his eyes off her face. It was a canvas for every wave of pleasure that washed over her, and he was immersed with an intensity he'd never experienced before.

He wanted this to last but he couldn't fight the roar of fire that burned, or the weakening of his defences her knowing touch and fevered moans elicited from him, and with one final cry he felt himself shatter into a thousand pieces.

Twenty-eight

Hayley stared at the ceiling of the old cottage and fought to catch her breath. Beside her she felt Luke's hard body, missing his weight and warmth despite the fact they were still touching. She knew they had chemistry—that had been obvious from day one—but this had been . . . beyond anything she'd ever experienced before.

'I wasn't expecting the morning to go quite like this,' she said into the quiet between them.

He gave a half-hearted snort, but turned his head to look at her. 'Me either, but I wouldn't mind if there were more like it.' He reached for her hand and threaded his fingers through hers. 'Do you have anything planned today?'

'Other than corrupting my sexy neighbour?'

'Yeah, besides that.'

Hayley scoffed but couldn't wipe the smile from her face. 'No, I don't.'

'You wanna come for a drive into town?'

'Sure. Why?'

''Cause I have to pick up some supplies from the feed store but I don't want to leave.'

'Aww,' she crooned, only half joking. His words actually melted her heart a little bit.

As they drove, Luke took her hand in his lightly, driving with one hand on the steering wheel. More than once Hayley had to mentally pinch herself to see if this was real. Were they actually here? Together? It all felt so . . . right.

When they pulled up in front of the feed store, Hayley stayed in the car while Luke went inside. A familiar car pulled up across the road and she climbed out of the ute and crossed the quiet road to meet Jason as he closed his car door.

'Hey, boss,' he greeted her, giving the area a quick scan. 'I didn't see your car.'

'No, I came in with Luke,' she said. 'I've been meaning to tell you, I found a good deal on an oven and stovetop package in Windsor. I was thinking of going over to have a look at it. Do I need to know anything other than the measurements of the hole its going in?'

He lifted an eyebrow. 'We need to work on your building terminology a bit, but no, as long as you take the measurements off the kitchen plan, you should be right. I'm heading over there to get some supplies on Wednesday if you wanted me to look it over with you?'

'Actually, that would be a great idea. That way if I buy the wrong size, I can blame you,' she smiled sweetly.

'If I'm there, we won't be buying the wrong size,' he assured her blandly.

Just then Luke appeared. 'Weaver,' he nodded, slipping his arm around Hayley's waist.

She saw Jason's eyes follow the action silently. 'Mason.'

Hayley felt the undercurrent between the two men. 'We were just talking about the old scullery kitchen makeover.'

'Sounds like you've been busy,' Luke said to Jason.

'We've got a big job ahead of us, but it'll be worth it, I reckon.'

'Mum showed me the plans you sent her,' Luke said, looking at Hayley. 'It's a big venture.'

She couldn't quite determine whether Luke's tone was politely curious or held a note of caution. Maybe it was a bit of both. She flashed him what she hoped was a confident smile. 'I guess it is a fairly big renovation, but as Jason said, the shed was already there and structurally sound, so it's not like we're building from scratch.'

'Guess that's true,' he said, although she suspected he was tossing up whether to say any more. She wasn't sure why his hesitation bothered her. She didn't need anyone's approval for anything she did now—but the fact she sensed a small amount of uncertainty about him irritated her.

'Did you end up finishing your manuscript, the one about the convict woman?' Jason asked, successfully diverting the attention from the building but unfortunately opening a whole other can of worms.

'You wrote about it?' Luke asked slowly.

'I wrote a book based on a local event, yes. And yeah, I sent it off to my agent the other day,' she smiled at Jason.

'I'm looking forward to reading it.'

He'd asked her about the book and she'd given him a brief summary of the plot and told him the story of Jane and Edward, minus the freaky stuff. Over the past few weeks working with Jason, Hayley had become pleasantly surprised by the change in him. It seemed they'd reached a point where he felt comfortable enough to let his guard down around her and she'd discovered a very different side to the man. He had a great sense of humour for starters—who would have thought? She genuinely liked him and enjoyed their playful banter.

She felt Luke's hand tighten slightly on her waist. 'Well, I guess we better get going,' she said with a bright smile.

'Yeah, me too. If I don't catch you back at your place, I'll call you about Wednesday to see what time you want to leave,' he said with a wave before he walked away.

'What's happening Wednesday?' Luke asked as they crossed the street.

'I was planning to look at some stuff for the kitchen and Jason offered to come along and check it out with me.'

'You didn't think I'd go with you?'

'Actually, it didn't cross my mind,' she admitted calmly, aware that his tone was becoming a little clipped.

They got into the ute and Hayley pulled on her seatbelt, looking up as she finished to see Luke staring out the front window quietly. 'What's wrong?' she asked cautiously.

271

'You're publishing the story about Jane and Edward?'

'I didn't plan on it, but the story just flowed out onto the screen. I think it needs to be told.'

'So he knows about everything?'

'About the visions, you mean?' she asked pointedly, somehow irritated by his refusal to acknowledge it.

'About what you *think* you saw.'

'No, I didn't mention anything about what *I saw*, or anything else that happened,' she added, eyeing him defiantly. 'I just told him what happened to Jane and Edward and that I was writing a book about it.'

'And you think that's a good idea?'

'Why wouldn't it be?'

'You've just moved to a new town and you're going to publish a story about how the locals murdered two people and covered it up? You really think you're going to win friends doing that?'

'It happened over two hundred years ago. I'm sure local people will be fine with it.'

'Really?' he said dryly. 'You think they're going to be okay with some stranger writing her own account of what happened involving *their ancestors*, an account that she can't even prove, I might add. You'll be slandering their family names.'

'The book is fictional and based loosely on actual events. I haven't used any real names. I am, however, putting up the story of Jane and Edward on my website for anyone who might be interested in reading about what inspired the back story in the book. I have no problems with that. If people don't like it, then too bad. I know it's true.'

'You can't prove any of it,' Luke said, turning to face her. 'Think about it, Hayley, you're going to write about local families who formed a posse to hunt down and murder a woman and a prominent local family's son to stop him opening an inquiry into the slaughter of Aborigines. *My* family,' he added pointedly. 'This has the potential to rip apart the family and any others involved. What happens if there's a backlash? What happens to my family's business? What happens to your new venture? If the reception centre and the restaurant go broke, you've just invested a shitload of money into renovating accommodation for nothing. You need to think about what you're doing.'

'Did anyone think about what they were doing when they told lies about an innocent woman or covered up all those deaths? Why the hell shouldn't someone give those victims a voice now? At least acknowledge the truth? Maybe no one cares about Jane or Edward or the women and children those men killed, but if someone knows the truth, they should tell it, and that's what I'm doing.'

'And how are you intending to prove it's the truth? Are you going to tell them it's because you *saw* it happen? You don't even know for sure what you saw.'

'That's why I'm going to talk to someone about it. Your gran gave me the name of a woman who might be able to help.' Up until this point she hadn't decided whether or not to contact the woman Pearl had told her about. She wasn't even sure why she'd said she was going to now, only that she was angry at him for being the cold voice of reason when she'd needed him to be her ally.

He gave a grunt of disgust. 'Well, I'm sure she'll help you get to the bottom of it. You're throwing your money away, but, hey, do what you want.'

'Thank you for your permission,' she said sarcastically before opening the door, then stopped abruptly. 'No. You know what?' she said without allowing him time to reply. 'Just so we're very clear, I don't need your permission, or your blessing, for any decision I make. Not my business. Not what I write about and sure as hell not who I choose to be around,' she added, tired of his disapproval where Jason was concerned.

'Where are you going?' Luke called out with a tired groan.

'I'll get a lift home,' she said, closing the door and crossing the street to where Jason was returning to his car. *Smile and blink. It'll be okay, just don't cry.* Only an hour or so ago they'd been deliriously happy and everything had felt as though it had fallen into place, and now she couldn't wait to get away from him. Why did he insist on being so intractable when it came to anything to do with Jane and Edward? What was he scared of?

Thankfully Jason didn't ask any questions when she requested a lift home. She saw him dart a quick glance across the street at a steely-faced Luke, but he didn't comment, just opened his door and got behind the wheel.

She spent the rest of the morning moping about the garden, hoping the sun would ward off her despondent mood. Luke's warning replayed in her head throughout the rest of the day. Could she be doing harm to Lochmanning? What if putting out her version of the truth did start something? What if it did somehow spark a backlash and people's lives were impacted? She still wasn't convinced anyone would get too excited by what she wrote on her web page. She had an alternative version of history and she was simply putting her theory forward. Maybe she couldn't prove it, but then again, there were no living witnesses to disprove it either. Surely Luke was just overreacting because he had his own issues to deal with.

Well, she thought, taking a deep breath as she dialled the number Pearl had given her, it looked like she would be talking it over with someone else after all. She just hoped this woman had some answers for her.

Twenty-nine

Luke ran from his house, the screen door slamming behind him as he covered the distance between his house and his parents' as fast as his legs would carry him. He vaulted over the verandah railing and pulled open the door, his breathing coming fast and heavy as he called out frantically. 'Gran?'

He heard her voice coming from further inside the house and hurried towards it, finding her seated in her favourite chair in the front room, turning cards over on the small coffee table in front of her.

'There you are. My, you were fast,' she said, looking up at him with a happy smile.

Luke stared at her, catching his breath. 'Gran, what's wrong? On the phone just then you said you needed me here. That it was urgent.'

'I did. And it is. Here, come and take a seat near me. You're really out of shape, aren't you? A short walk from your house to here shouldn't have knocked you up that much,' she frowned, eyeing him carefully.

'That's because I *ran* here, Gran. I thought something was wrong.'

'Why would anything be wrong?' she asked, eyeing him oddly.

Oh no, was she really losing her marbles, after all? 'Gran, you rang me,' he said hesitantly.

'I know I rang you, good grief, I'm not going senile,' she snapped.

Luke stared at his grandmother. *What the hell?* 'Then what was so urgent?'

'I need you here to pick some cards. I'm doing a reading for you.'

Oh, for frig's sake.

'You know the drill, pick me out three cards, there's a good boy,' Gran said, smiling sweetly.

'I'm not exactly in the mood, Gran.' Had he seriously just lost ten years off his life over some stupid card reading?

She lifted an eyebrow and waited expectantly, and with a long, drawn-out sigh, Luke reached across and plucked out three cards.

'Just as I thought,' she murmured.

'Gran, I really have to go. Are you sure everything's all right?'

'No, everything's not all right,' she said, staring down at the cards and looking troubled.

'Gran, I—'

'You've started remembering, haven't you?' she said, looking up and holding his startled gaze with a firm one of her own.

'What?'

'Hayley was here the other day. She remembers too.'

'Gran, what are you talking about?' He didn't want to know, not really, but he knew she was going to tell him anyway.

'Hayley remembers Jane.'

'Okay, that's it. I have work to do.' He stood up but felt a surprisingly strong grip on his arm.

'You're remembering Edward. I knew you would one day.'

And just like that, his world fell apart.

∽

The place Hayley pulled up in front of was nothing like she'd been imagining. She scoffed slightly. Sure, it was highly unlikely that the woman would be living in a tiny cottage in the middle of an enchanted forest, and yet somehow it felt as though she should be if she were authentic. The fibro house with a faded red tile roof and overgrown garden didn't give her much in the way of confidence.

Megan Johnson was listed on her web page as a past life regression therapist, and Hayley had been surprised to find so many listings for people who did similar things. Who knew it was such a big industry? She'd never heard of anyone going to their past life regression therapist appointment. It wasn't like, 'I've got a dentist appointment today,' or 'I'm off to my hairdresser's appointment.' 'Sorry I can't make it today, I'm about to go to an appointment with my past life regression therapist . . .'

She knocked on the front door and waited, listening as a rather surprising springy step approached on the other side of the door. Inwardly she rolled her eyes as she pushed away the image of a hunchbacked old woman shuffling towards the door.

Instead, a woman in her early forties appeared, her blonde curly hair pulled back into a messy bun and wearing a long flowing skirt and T-shirt.

'Hello, I'm—'

'Hayley,' the woman supplied, smiling. 'Please don't be nervous,' she said, lightly touching Hayley's arm. 'I'm Megan, but call me Meg. Pearl's told me a lot about you.'

'She has?'

She nodded. 'I've been hoping you'd call and make an appointment.'

'Did she mention what happened?'

'Not everything. Come on through to my office so we can have a chat,' she said, standing to one side and gesturing for Hayley to enter.

They walked into a room at the end of the hall and Hayley looked around the room curiously. There was no sign of a crystal ball set up under a draped tulle tent as she'd somehow imagined, and Hayley made a mental note to readdress some of the stereotypes she seemed to be carrying around with her. The walls were painted a gorgeous lime colour that felt fresh and clean. Two comfy-looking chairs with pastel upholstery were positioned facing each other in front of a desk. There were candles burning that gave off the most delicious scent, and Hayley started to feel a lot more at ease as she settled into her seat.

Meg took a chair opposite her and reached for the notepad from her desk. 'Pearl called a few weeks ago to tell me she'd given you my number, but all she said was that you might be looking for some kind of guidance in order to get answers to some dreams you were having.'

Hayley bit the inside of her lip thoughtfully as she decided how best to approach the whole subject, but thankfully Meg seemed to pick up on her hesitancy and jumped in to save her.

'How about we start with the dream you had. Would you like to tell me about it?'

'I'm not exactly sure that's what it was. It happened during the day, while I was awake.'

'So, more like a vision?'

Hayley nodded and drew in her bottom lip nervously. 'I saw a young couple murdered,' she started haltingly. 'It happened a long time ago, and I believe I know who they were. I did some research on them, only what history says about their deaths is very different to what I saw.'

'So you're here to find some answers about this event? About the deaths of these people?'

'I guess I am,' Hayley said haltingly. 'But I also want to know why I had the vision in the first place. Why I feel a connection to them.'

Meg nodded slowly, studying her in much the same way that Pearl had.

'Look, Pearl thinks it's something to do with a past life or something . . . I have to be honest, I'm not sure I buy that.'

Meg smiled gently. 'I understand, however in my opinion doing a regression is probably the only way we'll find out for sure.'

'What's a regression?' Hayley asked, half horrified, half curious.

'It's a form of guided meditation in which we explore the things that may be buried deep in your subconscious. I promise it's not scary—you are in complete control at all times. It's not like the hypnosis you see at those shows where they make people dance like a chicken. You can open your eyes or stop at any point and you'll be completely safe at all times. Would you like to give it a go?'

Would she? If someone had suggested she was about to go under hypnosis to reveal a past life, she'd never have believed them. She was open-minded to a point, but she just wasn't sure she could open her mind wide enough for this. And yet a part of her already knew that she believed it all. There was just no rationalisation she'd been able to come up with that explained it.

'Okay,' Hayley said softly. 'Let's do it.'

'Good, let's see if we can't find you some answers,' Meg smiled. 'If you'd like to take a seat over on the recliner, we can get started.'

Hayley gently rolled her neck in an attempt to loosen some of the tension she was feeling before leaning her head back against the neck rest and closing her eyes.

'Just breathe nice and slow, deep breaths, that's the way,' Meg instructed gently. 'Relax your body. Feel your hands relax, and your feet, your legs and your arms. Everything feels heavy. You're safe and you're in complete control. You can open your eyes at any time. Breathe in and breathe out. Long, slow breaths. Picture a bright light in the distance, it's warm and familiar. Walk towards it. Feel its gentle warmth wrapping around you as you walk deeper and deeper into the light. I'd like you to go back to the last vision you had, bring it back to mind. Tell me what you see?'

Hayley was instantly back at the old tree again. 'I see him standing by the tree. He looks worried,' Hayley said quietly.

'What's he doing now?'

'He's looking up, he's smiling again.'

'Where are you in this?' Meg's voice floated to her, 'Are you on the outside looking in?'

'No,' Hayley found herself saying, surprised. 'I'm on the inside. He's looking at . . . me,' she said, hearing her voice shake a little.

'That's good,' Meg said encouragingly. 'What's happening now?'

'He's running towards me. He's scooping me up and we're twirling around.'

She saw Edward's handsome face and for the briefest of moments everything was right. 'You came,' she breathed after he kissed her deeply.

'Of course I did. I love you, Jane. Always and forever.'

Meg's voice came to her, gently prodding, 'What's happening now?'

'I'm scared. I'm so scared. I want him to run. We need to leave,' Hayley whispered fearfully.

'What's Edward saying?' Meg asked.

'He's saying we can't run. We have to stay and prove it.'

'Prove what?'

'That I didn't murder Mr Mears in cold blood,' Hayley said. 'I'm trying to tell him they won't believe me. They'll send me away.'

'What's he saying now?'

'He's saying he can't leave, he's petitioned the governor about the murders and he needs to see that the guilty are punished.'

Hayley gasped.

'What's happening now?' Meg asked.

'They've found us.'

'Who?'

'The landholders.'

'What do the landholders want?'

'They want me. But they want him too. They're saying to give the girl up and prepare to die for his betrayal to his own family.'

'What betrayal are they talking about?' Meg's voice asked, but it sounded far away.

Her heart was beating frantically as she faced the men on horseback, their menacing guns pointed at her, the leering smiles sending her blood running cold.

'"My father will not condone this," Edward is saying. He's stepped in front of me and I want to hide behind him, but I'm shaking so bad I can't move. The biggest man is saying, "Your father sent us. You think a man like Wilfred Mason is going to allow his son to put him and all of his neighbours on trial for killing blacks?"'

Hayley stopped relaying the events as everything began happening too fast to keep up.

'You killed them in cold blood,' Edward yelled, fury making his words echo around them.

'We did what we had to do.'

'You did not have to murder innocent women and children. There is no excuse. I will see you all hanged for your part in it. Each and every one of you,' Edward declared.

'Edward, no, please, we need to run,' she whispered fearfully.

'We won't be the ones on trial, boy,' the large one said in a deceptively cordial tone as he lifted his long, evil-looking weapon.

'Jane, run,' Edward shouted, turning away to push her further behind him. 'I'll find you, run.'

'Edward,' she screamed seconds before the burning sensation filled her chest and sent her flying backwards into a dark, empty abyss.

Thirty

Hayley opened her eyes and gasped. The sensation of finding herself in the small room instead of out in a warm paddock was jarring. It felt like the slamming sensation as a rollercoaster ride comes to an abrupt halt at the bottom of a track.

'Hayley, look at me,' Meg instructed. 'You're fine. You're safe.'

'Oh my God,' she said, feeling slightly breathless. 'It's true,' she whispered. 'I was Jane.'

'Are you all right?'

Hayley looked up and managed a jerky nod. 'I think so.'

'You did very well.'

Hayley wasn't sure what to say. It had all felt so real. She lightly touched her chest, half expecting to find a large wound, but there was no pain. She'd smelled the gunpowder, heard the explosion, felt the burn of the bullet shattering her chest. Hayley felt clammy all of a sudden and closed her eyes once more.

'You'll be fine, just breathe in and out, slow breaths,' Meg advised gently as she got up and returned with a glass of water. 'Sip this.'

'It was so . . . real.'

'Yes, it can be. That was clearly a very traumatic regression, but we have something to work with now. We know why you're having the visions.'

'We do?' Hayley asked doubtfully.

'Past lives stay with us on some occasions because there were unresolved issues. Sometimes people come to me because they have phobias or because there's something that's holding them back from either happiness or success in their life—something blocking progress. Sometimes they're not even aware of any issues from a past life, they just have a curiosity and can uncover something unexpected.'

'I don't think I have any phobias or blockages.'

'It sounds like there was quite a lot of trauma involved in your death, not to mention the death of a loved one. I would be very surprised if that didn't have some kind of impact on you.'

'Like what?'

'I don't know, it could manifest in a number of ways. Do you have trouble letting people in your life? Trust issues?'

Hayley gave the woman a sidelong glance. Of course she had trust issues, her husband and best friend had been having an affair behind her back.

'No one believed Jane—she was a convict accused of murdering a man and her rich, landowner lover. Do you have any incidences in your life where you felt betrayed maybe, or as though you were alone and no one would believe you?'

'Does having my vision count?' she said dryly but was surprised when Meg answered.

'Yes, it could, but I'm thinking there could have been other times in your life you've experienced that kind of helplessness.'

Other than Paul's betrayal, she couldn't think of anything she was conscious of. She felt a ripple of scepticism stirring in her until she recalled what she'd just gone through. It had been too real for her to have imagined it.

'Where were you when you experienced this vision?'

'I was out walking. Near an old tree on my property. I think it was the place where it all happened.'

Meg nodded. 'Maybe the location set it off.'

'It doesn't make any sense. If this past life thing really exists, what are the chances I'd end up in the very same place over two hundred years later?' Hayley said, eyeing the other woman doubtfully.

A slow smile spread across Meg's face. 'There's no *chance* involved, my lovely,' she said gently. 'Everything is preordained. You were destined to return to this place one way or another. Nothing in our lives happens without a reason.'

'But I didn't even think about moving here and buying Abby Cottage until I saw it pop up on my computer screen one night.'

Meg gave a brief shrug. 'Destiny works in mysterious ways.'

'Isn't that saying supposed to be *God* works in mysterious ways?'

'God, fate, destiny, call it what you like.' She paused and closed her eyes briefly, seeming to hesitate a moment before opening her eyes again and saying, 'Let's go back to Edward. You mentioned before that you thought you knew who Edward was. That you felt that connection to someone.'

She'd asked earlier if it were possible for two people to reconnect again from a past life, but hadn't told her that Luke had experienced similar flashbacks. Hayley gave a jerky nod. 'Is something like that possible?'

'Absolutely. In the same way you were drawn back to the place it happened, souls can also draw one another back. I have to say, though, it's not always for the better. Sometimes the bond that connects you can be what holds you back from living a fuller life. In the same way that past trauma can re-emerge in another life and affect you, so too can a past love. Sometimes it's destructive.'

'So what do you do about it?'

'It depends on what's happening in your life now. Sometimes we don't align with our true soulmate in every life, but that bond can remain and hold you back from finding a satisfying relationship in some form—for example, you could be subconsciously waiting for someone to turn up and sweep you off your feet but, in the meantime, you're letting other opportunities slip by. If that's happening, then cutting that bond will allow you to move on in this life.'

'But if you cut that bond . . . what happens if your soulmate *does* turn up in that particular life at some point? Does it mean you won't find each other?'

Meg's smile held a tinge of melancholy. 'Fate will decide.'

Hayley let that sink in for a moment, the silence only broken by the soft Celtic music drifting over to them from a small speaker in the bookshelf. 'So what happens now? Am I cured?' she asked, striving for a lightness that belied the intensity of what she'd experienced.

Meg placed her hands together and smiled gently. 'There's no cure. There's only understanding and acceptance, but I would suggest we do another session to cleanse your aura, cut ties with past lives and release any unhealthy attachments that may be holding you back in this life.'

And what would that solve? It didn't give her any answers about repercussions for people she cared about if she published her book. It didn't fix the issue Luke had with accepting what had happened to her. It didn't give her any peace of mind that setting the record straight about Jane was actually going to *do* anything.

'If I cut ties with the past, will I stop having the visions?'

'Hopefully,' Meg said in the noncommittal tone she seemed to favour. 'Once the ties are cut, I believe it will at least free you from the promise that held you tethered to Edward all these years,' she said, touching her arm.

Always and forever.

Thirty-one

Over the next few weeks the remainder of the calves were born and Hayley found comfort in them. Leaning against the fence with a coffee, she watched as they grew stronger each day. Flossy's calf, the eldest, waited impatiently for the smaller arrivals to be able to stand steadily enough and run so he could play with them. In no time the seven calves had formed an entertaining little gang, harassing their long-suffering mothers who tried to eat in peace in order to produce the milk to feed them. They played a form of calf tag, racing in and around the tolerant mothers at surprising speed for animals born barely weeks before.

The building was moving along equally quickly. The renovation of the old shed had commenced and the transformation was amazing. There were already three separate rooms framed now, and inside looked nothing like the empty machinery shed it had started out as.

She'd only caught glimpses of Luke since the day she left him in town. He'd come over a few times to check on the cattle. She'd wanted to go out and talk to him but each time nerves got the better of her, so she'd stayed inside the house, trying not to feel as though she were hiding like a frightened mouse, until he'd gone. It wasn't a solution. They were partners in the cattle and at some point they'd have to talk to each other.

That time was coming closer each day. Sophia had raved about the new manuscript, which had lifted a considerable weight off Hayley's shoulders. Maybe now she could take a small break and allow a new story to unfold at its own pace without the pressure of a looming deadline.

Sophia wanted to come up for the day to discuss the new book and some possible overseas prospects. It would, of course, have been easier to go to her, but she'd been dying to see Hayley's new place. She'd asked to go someplace nice for lunch, and although Hayley had offered to host lunch at Abby Cottage, Sophia had automatically brushed the notion away. 'Darling, what good is having an expense account if I can't use it? Besides, I want to see what this place has to offer.'

Naturally the only place that would meet Sophia's high expectations was the restaurant at Lochmanning.

'Oh, this is just divine,' Sophia said as they walked into the restaurant. 'It's so . . . rustic and gritty.' In her enormous Audrey Hepburn sunglasses, tight skirt and high heels,

Sophia blended into the rustic setting as seamlessly as the Pope at a nudist beach.

Hayley's gaze darted around the room, but she wasn't really expecting to see Luke in the middle of the day. She'd been more nervous after parking the car and walking inside in case she happened to run into him out there. It was a relief not to see him, and after ordering a drink from Grant she finally began to relax a little.

A table further across the room seemed a hive of activity, with much laughter and drinking going on. The table of seven women seemed to be having some kind of celebration, drinking wine, she noticed absently, instead of the boutique beer.

'I have to say, Hayley, I think this is some of your strongest writing yet,' Sophia said, sliding her glasses on top of her head and folding her elegantly manicured hands in front of her on the table. 'There's just something about this one. There's a different feel to it. I love the convict woman's storyline. Fascinating. How on earth did you come across it?'

Hayley toyed with the edge of the menu. 'Oh, you know . . . research. I heard something about it and decided to look into it.'

'You did a marvellous job. The scenes are so full of detail. You must have been very thorough with the research.'

'Yeah,' Hayley agreed weakly. 'I'm just relieved the publishers like it.'

'They love it. Here's to a fantastic book and big things on the horizon,' Sophia said, and raised her glass to gently tap Hayley's. 'What's wrong, Hales?' Sophia asked after a moment, eyeing her over the top of her beer glass as she watched her gazing at the table of happy, somewhat drunk women across from them.

'Nothing,' Hayley said, forcing a smile to her face. And that was the truth. There was nothing but good things happening in her life everywhere she turned, and yet a heaviness continued to hover about her. So much had happened since arriving here that sometimes she felt drained just trying to process it all.

Her vision no longer freaked her out—after seeing Meg she'd accepted what it was, and writing Jane's story seemed to have helped too. She'd exhausted every avenue of rational explanation trying to explain it. In the end acceptance had been surprisingly liberating.

She'd learned more about Jane since her regression therapy. Tiny snatches of memory had been resurfacing—the oddest things: walking along the cliff tops of her homeland and watching the raging ocean far below. The smell of wood smoke, and the sensation of wearing long swishy skirts. She saw a small town and remembered the experience of going to some kind of fair, where people smiled and children ran, laughing as they darted in between their parents' feet.

Sometimes the memories came to her while she was doing the most mundane things, like cooking dinner or vacuuming; other times they came to her while she sat in the garden enjoying the warmth of the sun. She couldn't explain it, but she knew they were memories of her life as Jane, back in her village on the west coast of Ireland.

They were as familiar as the memories of the childhood she had now.

There was only one thing missing.

'Well, would you take a look at that,' Sophia drawled. 'You don't get them back in the city,' she murmured as she followed the man who had walked in from the brewery into the restaurant.

He was dressed in jeans, a light blue work shirt and boots, and Hayley felt a stab of familiar longing as her eyes locked with his. To his credit, Luke hid his surprise at seeing her there well; only the slight hesitation in his step gave any indication he'd been affected as he continued across to the rowdy table of women. Hayley watched as a tall blonde woman gracefully stood at his approach and greeted him with a hug.

Hayley dropped her gaze quickly. It was none of her business, she reminded herself firmly as she tried to concentrate on the meal before her. Sophia, always guaranteed to hold the conversation, kept up a steady flow of gossip about people they both knew, and Hayley managed to nod and say the appropriate things in the right places, but her mind was racing as she tried not to watch the other table.

'Hayley?'

Hayley snapped her gaze up to her friend's face and realised she'd stopped listening. 'Sorry?'

'I asked if you knew that fine specimen of manhood who just walked in?'

'Ah, yeah, kind of. He's my neighbour. Why?' *Do not look over at him.*

'Because he's been sliding you sideways glances ever since he came in and now he's coming this way.'

Hayley dropped her fork and the sound of its clattering seemed to echo around the large room.

'Hayley, nice to see you.' Luke's deep voice sounded close and she could see him in her peripheral vision as she summoned the courage to look up.

'Luke,' she acknowledged, relieved when her voice sounded reasonably normal. 'This is my friend and agent, Sophia. She's driven up for the day and I thought I'd bring her over here for lunch.'

'Nice to meet you, Sophia,' Luke said smoothly. His charm seemed to be working, judging by her usually unflappable agent practically melting in her seat. 'I hope we're managing to impress you.'

'Oh, I'm impressed right enough,' she crooned, and Hayley couldn't help rolling her eyes at that remark.

'When you get a spare minute, I need to talk to you about an upcoming market. We need to go over some things,' Luke said, leaning down, his hand on the back of her chair, almost touching her but not quite. She could practically feel the heat of his body and it was playing havoc with the internal war she was fighting to remain unaffected by the man.

'Sure, maybe tomorrow sometime,' she said, seeing Sophia's speculative interest from the corner of her eye and anticipating the inquest that would follow once Luke left.

'Luke, I'm ready,' a silky voice said, making Hayley glance up. The tall woman from the other table had come to stand at Luke's side, slipping her arm around his waist.

She watched as Luke straightened and introduced the newcomer. 'Hayley and Sophia, this is Lucinda. Hayley bought Abby Cottage,' he added for the woman's benefit.

'Oh, I love that place,' Lucinda gasped, pressing her hands to her mouth. 'Do you remember we talked about buying it some day?'

Hayley felt her heart sink. This was *that* Lucinda ... Luke's ex-fiancée ... girlfriend ... whatever they were. The one who'd broken his heart.

Luke seemed uncomfortable as he shifted his weight slightly from one foot to the other. 'That was a long time ago.'

His short reply sent a flash of hurt across the woman's perfectly made-up face but she quickly covered it with a bright smile. 'Yes, I suppose you're right. It's too quiet out here for me anyway,' she said with a shrug before looking down at Hayley. 'I hear you're an author.'

'Yes, I am.'

'I don't read, never had the patience to sit around all day.'

Alrighty then. 'Well, it's not for everyone,' Hayley murmured with a smile.

'Lucinda's here for a wedding tomorrow,' Luke explained, seemingly a little unsure of how to proceed.

'How nice,' Sophia commented. She was giving Lucinda her smiling assassin's smile, the one Hayley had seen her use on publishers right before she launched into a list of demands. 'Not yours, I take it.'

'Oh God no, I'm just in the wedding party,' she said with a wave towards the table of women. Her smile slipped and twisted into something more fatalistic. 'No, I had my chance. I was foolish enough to let him get away,' she said softly.

'We better let these ladies finish their meal in peace,' Luke said, clearing his throat, and his arm went quickly around Lucinda's waist to usher her away.

'Yes, you promised to give me a private tour of the new brewery,' Lucinda agreed, and Hayley saw her smile brighten measurably.

'I'll catch up with you tomorrow, Hayley,' Luke said, looking over at her sheepishly.

'No hurry,' she said, dropping her gaze back to her plate. 'Don't rush your tour.'

'It makes sense now,' Sophia said slowly once they were alone again.

'What does?' Hayley asked.

'You,' she said simply.

'I have no idea what you're talking about.'

'There's something different about you, and I've been trying to figure it out all day. Now it makes sense. You're in love.'

'I am *not* in love,' she glared.

'Whatever you say,' Sophia shrugged. 'But in case you're wondering, there's no way that man is interested in the fair Lucinda.'

'She seems pretty interested in him,' Hayley said reluctantly.

'Too interested. She's obviously trying *too* hard.'

'Well, it doesn't matter anyway, he's just my neighbour. I'm not interested in his personal life.'

Sophia gave a rather unladylike snort. 'Fine, lie all you like to yourself, but it's not fooling anyone. Even Lucinda could tell there was something going on between you two.'

'Oh please, now you're being ridiculous.'

'Am I? Maybe you two are oblivious to it, but you'd have to be blind not to see the electricity between you.'

'There might have been a thing . . . briefly . . . but it's over now.'

'Oh honey, whatever it was between you both is *not* over . . . not from where I'm sitting.'

Hayley had a moment of hope at her friend's words, but it plummeted quickly when she recalled Luke's hand on Lucinda's waist as they'd walked away from the table.

'What happened between you two?'

'It just didn't work. We had different . . . beliefs.'

'Beliefs? I didn't think you were ever terribly religious?'

'Not that kind of belief.'

Sophia's eyes widened, 'Is he into something kinky? I bet he is,' she said, leaning across the table with relish. 'Tell me.'

'No, he's not,' she said, exasperated. 'Look, we tried. But you can't make someone change their mind about certain things, and he and I have very different views about . . . stuff.'

'Well, that's a shame. If the amount of chemistry between you two isn't enough to make things work then there's no hope for the rest of us. Something like that doesn't come along very often. Trust me, I know, I'm still waiting.'

Hayley considered her friend thoughtfully. 'Do you believe in destiny, Soph?'

'I believe that if you want something badly enough, you have to get off your backside and go out and get it. Destiny doesn't hand-deliver your heart's desire.'

Hayley thought about Sophia's words as their dessert arrived. What if destiny sometimes got it wrong? Surely if she and Luke were supposed to be together they wouldn't be going around in circles the way they had been since day one. What was she supposed to do? Forget everything she'd discovered? Did it mean that if she wanted to be with him, she had to agree to his terms? That was no way to live, and she certainly wasn't about to allow another controlling man to determine the choices she made. He may not want to believe in any of it but was it really that difficult to accept someone else's beliefs? Clearly it was for Luke.

Thirty-two

The saying *Could have been knocked over with a feather* had never seemed more apt than this afternoon when he'd walked into the restaurant and found Hayley there. As if he hadn't had enough surprises to deal with. He'd been agitated all morning, ever since Grant had called to warn him of Lucinda's unexpected visit. He was fairly sure she was hoping to rattle his cage a bit. She would have known about the wedding for months, so why hadn't she told him she was coming? Or, for that matter, why did she even bloody accept in the first place if she knew where it was going to be held?

His mother had cornered him outside, giving him a rather pointed lecture on behaving. He may not want to see her but she was part of a bridal party and the bride was a paying guest. Under no circumstances was he to make a scene.

Truth was, he had no intention of causing a scene. He was irritated that she'd shown up here, yes, but other than that, he didn't feel anything really. The hurt he'd felt after their break-up had gone, becoming only a dull memory of another time in his life. He'd wanted to go in and face Lucinda and get it over and done with. He'd wanted to show her that she no longer held any power over him. As he'd walked through the door, though, his gaze had fallen on a familiar face and his heart had momentarily skidded to an abrupt halt. Hayley.

Thankfully he'd regained his composure quickly and walked over to Lucinda's table. He could deal with his ex, he had no doubts about that whatsoever, but he wasn't ready to deal with Hayley. This thing between them was far from over. He doubted it would ever be over.

Somehow he knew that a part of him would always be pining for her and the thought made him sad. Why couldn't they just be normal? Why had his gran's stupid stories spilled over and infected them? If only he'd kept her away from Gran and her belief in fate and destiny, maybe she would have let the whole Jane and Edward thing go.

God, but he was tired. He'd been working long hours, both from necessity and as a way to keep his mind off Hayley, but it was catching up with him. All he felt like doing was going to bed and sleeping for a week, but he knew that even if he could go to bed right now he'd only end up thinking about Hayley and feeling sorry for himself.

Grant had called him an idiot for not getting over whatever was eating him and asking her to forgive him. It wasn't as though Luke hadn't thought about it himself, but he was still angry that she'd left him to go home with bloody Weaver. He knew deep down that she hadn't also jumped into the guy's bed, but it made it easier to hold on to his anger and stay away from her if he let the notion at least run through his mind.

Besides, he might not know much about relationships but he knew enough to realise you couldn't tell people what to do or make them be something they weren't. That's what Lucinda had tried to do to him. He couldn't do it to Hayley. If she decided to embrace Gran's way of seeing the world, to believe in past lives, and tarot, and visions, he couldn't ask her not to; that wouldn't be fair. But he wasn't sure he could live with it either.

Lucinda hadn't changed—she was still beautiful—but now he could see past the perfection. It was almost as though time had given him a fresh set of eyes to see her with. He heard the note of insincerity in her tone as she spoke with the other women at the table, the people who were supposed to be her friends. Her whole world revolved around an image of perfection, but it was all fake. He felt sorry for her.

Life wasn't perfect. People weren't perfect. His gaze drifted across to Hayley. Maybe he was wrong. She was pretty darn close. Her curly hair the colour of malted barley; the warm blue of her eyes. He could see every detail of her face with his eyes shut. He had in fact been doing so for the last few weeks, because other than catching the briefest glimpse of her when he'd gone over to check the cattle, he hadn't actually gotten to see her face in way too long. Everything would have been perfect if it wasn't for . . . He paused.

Was he just as bad as Lucinda, only wanting Hayley if she believed in the same things as he did?

Damn it. He wanted her in his life. He wanted to see her smile as she watched a newborn calf running in circles around its mother. He wanted to hear her laugh—a sound that sent a warm rush of happiness through him every time he heard it. He wanted to hold her and comfort her when she cried over the death of a sick cow or an injured animal. He wanted to be there to experience everything with her.

He didn't know what Lucinda was up to, but if she thought there was any chance of them getting back together, she was mistaken. There was only one woman he was interested in and it wasn't Lucinda.

∽

Hayley prepared to leave, having said her goodbyes to Sophia at the restaurant, but she turned when she heard Jason call her name.

'Hi,' she said, and realised she probably looked as surprised as she felt seeing him here of all places.

'A potential client asked me to meet him here, but he just called to say he was running late. Do you have time for a drink while I wait?'

Hayley gave her wristwatch a brief glance and shrugged. *Why not—she had nothing else to rush home for.* 'Sure. So, this new client, is he local?' she asked as they took a seat at the end of the bar.

'Some big nob with a weekender he wants fixing up,' Jason said, giving his order to Grant as he approached.

She saw Grant nod briefly at Jason in greeting before sending her a sidelong glance. She tried not to read too much into the look. She wasn't doing anything wrong, and if Luke's brother thought there was something odd about her having a drink with another man then he could just mind his own damn business.

'Good thing I got you early before you became in such demand,' Hayley said, forcing her attention back on Jason.

'Nah, it's not quite like that yet,' he said, picking up a coaster and turning it in his hands. 'But word of mouth seems to be spreading, and I have you to thank for it,' he said, holding her gaze seriously. 'No one was willing to give me much of a start before you came along. So thanks.'

His gruff words touched her unexpectedly. 'Your craftsmanship speaks for itself. I'm glad you're getting plenty of work.'

From the corner of her eye she saw Luke coming back in with Lucinda and felt the smile slip from her face.

'What's that all about then?' Jason asked, following her line of sight.

Hayley snapped her gaze away and tried to look blasé. 'Luke's ex-girlfriend is back in town and he's showing her around.'

'I see. And you're fine with it?'

'It's none of my business.'

'Really? I thought you two were a thing?'

'Nope,' Hayley said, forcing a bright smile to her face.

'I see,' Jason said slowly.

'There's nothing *to* see,' Hayley told him firmly. 'We had a brief . . . thing and it ended. He's free to see whomever he likes. Besides, I've got far too much on my plate to be even thinking about a relationship right now.'

'Okay,' Jason said with a shrug. 'I believe you.'

'I'm serious.'

'Okay,' he said again. 'I hear you. There's no *thing*.'

His dismissal of her protest annoyed her for some reason. When her drink arrived, Hayley took a sip, feeling self-conscious as she noticed Luke had now spotted them from across the room.

'For a guy who's not supposed to be into you anymore, Mason sure is looking very interested in the two of us sitting here,' Jason said, casually facing her as he leaned one elbow on the bar, watching her.

His attention gave her a moment of concern, and when he reached out and touched her face, she blinked in surprise at the overly familiar gesture. Moments later Luke brushed past them and headed outside without a backward glance.

'What was that?' Hayley asked, narrowing her eyes at Jason.

He dropped his hand and gave her a small grin. 'Just testing a theory.'

'What theory?'

'The theory that Mason's still got it bad for you.'

'I told you,' she started, but her words were cut short when Jason leaned in and kissed her, stunning her more than if she'd suddenly had a bucket of ice tipped over her head. When he pulled away, Hayley blinked and swallowed, unable to think of a single thing to say, despite having a million things running through her head.

Jason slowly sat back, picking up his beer and taking a sip.

'And *that* was?' Hayley asked pointedly.

'Another theory,' he said. 'One I have to admit I've been debating about testing for a while.'

'Well, by all means, feel free to test whatever theory you like,' she said, waving a hand in the air blithely.

'If it's any consolation, I was right.'

'About what?' she asked, flabbergasted by the unexpectedness of it all.

'Didn't feel a thing,' he said nonchalantly.

Hayley felt her mouth open in disbelief. *He didn't feel anything?* Was she losing her touch? Did she even have a touch to begin with? Then she found herself becoming indignant. What the hell? He didn't feel *anything?*

His chuckle made her close her mouth abruptly and she glared at him.

'I'm just messin' with ya,' he finally said.

'Jason,' she started but he shook his head.

'I shouldn't have done that and I'm sorry,' he said sincerely. 'But weren't you at all curious?' He lifted an eyebrow at her. 'Just a little bit?'

Hayley felt her face flush slightly at the memory of watching him work bare-chested. Okay, so the guy was kinda hot, and no, she couldn't deny there was a touch of something like attraction. The kiss had been nice—but not earth-shattering the way Luke's was. *Used to be,* she corrected firmly. Luke's kisses *used to be* earth-shattering. 'I really like you, Jason,' she started and he gave a fake groan.

'No, stop. Don't do it,' he said with a theatrical shake of his head which drew a reluctant smile from her.

'I'm sorry,' she said with a small shrug.

'It's okay,' he said, cupping his hands around his beer glass. 'If you want to know the truth, I really only did it to piss Mason off,' he said, sliding her a cocky grin and tossing his head towards the glass door that led to the brewery.

Hayley automatically turned her eyes towards where he'd indicated and gasped when she saw Luke turn away and disappear out the back. Oh God, it felt like a bad sitcom, only it wasn't funny and it wasn't make-believe. How on earth had she managed to get herself into this mess?

Thirty-three

Hayley hadn't slept well. It was hard to distinguish between dreams and memories lately, but she suspected the ones that involved Luke were merely wishful thinking. She was up early, coffee in hand, leaning against the timber railing of the fence as she watched the sunrise. She loved how the thin veil of night slowly lifted inch by inch to reveal the bright new day in soft shades of pink, orange and yellow.

The sound of a vehicle drawing closer made her ears prick, and she fought an attack of butterflies in her stomach as she recognised the ute.

'Hey,' Luke said as he climbed out of his vehicle, shoving his hands in his pockets.

'You're here early,' she said for want of anything intelligent to say.

'Sorry I didn't call, but I didn't want to wake you up. Thought I'd get a bit of a head start on things. I need to draft off a few of the steers.'

'That's okay. You don't have to call to ask to come over. I was just up watching the sunrise.'

She felt the tension hanging between. 'Listen, about yesterday,' she started but was interrupted.

'What you do and who you do it with isn't any of my business,' he said shortly.

It felt like a slap across the face and Hayley was momentarily lost for words before indignation came to her rescue. 'Exactly. Just like it's none of my business who you give private tours to.'

She really wished she could have been the bigger person and kept her mouth shut.

'I didn't know Lucinda was coming,' he said finally, surprising her with his willingness to discuss it at all.

'Then that must have been a surprise.'

'Almost as big a surprise as seeing you and Weaver there together,' he said stiffly.

'We weren't there *together*. He was there for a meeting. I was just having a drink with him.'

'Looked like more than a drink to me,' he said, looking down at his boot as though it was the most fascinating thing he'd ever seen.

'Maybe if you decided to give Jason a break instead of antagonising him, he wouldn't feel a need to try to provoke you at every opportunity.'

'*Me* give *him* a break? I told you, I tried to help him and he almost broke my bloody jaw.'

'He's really trying to get his act together, Luke. And you were right, he did have issues—how could he not after everything he'd been through? But he needs a friend now more than ever. I know he hurt more than your jaw that night,' she said softly. It must have wounded Luke to have a childhood friend turn on him so violently. 'But he's truly sorry for what happened. I'm just not sure he knows how to say it.'

Luke gave a snort and dismissed her words with a shake of his head, but she saw something flash across his face and knew she'd hit a nerve.

'Sounds like you're worrying about his wellbeing a bit more than is warranted for a guy who just does odd jobs around the place.'

'He's a friend. There's nothing else to it.'

'You kiss all your friends like that?' he shot back.

'This isn't about Jason. It's not even about you believing I'm going to ruin businesses with my book or send Lochmanning broke.'

'Interesting that you can dismiss my family's business viability so casually,' he cut in sarcastically.

'My book isn't going to have any detrimental effects on anyone. So what if it sparks some controversy? If anything it'll be *better* for business if it brings people out to take a look around. Stop snatching at straws and face the real reason. It's about Edward and Jane. Isn't it.'

She saw his expression shut down and harden the features she'd come to know like the back of her own hand. 'Why does it bother you so much? You've lived around Pearl your whole life. Why is it so hard for you to accept what I've experienced? What are you afraid of?'

'Maybe I've just had enough of this crap being forced down my throat all my life, without having someone I—' He stopped abruptly. 'What if I believed that what Wilfred Mason did was justifiable?'

Hayley stared at him. 'But you don't,' she said simply.

'But what if *I did*, Hayley? What if what I believed was just as unshakable as what you believed? Could you live with someone whose beliefs were so different to yours?'

'You're comparing me to a cold-blooded murderer?'

'I'm comparing you to a man who was adamant until the day he died that he'd done nothing wrong,' he shrugged. 'That was his *belief.*'

It was clear then that Luke had no intention of accepting her and they had no possible future. 'I better leave you to it,' she said, turning away sadly.

'Hayley—'

She turned, watching him expectantly. *Say it,* she pleaded silently, grasping at what little hope she had. *Hayley, I want us to start again. It's okay about the book . . . I don't care that we don't agree on the same things . . .* But he wasn't going to say any of that. Slowly she turned away again. As she moved past, she held her breath. *Say something to make me stop,* she pleaded silently, but the only noise she heard was the calling of birds high in the trees and maybe a long, sad sigh.

Once safely inside the house, she touched her fingertips to her cheeks and realised that she was crying. No. She was not going to cry. She had no reason to. Luke was his own person, they weren't a couple, they never would be. All they'd keep doing was disappointing and hurting each other. She could see it, like one endless loop, repeating the same frustrating pattern.

She had to put a stop to it, she couldn't go on living next door to the man, loving him like she did and continuing this on again, off again thing they had happening. She had to end it once and for all.

∽

Luke was in a bad mood when he arrived back home and it didn't improve for the remainder of the day. He should have said something. He'd wanted to. Desperately. The words he wanted to say burned inside him, but he couldn't get them out. What was wrong with him? He tossed down another beer and stared moodily at the empty room. What was he doing? He was thirty-one years old and he was sitting all alone in an empty house, pining for a woman he *could have* if he'd just shake off this stupid fear inside him.

He'd always known about Edward. It had been part of him. As a child he remembered things about growing up here at Lochmanning—things he shouldn't have known because they happened a long time before he was born. He'd never thought anything of the memories until he'd gotten older and somehow understood that it wasn't normal to talk about the things he'd lived through before.

His name had been Edward, before. And he'd died.

Gran had been the only one who understood. His parents had ignored his odd comments for the first few years, but one day when he was about seven, he told his father that he felt bad for the things that had happened to the local Aboriginal people who had lived here before they'd been chased away. His father lost his temper. 'You are *not* Edward Mason. Your grandmother has filled your head with this rubbish and it's time you bloody well grew up and stopped all this rot. Enough is enough. If you want to be a farmer, you better start acting like a man or you can forget about working here one day.' He could still recall the sharp sting of embarrassment and shame that had followed his father's outburst.

His dad was his hero; all he'd ever wanted to do was be a farmer just like him and make him proud. To suddenly hear that he was an embarrassment to the man he worshipped almost gutted him with shame. Nothing was more important to him than being a farmer, and if that meant he had to stop remembering then so be it. So he had. He never thought about Edward Mason again, and somewhere along the line he forgot about his other life. Until a woman with dark hair and cornflower blue eyes came back into his life.

Luke went in search of another beer but the fridge was empty. He needed to escape this empty house. There was too much quiet, and memories liked quiet places.

He headed down to the bar, glad to find it wasn't overly crowded. He walked behind the counter, taking a beer from the fridge before wandering around to sit at the bar and drink.

'What's going on with you?' Grant asked after he finished serving a customer up the other end.

'Why?'

'You're in here drinking for starters.'

'I didn't know there was a law against it.'

'You're never in here drinking alone.'

'I ran out of beer at my place.'

'Fair enough. But I think you chose a bad night to renounce your hermit lifestyle.'

'What do you mean?' he frowned across at his older brother and saw him nod towards something behind him. Luke turned in his seat and groaned as he saw a table of party-goers and one in particular who was very familiar. He turned back and continued drinking his beer, hoping he might go unnoticed.

'Hey, cowboy, can I buy you a drink?' Lucinda's smooth tone, which he'd once loved, now felt like fingernails on a chalkboard.

'I'm good thanks, and I get them free,' he said, holding up his beer. 'I thought you were at the wedding.'

'It was an early wedding, with the reception at lunchtime. Who even does that?' she asked, leaning both arms on the bar to better show off her cleavage. 'Anyway,' she continued in that bored tone, 'the reception's over and the night is still young.'

'I'm sure you and your friends will figure out something to entertain yourselves with.'

'You should come over and join us.'

Luke slid her a dry glance. 'No, thanks. I seem to recall I never got on with your kind of friends.'

'You'd like these ones.'

'I doubt it, Cin,' he said, taking another long pull of his beer and feeling the slight buzz from the previous ones starting to kick in.

'No one calls me that anymore,' she said softly, and he caught a rare vulnerable look on her face. For a moment it caught him off guard. It hadn't all been bad, just the last part.

'Let's have a few drinks and a couple of laughs, for old times' sake,' she said with a smile, ordering two more beers and handing him one before gently tapping their bottles together.

He took a long swig of the beer and let her lead him across to the table of people waiting for her. What the hell, he thought, taking another drink. She was going to find out sooner or later that he hadn't changed and give up whatever her game was, but it had to beat sitting at home alone thinking about Hayley.

Thirty-four

'I need you to cleanse whatever it is you cleanse and cut the ties to Jane and Edward.'

Meg didn't seem particularly fazed to find a distraught woman standing on her doorstep. 'Are you sure?' Meg asked, watching Hayley closely.

Hayley managed a nod and tried to ignore the emptiness that opened up at the thought. She followed Meg into her room and sat in the recliner as Meg took her through the relaxation techniques. Without even trying, Hayley stepped back into the past and instantly felt the fear and apprehension as she ran towards Edward at the tree. It was like Groundhog Day—nothing changed, it always ended the same way.

She saw Edward turn to her and tell her to run—that he'd find her.

She heard Meg's words floating to her like a whisper on the wind. 'Tell me what you're feeling.'

'I'm scared, I know neither of us will escape the men. I know he's only telling me he'll find me later to give me some kind of hope . . . but part of me believes him.'

'You've been waiting for him to find you?'

'We keep losing each other. We never find each other at the right time. I want him to stop trying to find me. It's never going to be the right time. We're not meant to be.'

'If you're ready to cut the cord, I want you to picture a rope linking you and Edward. I want you to remember back to the moment by the tree.'

She looked into his eyes, those same eyes she knew so well. Luke's eyes. She saw love reflected in them, behind the fear and the terror. The kind of love that would follow her for a lifetime.

Hayley felt that familiar pressure against her chest as Meg talked her through visualising the cord being cut and the pain and the sadness being removed. Lightness filled her as the last of the sorrow dissolved, and Hayley found herself standing in front of the tree.

'Goodbye, Edward,' she whispered, feeling the burn in her chest followed by the sensation of being dragged backwards into the dark once more. When she opened her eyes this time she found that her cheeks were wet and her chest felt heavy with grief.

'It's all right, Hayley, just breathe, long and slow.'

Hayley hardly remembered what Meg had said to her afterwards; she remembered they'd spoken, but she'd been too wrung-out to contribute much. She drove herself home and ran a bath, letting the warm bubbles surround and comfort her. She closed her eyes and wept. She didn't bother with dinner, she simply climbed into bed and fell into a deep, dreamless sleep. The first in a very long while.

∽

The morning ritual of throwing the donkeys their fresh hay before letting the chooks out of their coop and feeding them was a balm to her bruised soul. There was something soothing in stepping outside in the early morning air to be greeted by her small menagerie.

Her phone rang and she dug into the deep pockets of her cargo pants to locate it, seeing Sophia's name on the screen.

'Hales! How are you?'

What was she doing calling so early? Hayley glanced at her watch and realised it was almost ten o'clock. She'd been sidetracked after feeding the animals into watering the fruit trees and had lost track of time.

'Sophia, hi. I'm great.'

'Well, be prepared to be a lot *more* great. I've just got off the phone with Theo and they've finally got all the funding for *Chance is a Fine Thing*,' Sophia said triumphantly. 'They've already got interest from some pretty major Hollywood heavyweights to play Chance, and they're ready to talk to potential screenwriters. I'm going to push them for a script consultant role for you.'

'Seriously?' When they'd sold the option for her first book she'd been super-excited, only to discover that contrary to what she'd always imagined when your book was bought by a movie producer, it didn't necessarily mean it would ever get made. It had been so long since she'd heard anything about it that she'd pretty much learned to stop thinking about it, and now, out of the blue, it seemed it was going to happen after all.

'Seriously,' Sophia assured her. 'They're talking cast and location, and all sorts of wonderful things. It's really happening.'

'Holy cow.' Hayley was too shocked to say anything more coherent but she was soon snapped from her stupor when Sophia mentioned Sydney. 'Sorry, what?'

'I need you down here for a few days. We have a few things to sort out.'

'When?'

'Tomorrow if possible.'

'I'm not sure I can. I have animals . . .'

'I seem to recall you have a certain sexy neighbour who I'm sure would be more than happy to pop over and feed them for a few days.'

There was a conversation she was pretty sure she didn't want to get into. 'I'm not sure. I'll have to find out. I'll need to get back to you.'

'This is important, Hales. Do what you have to do, okay?'

'Okay, I'll call you back.' She disconnected the call, her initial excitement dampened slightly by the thought of calling Luke.

She stared at the phone thoughtfully for a minute before scrolling through her contacts. 'Hey, Jason. It's me. No, I haven't changed my mind,' she said, rolling her eyes, 'but I do have a favour to ask.'

∽

Sydney had grown in the five months she'd been gone. It had to have. Surely it was never this big or busy before? There seemed to be more traffic, more construction, more noise, more people . . . more *everything*. It was a relief to step into the cool and quiet of Sophia's office.

'Oh dear, I take it things aren't going any better with the cowboy then?' Sophia said as she eyed Hayley from across the desk.

'Why would you say that?'

'Honey, not even makeup can hide a broken heart.'

Hayley closed her eyes briefly. Was she really that easy to read?

'I can't do anything to fix it,' Sophia went on gently, 'but I can help make this movie happen. It may not be a cure for a broken heart, but having your book made into a movie sure as hell must come pretty damn close.'

Hayley gave a chuckle despite feeling miserable. She had a point.

After that the morning flew past, and Hayley was grateful for the distraction. They discussed the details of the contract and went over anything they wanted to add before it was time to bundle into a taxi and drive to a meeting in the city.

The producers who were making the movie were based in the US and Hayley wanted to be sure they'd be true to her vision for her book series. Even though she'd have liked the movie to have kept the book's Australian roots, the sad reality was that there was a lack of funding to produce quality Australian films. Changing the book's location and giving her characters American accents would be a shock to the system, but it wouldn't fundamentally change the storyline. As long as Chance remained a sharp-tongued, arse-kicking woman with a heart of gold and a soft spot for damaged but decent men, she could live with the location change.

After the meeting with the production company, Hayley's head was swimming with details, but she felt confident they'd make a decent job of it. Bringing her books to life on the big screen was the icing on the cake, but it wasn't what was most important to her—that was the books themselves.

She knew from personal experience how important books were. As a lonely kid, to her they were more than just an escape, they were a salvation, a way to forget the misery of her real life and live in a world where, even though things got dark, there was always a way out—a happy ending, good triumphing over evil. That was why she wrote her Chance Delaware books. Because she knew that somewhere out there was someone else who needed a heroine—someone to believe in even if it was just for a few short hours.

The view of the sparkling harbour before her and expensive menu should have been a distraction, after all they were celebrating—Sophia had insisted. *How many times have I been to this place over the years?* she wondered briefly. She'd lost count. She had smiled serenely when Sophia had told her she wanted to bring her here to remind her what she was missing, being out there in the sticks, but the truth was, as beautiful as the harbour and the restaurant and the city itself was, she didn't miss it—any of it. What she missed was her animals and her little cottage. She missed home.

Thirty-five

The phone in her hotel room rang and Hayley reached for it without taking her eyes from the computer screen where she was busy working on rewrites the producer had asked for.

It was reception informing her she had a visitor in the lobby.

'A visitor?' she asked, surprised. Who even knew she was here?

'Mr Luke Mason.'

Hayley felt her mouth drop open and quickly closed it. 'Um. Okay. Can you ask him to wait in the bar, please? I'll be down in a few minutes.'

What the actual hell? What was Luke doing here? She snapped out of her daze long enough to remember to change out of her tracksuit pants and old jumper. The ride down in the elevator seemed to go way too fast. She'd been hoping to use the time to compose herself and figure out what to say to him, but before she knew it the doors had opened and the doorway to the bar was directly opposite her.

She walked cautiously towards the lone figure seated at the bar. When he looked up, Hayley felt a flutter inside her chest but she pushed it away firmly.

'Hi. I'm sorry I didn't call ahead and let you know I was coming.'

'What's wrong? Is everything okay? Is it Pearl?' she gasped. Her mind was racing with a thousand possible reasons for his visit.

'No. No, it's nothing like that. Everyone's fine,' he said, and a small smile tugged at his lips before he swallowed and looked nervous again.

'How did you know where I was?'

'Sophia told me.'

'Oh right. So you and my agent are now besties?'

He gave a crooked smile and shook his head. 'I rang her and pleaded my case. She felt sorry for me and told me where you were staying.'

Traitor, Hayley thought irritably.

'In all fairness, I made it very hard for her to say no.'

'I'm sure you did.' She could picture her drooling agent, with a weakness for country men, tripping over herself to do whatever the hell he asked.

'I saw Jason yesterday,' he said. 'I went over to talk to you but found him there feeding the livestock. He said you'd gone away for a few days.'

She was sure that particular visit would have gone over well.

'He cleared the air about what happened at the bar. You were right, he was only trying to stir me up,' he said with a slight wince. 'And we sorted out . . . the other stuff.' He cleared his throat.

She tried to picture Luke and Jason having a deep and meaningful and came up blank. But as the shock of the unexpected news settled, relief set in and she felt herself relax. 'That's good.' She eased up onto the bar stool next to him and ordered a drink from the bartender.

'I've done a fair bit of thinking lately. You hit a lot closer to home than you probably realised the other day when you asked me what I was afraid of.'

Hayley bit back the questions on the tip of her tongue. She knew whatever it was, he'd fought hard to keep it hidden, and this was no easy step, coming here to tell her.

'I'm sorry,' he said, looking up and pinning her with a solemn gaze that almost stopped her heart. 'I let my own hang-ups and fear get in the way of *us*.'

'Fear?' Hang-ups she understood. Living with his gran had turned him off everything to do with the supernatural, she got that. But fear? What could possibly frighten him?

'When I was a kid . . .' He paused, as though trying to find the words to explain. 'Gran once told me that kids often remember things about past lives more than adults . . . it's still fresh or something,' he shrugged awkwardly. 'Anyway, I guess that was the case for me.'

He looked up at her slowly, his face serious, and her breath caught.

'I remembered everything about Edward Mason's life. When I was a kid,' he added.

Hayley felt her pulse pound frantically but forced herself to remain silent and hear him out.

'When I was five, I drew the tree and the horses and men with guns. I used to have nightmares about it. My parents brushed it off as a developmental phase, but Gran knew better. She knew that I was remembering my past life as Edward Mason.' He stared down at his drink silently for a few moments. 'I'd forgotten about it. I don't know how, maybe because Dad freaked out at me one day and it really scared me. Maybe I outgrew it, I don't know, but at some point I stopped believing in it and it all went away.'

Hayley was fairly sure if she hadn't already been sitting down she would have fallen down. For a long time she could only stare at Luke, completely stunned.

'The very first time I saw you, standing in that dam, I felt as though I knew you. I knew I'd never met you before, but I recognised you. Then the night we first kissed, it triggered something. I couldn't put my finger on it but I knew there was something important I needed to remember, only the more I tried to figure out what it was, the more frustrated I became. And then at the cemetery it got worse. I knew whatever it was, I didn't *want to* remember. It wasn't until you'd visited with Gran and told her about your visions that my own memories came back, and it scared me, Hayley. More than I care to admit as a grown man.'

Hayley swallowed past the lump that had formed in her throat. Slowly she reached out and placed her hand on top of his. She knew exactly what he'd gone through. 'Why didn't you tell me all this before?'

'I spent most of my life forgetting it. It worked too. To a certain degree. I managed to bury most of the detailed memories by the time I was a teenager. I guess hormones pretty much overtook anything else—it's easy to forget stuff when you're preoccupied with girls and sex and farming,' he said with a grin. 'Not to mention when you're trying extra hard to not be weak and pathetic.'

'Weak and pathetic?'

'That's what my dad said once when he was arguing with Gran. I overheard him. Gran was saying that the more sensitive a person, the more likely they were to be able to connect with things like past lives and angels and God only knows what else. I can still hear the disgust in Dad's voice,' he said, and a hard look entered his eye. 'He told her to stop filling my head with nonsense and he wasn't going to raise a weak and pathetic sissy for a son.'

Hayley squeezed his hand in sympathy.

'I guess my hang-ups have controlled me more than I cared to admit. I'm sorry I made you feel like crap about it all, Hayley. I more than anyone should have realised how that would make you feel. I'm not proud of myself.'

'At least I wasn't a kid,' she said.

'It's still no excuse. I'm sorry.'

'Apology accepted. Can we put it all behind us now?'

'Do you think we can?' he asked with a frown.

'Yes, I do. I already have. I was scared of it before too, but now I think I was incredibly lucky to have experienced it. That doesn't mean I'm going to go looking for it though. I don't want this thing to define me.' She fiddled with the coaster on the bar in front of her, idly. 'You were so sure that I was going to turn into someone like your gran, but I'm not. I never was,' she said looking up at him. 'I'm the same person I was before this happened—maybe I'm a little more open-minded but I'm still me.'

'I should have faced it like you did. I was an idiot.'

'You had your reasons, I don't blame you for that. I'm in a better place about it all now. I've moved on and so should you.'

'I don't want to move on,' he said after a moment of silence. 'I'm in love with you, Hayley.'

Just when she thought the man couldn't surprise her anymore.

'I want to try again. With you. If you want to,' he added uncertainly.

'Maybe you should wait until you've seen Meg and dealt with all the Edward stuff.'

'You think I'm in love with you because of Edward?' he asked, wearing a frown.

'Maybe,' she shrugged. 'I mean, that's where it started. Maybe it's just leftover emotion or something.'

'What I feel has nothing to do with Edward.' He shook his head. 'I may have acted like a bloody idiot, but how I feel about you was never in doubt. It has nothing to do with the past.'

'It's more than that, Luke,' she said wearily. 'I'm going ahead with publishing the story.'

He stopped at that, seemingly a little taken back for a moment. He gave a brief nod. 'Well, you must have taken everything into consideration before you made the decision, so I guess we see how it all plays out.'

'You're okay with that?' she asked doubtfully.

'I'll stand by you. You haven't published anything that isn't true,' he admitted. 'I'm just a little concerned about the backlash you might cop over it, that's all.'

'I can handle whatever happens.'

'*We'll* handle whatever happens,' he said, reaching for her hand and taking it in his. 'I mean it, Hayley. I'll stand behind you, whatever you do. Now and for always.'

Her heart flittered a little at the sincerity she read in his eyes. Could she trust this was going to work? What happened when the next test came their way, and there was sure to be more than a few? Would he walk away like he did before? As she released a long slow breath she was filled with a calm stillness, the same feeling she'd had when she'd decided to buy Abby Cottage and move from the city. It felt . . . right.

'I don't want you to stand behind me,' she said, and his expression fell. 'I want you to stand beside me. We're partners, aren't we?'

His smile widened and her breath caught as he leaned across and kissed her. She still felt the power of it and a little piece of her breathed a sigh of relief. It wasn't gone, this attraction between them.

'We sure are,' he said, resting his forehead against hers gently.

Hayley pulled back and looked up at him seriously, 'You do know that I come as a package deal, right? Me, four cats, the chooks, Errol and Flynn, and a herd of miniature Galloways.'

'Yes, I know. You and the whole damn circus,' he groaned, 'but you realise you're not just taking me on, right? You get my parents and a fan-girl sister-in-law on top of a crazy grandmother. Are *you* sure you know what *you're* getting into?'

'Absolutely,' she smiled, kissing his lips gently. 'I wouldn't have it any other way.'

Epilogue

Luke parked his ute in front of the old limestone cottage and grabbed his hat from the passenger seat, jamming it on his head as he opened the door. It'd been a long day. He and his dad had spent it installing solar-powered cameras in most of the paddocks to check on stock.

He smiled thinking back to the weekend he and the old man had just spent at a conference on digital agriculture technology. He still couldn't believe he'd managed to talk him into going with him. For the first few minutes Patrick had sat, arms folded, mumbling under his breath as the presenter, who even Luke had to admit hadn't looked older than seventeen, launched into a talk about robotics, drones and smart phone advancement. But within a short space of time he'd seen his father taking a real interest. He'd been fairly quiet on the trip home, which was unusual in itself, but even more surprising had been the phone call he'd gotten the next day, informing him that his father had just ordered a couple of those *remote camera things*.

It turned out that, in his father's exact words: 'Maybe it wouldn't hurt to cut down on a bit of the workload by checkin' stock via cameras.' Luke knew better than to remind his father that he'd been suggesting this for a while now, instead he told him it sounded like a great idea and kept his mouth shut. He hoped it was the start of a shift in their relationship.

Luke had been making a bigger effort to take his dad's advice, realising that maybe he'd been trying too hard to show him he had everything under control. The truth was, while Grant and Luke had gotten so wrapped up in the restaurant and the brewery, and his mother was focused on the wedding business, no one had realised that their father was feeling a little redundant and very much on the sidelines of the farm he'd run pretty much single-handedly for over fifty years.

It was baby steps, but he was feeling confident that it wasn't too late to try for a better relationship with his dad.

A sound caught his ear as he walked inside and tossed his dusty hat onto the peg inside the back door. He frowned, cocking his head slightly as he tried to work out where it was coming from.

'Hayley?'

'In here,' he heard her calling back in a hushed tone.

He followed her voice into the laundry and stopped in the doorway, shaking his head. 'No, Hayley. No way.'

Seated on the floor was his wife of six months and a long-haired golden retriever she'd brought home only two weeks earlier . . . and an armload of wriggling, squeaking newborn pups.

'Okay,' she started explaining, 'so, plot twist.' She grinned up at him. 'Turns out Molly wasn't just fat after all . . . she was pregnant.' Hayley wasn't even bothering to hide her glee.

'I told you to get the vet to double check she'd been desexed,' he sighed.

'I was planning to. I just hadn't gotten around to it,' she shrugged, holding up a tiny blond-coated pup. 'Aren't we lucky?' she said. 'Seven puppies.'

Luke gave a fatalistic laugh, but looking down at her vivacious smile and bright eyes, he forgot whatever logical argument he had against having eight dogs in the house and felt his heart melt—not over the puppies, but over the woman who owned his heart lock, stock and barrel. They *were* lucky. More than lucky. He'd won the whole damn lottery the day he'd stumbled on a woman trying to pull a donkey out of his dam.

He crouched down in front of her and took the pup from her hands, a reluctant smile tugging at his lips. 'What are we naming them?' he said with a resigned sigh.

'I'm not sure yet. I'm waiting for them to tell me what their names are,' she shrugged. 'I missed you,' she smiled, leaning over and kissing him lingeringly, just like she did every afternoon when he walked into the house.

'Missed you more.'

She returned the tiny puppies to their mother, giving her a loving pat before standing up and leaving her to get acquainted with her litter.

'Did you get all the cameras installed?' she asked, slipping into his arms and tipping her head back to gaze up at him.

He still felt that familiar kick in his gut when she looked at him like that; it was probably ridiculous, but he kind of hoped it never went away. 'Yep. All done. I left Dad in front of the computer, shaking his head and muttering, "Bloody ingenious" as he clicked between all the feeds.'

She laughed at his imitation of his dad and he found himself smiling too.

'What?' she asked, watching his expression soften.

'I was just thinking how different my life was a year ago.'

Her smile tilted. 'It didn't include eight dogs, a herd of miniature cattle, two donkeys, a bunch of chooks, four cats and a wife, did it?' she agreed.

'Nope. But I wouldn't change a thing.'

'Really?' she asked. 'Because Ernie was telling me there's an old lady who can't take care of her two Shetland ponies and thought I might—'

Luke groaned and kissed her, effectively stopping what he knew she was about to say. He grinned against her lips when he felt her respond and knew for at least a few more minutes he had her complete and undivided attention. He was smart enough to realise it was only delaying the inevitable, though—by this time next week he'd be calling in Jason to start building a set of stables for the damn Shetlands. As her arms slipped around his neck and her body pressed tightly against his own, he realised right at this very moment he couldn't care less how many animals she brought home, as long as she was here beside him.

They didn't talk about Edward and Jane anymore. They didn't have to, they had each other, here and now, and that was all that mattered. Whatever fate had stolen from them in their past, this was their happy-ever-after, and he for one wasn't going to take a second of it for granted.

He moved her towards the bedroom and kicked the door shut with the heel of his boot. Right now he had a wife who needed some serious distracting before they ended up with any more stray animals, and he planned on distracting her for a very long time.